ROTTEN IN DENMARK

'I really enjoyed this book. Jim Pollard knows what he's talking about.' – Nigel Williams

'Rotten In Denmark is funny and fast-moving, taking a close look at both the music business and the business of growing up. Jim Pollard is a knowledgeable and thoughtful guide on both subjects. He's a talented new writer: one to watch' – Mark Illis

'Strong storytelling with surprising twists; a true portrayal of friendship and rivalry' – Jane Rogers

Jim Pollard was born and grew up in south London. A freelance writer, editor and photographer, he has an MA in Writing (Novel and Scriptwriting) from Sheffield Hallam University.

He is author of three health books including the acclaimed *All Right, Mate? – An Easy Intro To Men's Health* published by Gollancz Vista in 1999.

Rotten In Denmark is his first novel.

ROTTEN IN DENMARK

Jim Pollard

Smith/Doorstop Books

Published 1999 by
Smith/Doorstop Books
The Poetry Business
The Studio
Byram Arcade
Westgate
Huddersfield HD1 1ND

ISBN 1-902382-20-X

A C.I.P. record for this book is available from the British Library.

Typeset at The Poetry Business
Cover design by Blue Door, Heckmondwike
Printed by Redwood Books, Trowbridge

Represention: Signature Book Representation Ltd, 2 Little Peter Street, Manchester M15 4PS, tel 0161 834 8767
Distribution: Littlehampton Book Services Ltd, 10-14 Eldon Way, Lineside Estate, Littlehampton BN17 7HE, tel 01903 828800

The Poetry Business acknowledges the financial help of Kirklees Metropolitan Council, Yorkshire & Humberside Arts and the Arts Council of England.

Back cover photography © Julian Brown
Author photograph © Andrew Gillman

for my Mum and Dad

Acknowledgements
I'd like to say thank you to, in no particular order: the staff and students on the Sheffield Hallam University MA in Writing, particularly Jane Rogers for her tutoring, encouragement and advice; my editors and publishers at Smith/Doorstop Books for their confidence in me and the novel; Amanda White for being a fantastic agent and Serafina Clarke for taking me on; Andrew Gillman, Julian Brown and Friedl Gamerith for the cover photos; Jill Dawson for friendship and encouragement; Dr. Ronnie Cummings for the medical bits; The Unknown, The Lemmings (Who Bottled Out), Just Good Friends and Spoilt For Choice for refusing to be bound by the shackles of musical talent, technique or theory; and Bela Maria for believing in me.

Editor's note

The recent history of Frankie Dane has, of course, been well-documented in the media.

This volume contains his full, unedited manuscript for *Rotten In Denmark* which, in keeping with the technique he adopted throughout the text, has been supplemented with two topical newspaper cuttings chosen by the editor.

Cal Carter died in 1979 , not yet twenty one. We were at the height of our fame.

He might have argued that Mrs. Thatcher's election alone was reason enough to take an overdose. As it was, there was a number of factors cited at the inquest including the state both of his mind, 'disturbed', and, of his amphetamine sulphate, 'adulterated'. Whatever it might say elsewhere – and let's face it, these things are always shrouded in mystery (look at Jim Morrison, Kurt Cobain, old Sid Vicious) – whatever it might say, I know Cal did not intend to die.

To him this book is dedicated.

Please allow me to
introduce myself ...

1
---

*Nothing is subtle in the synthetic city. There is the perpetual scream
of the houselights rendering even a west coast tan, wan yellow. There
are the jewels, flashing blades of brilliance, set in awkward
billowing necks. There is the clatter and the rumble of the not-so-
far-away fruit machines. And there is the smell – a smell where
perfume ends and disinfectant and incontinence begins.*

*This could be a bingo hall. With a little imagination. They don't
play in tiara and fur in south-east London but perhaps here. Big
enough to house an aircraft. From the lighting balcony at the back,
a technician sweeps the supertrouper across the vast stage like a
searchlight.*

*The men are in dinner-dress: standing, civilised, easing back
chairs. Big-shots or bouncers, it's hard to tell. The women are plucked
from the pages of a hundred magazines, the stuff of white dreams.*

*By a side-door, a young man with hair a cheerleader would kill
for is playing his hunches. A doorman distracted by a lick of lamé,
the young man marches in – adjusting his tie, nodding his hollow
hellos with purpose. In his pocket are a handful of dollars. Tickets
tonight cost hundreds. Anyone watching would see that he is an
intruder and no master of disguises: hunched at the bar over
another man's bourbon; then standing at the door with a tip-me
tug of his golden forelock; then crouched at the side of the stage
scribbling into a notebook. Anyone watching could tell that he is*

an impostor but nobody watches. The crisp English cut of his suit is adequate, even appropriate. Cal Carter is wearing it for the first time, Elvis Presley his shimmering jumpsuit for the umpteenth. It is Las Vegas, it is 1976 and rock'n'roll has gotten fat.

Out of the darkness, a single spotlight targets the microphone. Presley appears. Applause. The lights lift as the orchestra clicks into a crisply concluded crescendo. Two bars. Cal has done it: gatecrashed the King. Imagine him glowing inside with a sip of Jack Daniels and a surge of pride.

'I'm...' The orchestra comes back as Presley sings: '...hurt' – the word straddles a beat, a backbeat, a bar and another.

'...to think that you lied to me.'

'Hurt.' Shorter this time. The first wiggle of the hip and shudder of the lip. 'Way down deep inside of me.'

'And that was it,' Cal would say. 'Down deep. Like a voice from a cave. Like buried treasure.' Unless you really knew him and how fast his mind worked, my best friend's sentences appeared to come in prepacked, ready-to-speak slices. Whenever he told this story – and I heard him tell it several times to the band, to reporters, to fawning girls and buck-skinned boys – he always described the moment thus: like buried treasure. That was the moment Cal Carter believed he saw our future.

The first time I heard the story we were sitting five thousand miles away from Las Vegas in the far from glamorous public bar of The Roebuck, our special seats round the corner out the way of the dart board where we always sat when the information to be exchanged was serious stuff. He'd arrived back from America that morning and had jet lag scratched scarlet across his eyes.

I watched him standing at the bar. Shaking his head and waving his hand as he ordered bourbon and was offered scotch. We were neither of us whisky drinkers but Cal's return was already working great changes in our lives. I was eighteen, a smoker of Players No.6 and a drinker of keg bitter. I was a member of Her Majesty's Civil Service and a lowly one at that. Licensed to bill. Elvis Presley at the Hilton Hotel, Las Vegas was another world, another language.

Cal returned with more pints and two whiskies which he

1

Nothing is subtle in the synthetic city. There is the perpetual scream of the houselights rendering even a west coast tan, wan yellow. There are the jewels, flashing blades of brilliance, set in awkward billowing necks. There is the clatter and the rumble of the not-so-far-away fruit machines. And there is the smell – a smell where perfume ends and disinfectant and incontinence begins.

This could be a bingo hall. With a little imagination. They don't play in tiara and fur in south-east London but perhaps here. Big enough to house an aircraft. From the lighting balcony at the back, a technician sweeps the supertrouper across the vast stage like a searchlight.

The men are in dinner-dress: standing, civilised, easing back chairs. Big-shots or bouncers, it's hard to tell. The women are plucked from the pages of a hundred magazines, the stuff of white dreams.

By a side-door, a young man with hair a cheerleader would kill for is playing his hunches. A doorman distracted by a lick of lamé, the young man marches in – adjusting his tie, nodding his hollow hellos with purpose. In his pocket are a handful of dollars. Tickets tonight cost hundreds. Anyone watching would see that he is an intruder and no master of disguises: hunched at the bar over another man's bourbon; then standing at the door with a tip-me tug of his golden forelock; then crouched at the side of the stage scribbling into a notebook. Anyone watching could tell that he is pointedly and, I discovered only years later, inaccurately, referred to as 'chasers'. Then he was off again, back there again. 'At first it was just a bit of a fun. Seeing how many Bourbons I could lift. It was just a scam. You know, Presley, Christ...' He paused over his beer. 'It was four lines in, Frankie... Buried treasure.'

He shook his head and smiled again. 'And I could barely hear it beneath the applause and rattling of jewellery.'

I probably smiled back. I certainly lit a cigarette. He shook his head when I offered him one and produced an American soft-pack from the breast pocket of his denim jacket. He tapped on the top and a cigarette emerged, sliding upwards, humbling gravity. Although Cal went on about it for another half-an-hour that, I think, was the moment when he convinced me. You could put it down to the power of Presley but those soft-packs were something else.

'It was better than any amount of money.'

My eyebrows barely moved and he may have sensed my interest waning. 'It was better than sex.'

I smirked. 'Presley singing was better than sex?'

'Better than sex.'

Cal and I had grown up together. He understood the expressions on my face, the way I fiddled with my hair. He smiled and pushed a tumbler of scotch towards me.

'More than that,' he said. 'It was better than you thought sex would be when you were fourteen.' I looked up at him . Now that was a wholly different ball game of soldiers. He was in the process of sitting. He leaned across the table, his eyes inches from mine, his breath flecked with whisky.

There was a pause before I shook my head. 'I thought we'd finished with that schoolkids stuff. Isn't that what Jon said?'

'But you never had the vision before,' said Cal. 'I never had the vision. Any of us. It's all very well to want to make money, shag women and take drugs, but...'

'I thought there might be a but.'

'But you have to see it, feel it. Take it and twist it.' In his eye there was a twinkle like a safety pin in the sun.

I wasn't too sure what he was talking about but I could feel a schoolboy's grin tighten across my face, a sensation I hadn't felt for

15

at least a year. The grin Wendy Carter said was cute when she was twenty and I was fifteen and a half.

Potential is just that. Unrealised. But I am as close to certain as it is possible to be that when Cal died his best moments were yet to come, his best songs were yet to be recorded. Today he stands next to me just a stage width away from Elvis in some rock'n'roll waxworks museum they've got for the tourists up in town. They've made Cal three inches taller than he really was. I'm the right height but I'm told my eyes are hollow, empty and robbed of the sparkle of life.

I knew him – the supposed new McCartney to his new Lennon. I can say, hand on my rock-hardened heart and without an ounce of the all-American sentimentality that once inspired us that my story is nothing without the story of Cal Carter.

And when I think of him now, it's often of that cabaret moment. Not of any of the umpteen millions of moments when we were together but of that one in Las Vegas when Elvis Presley sent a chill down his spine. And sometimes, I can see it as big and as bold and as bright as Presley's white sequined suit. And sometimes I can hardly imagine it at all. Perhaps that is because I can't imagine *me* there. Sore thumb me but Cal fitted.

2

Beech Park, 1969

So far as I can remember I've only ever seen a bowler hat on television. And Oliver Hardy has usually got his foot through it. Neither the white heat of technology nor the black hat of respectability ever quite made it to the bit of Beech Park where I grew up. Ours were neat but not noteworthy streets. Neither garden suburb nor concrete jungle. Halfway houses.

I spent much of my childhood, or so it seems to me now, sitting in the window of the railway station. Beech Park was a two platform affair, in and out of Charing Cross, every half-an-hour. 'Charing Cross, in the heart of London's West End', as it always said in the newspapers. At the age of ten I was well aware that I lived a full four stops away from where life was being lived. They never mentioned Beech Park in the newspapers. Not even the local one.

The station was a simple concrete building, sufficient to accommodate the ticket office, Mr. Parker, Mr. Parker's confectionery stand, a cantankerous old dog belonging to the ticket clerk and two wooden staircases down to the respective platforms. It was finished with a solid Victorian surety and discreet flourish. The circular window between the in-door, which said 'To The Trains', and the out-door, which said 'Missing. Small Ginger Tom. Answers To The Name Of Rusty', had a concrete window ledge that was at least a foot deep. That was where I sat: feet up, my school bag under my knees, my back nestled in the curve of the white ledge.

I used to sit in it on the way to school and chew watermelon flavoured bubble gum. Only when the flavour had all gone, well and truly, would I walk on. I had no idea what watermelon tasted like or even looked like but the gum, which came in green balls slightly larger than a marble, was my favourite. My father, a man who disapproved of so many things – a man, indeed, whose defining quality was disapproval – disapproved of gum chewing so I kept the stuff out of the house. Anyway, the station window was a more comfortable place to sit and chew than our garden wall: our garden wall being shaped like the battlements of a castle. It's a shame that now I have tasted watermelon, and even fished it out of a cocktail glass, I can no longer remember what the gum tasted like.

At first, it was all I could do to climb up into the window alcove. Gradually, it got more comfortable. I liked watching the people, the men, getting on and, more rarely, off the train. I was fascinated by their briefcases – full of things to do. Black ones and brown ones, pristine and battered ones. I used to imagine what was in them and where they were going with them. Didn't know then that one day I'd be joining them with a briefcase of my own and nothing more interesting inside it than a cheese and pickle sandwich.

At first, I only had sufficient gum for one ball on the way to school and another on the way back but then I started to get more pocket money, and I started to hear the school bell ringing at the top of the hill with me still sitting in the window chewing. Ball two, ball three, like an American baseball umpire counting someone out.

It was at about this time that my parents paid their first visit to the school to see about, as my mother put it, quoting from my report card, my 'lack of satisfactory progress' or, as my father put it, to get them to 'knock some bloody sense' in to me. At home the word 'comprehensive' assumed the whispered status of a profanity like 'bloody' – muttered with stifled anger and not for my ears. Increasingly, the two appeared in tandem. As in 'bloody unions' or 'bloody Alf Ramsey': 'bloody comprehensive'.

My father got quite excited over the eleven-plus which he made sound like an educational version of penicillin – the cure for everything. To me, sitting down at the station window, watching our insignificant little world go by, became ever more attractive.

One day I was sitting there on the way home. It was early and apart from that stupid dog yapping the station was silent, deserted. I was so bored that I was rooting through my schoolbag looking for something to do or even to read.

'Want to swap bags?' came a still-in-short-trousers sort of a voice.

I looked down. A little blond haired kid from the posh school – the one where the teachers were called masters. 'Masters because they've mastered their subject,' my father had explained. 'Not like those half-trained bloody monkeys down your place.'

I was chewing bubble gum. The titchy kid was eating a bar of chocolate.

'Is it your birthday?' I asked.

He regarded me for a moment as if I were mad. He was a good foot shorter than me and I could have flattened him had I wanted but there was an assurance and confidence in his piggy eyes that I found appealing. Desirable. I realised it was an absurd question even as I was asking it but to me Mars Bars were the stuff of special occasions – the pantomime, cinema or birthdays. He looked up, fixed his eyes first on mine and then lowered them steadily towards my bag. He seemed to find it more interesting than my face.

I looked at his bag too. It was proper leather. He was carrying it like a satchel but with very little imagination it could have been a briefcase. That made me feel self conscious about mine. It was an old blue linen holdall with sparse dewlap trimmings in which my father had once kept his tools for the Morris Traveller.

'Yeh, all right,' I said, answering his original question.

The contempt which had slowly drained from his eyes returned in a flash. Without blinking, he began laughing, a laughter louder than his size should have permitted. I zipped my bag up. The smell of engine oil was beginning to make me feel nauseous.

'My dad's a publishing magnate' he began.

I shuffled, my window seat beginning to feel uncomfortable.

'He attracts money.' He erupted into grating laughter again. But it's the way you tell them and Cal could always do that. Even through puberty Cal kept his confidence when, amidst the confusion of broken voices, volcanic acne and wayward testicles, all around were losing theirs. This despite the fact that he wasn't gaining the inches that to the rest of us were the compensation for surviving adolescence.

He held his satchel up to me like an offering. It smelled of my mum's best handbag – the one she kept in the top drawer of her dressing table and only took out on special occasions or when we went to see Aunty Anne.

'I don't want your bag,' I said.

'Can't have it, so,' he said, snatching it back. His eyes were keenly fixed on my bag now. 'That's what bank robbers use, that is. Or the perpetrators of major heists or Mafia.'

I spat my gum out to near where he was standing.

'Gum's bad for you,' he said. 'It's just glue, you know. It's made out of animals' bones. If you swallow it, it sticks your intestines together, the long one and the small one and you die a long, lingering and extremely painful death.'

There were another five balls of gum in my blazer pocket and I jiggled them around uneasily as I looked to get down from the window. I am sure that I had had cause to doubt my father's wisdom on previous occasions but this is the first such moment I recall, the moment my memory has ascribed a significance. In his campaign against my chewing habit, why had my father never informed me of these facts?

I looked Cal up and down. The half-pint kid with a gold top. It didn't take long.

My blue blazer was frayed and threadbare in places from a wash or two too many, his was shop window clean, his gold braided school badge demanding my attention like a stuck out tongue. My sleeves ended just beyond the elbow, his covered his shirt-cuffs like a suit. My shoes were scuffed from playground football and walking in the gutter, his were gleamingly polished and, I fancied, like his satchel, real leather.

But, I told myself, he was a shrimp, and I, as my father would say, was a good deal bigger and stronger. I jumped down close to him, narrowly missing the masticated blob of gum on the pavement. This, with an emphatic swing of my considerably longer than his legs, I kicked into the road where it stuck to the door of a parked car.

'Bet you can't get up there,' I said to Cal, gesturing at the window.

As I walked off, taking big, tall strides, I looked back over my shoulder to watch him trying and failing. After perhaps half a dozen attempts, he looked back at me and then walked off in the opposite direction, his satchel over his left shoulder and against his right hip. On properly, like a snob school kid. I kicked a stone along the gutter and pretended I was Jimmy Greaves.

A few months later, when I passed the eleven-plus, all was happy, joyous celebration in the Dane household for a period of approximately a day and a half.

My enthusiasm for the exam had blossomed when I learned that it was the difference between travelling several miles on a couple of buses (if you failed) and walking a few hundred yards (if you passed): the difference between leaving the house at eight and eight thirty. I didn't yet appreciate, as I constantly tried to convince myself during my teens, that the exam was a measure of intellectual capacity. It seemed more like the puzzle page of *The Wizard*.

When Cal passed the eleven-plus, his mother and father were sufficiently confident of Beech Park Grammar to allow their son to return to the state system. We bumped into each other on the first day or rather, Cal sought me out. It was in the main assembly hall. I was with the other kids from my primary school concentrating on waiting patiently. There weren't many of us and none of them were particularly friends of mine. I was trying to make conversation with a fat boy with whom my only previous contact had been to yell, 'out of the way, gut-bucket' on the occasion he had strayed onto our playground football pitch.

Cal came up and poked me in the ribs. 'Got any bubble gum?' he asked. A good six months had passed since our first meeting – an eternity at that age – but I remembered him immediately. He did not appear to have grown any.

He still had that leather satchel only now he was carrying it like a briefcase. He also had a new blazer. I tried to ignore him. I switched my fountain pen from one blazer pocket to the other, hoping it might hide the stitching marks left behind when my mother replaced my primary school badge with the new one.

'I know your name,' he said. 'It's Frankie.'

His voice was becoming loud enough to attract attention. The teachers were standing up the front of the hall, taking it in turns to step forward, read out the names of their forms and then lead their charges off to their classroom. There were only enough kids left now for two, maybe three, classes and I was beginning to worry that I had missed my name. There had been a Dean called but the teacher had had some sort of accent. Perhaps he meant Dane.

'Ssh,' I said.

'Got any gum?' he asked again.

I put my hand in my blazer pocket and, keeping my eyes fixed on the front of the hall cupped my hand around a bubble gum ball. I released it into his outstretched hand. The stupid little sod dropped it, of course, and to make matters worse got down on all fours to pursue it like a hound as it skated across the hall.

It completed one tight parabola before rolling across the polished floor like a little green jet propelled marble. At the front of the hall, Mr. Blake trapped it, flicked it up with the toe of his slip-on shoe, caught it and dropped it in the bin. A suppressed titter rippled round the hall. He cast a hard stare in our general direction. I looked ahead like a squaddie. Then Mr. Blake started reading names out. From the corner of my eye, I was aware of Cal smirking, trying to stop himself laughing.

Mr. Blake called my name and, as I followed him out of the hall, I was relieved to see that Cal, whose name I still did not know, was not tagging along.

'So,' said Mr. Blake, dropping back to walk next to me. 'Like bubble gum do we, Mr. Dane?' Once again Cal's advice on the dangers of chewing gum flashed red across my mind. Advice I realised he no longer himself heeded.

The word in the playground at break was that the classes were called out in reverse order and therefore I was in the second from top class. The fat kid told me this while we were waiting to be picked for a football game. After two hours in which we appeared to have done nothing but tell people our names, write our names and spell our names, secondary school had already taught me what six years of primary school had failed to do: the fat kid's name was Hawkins. Obviously nobody was going to pick him for their team but they seemed to have decided that as I was talking to him, I was his friend and so I must be rubbish at footie too. I shuffled along the wall. If they picked him before they picked me I might as well throw myself under a train.

Kids were bagging position. Some were taking off jumpers and blazers, making goalposts and measuring out goals. The bigger kids were juggling with the tennis ball impatient for the game to start. Captains were scratching their heads. I was still standing against the wall.

'Him,' said a boy who was captain because he didn't have a proper school uniform or a tie. He was also bigger and broader than the average first year. I resisted the temptation to look over my shoulder. I smiled. He was picking me. His name was Terry Chambers. I hadn't realised he was at Beech Park because he hadn't been in assembly that morning. Must have sauntered in late as usual. He'd also come from my primary school and he was hard.

'You can go in goal,' he said, turning away.

Now, I am crap in goal. Always was. Still am. My palms were already sweating when a voice piped up, 'I'll go in goal'. It was Cal.

'We've got this kid,' I yelled to everyone bar Cal himself. The game was already under way.

The captain was unsure. 'He's a shrimp,' he said.

'They've got one more player than you have,' said Cal as the ball flew past his right ear. He put out his left hand to try and stop it, flailing a bit like a girl hitting you. He missed it by miles and the ball continued goalward.

'No goal,' shouted Cal. 'Over the post.'

'You've moved the post,' said someone from the other team but Cal had already restarted the game by throwing the ball out to our captain and the incident was over. I think we won the match. I played terribly, even missing an open goal and tripping over a duffel bag but the reason I am sure that we won is that our goalkeeper had moved our goalposts some three feet closer together. Cal, I realised, was in the top class.

Frankie Dane's entry in the most recent edition of The Encyclopaedia Of Rock

Frankie Dane
English, singer-guitarist-songwriter
Born 1959

First exploded onto the London punk scene as one of the Go-Karts. On strength of excellent debut album *Rotten In Denmark* (1978), he and songwriting partner Cal Carter were hailed by the critics as the bards of the new wave – 'the thinking men of punk'. After Carter's untimely death the following year, Dane moved initially to France and disappeared from the rock scene. He returned with one of the biggest popular and critical successes of the 80s in *Stolen Moments* (1984). It went platinum – an achievement he matched with *Phoenix* (1989). His strength is in his unswerving approach unaffected by fashion – both solo albums display the Go-Karts hallmarks of dual guitars, infectious melodies and kitchen sink lyrics. His lack of pretentiousness throughout the 80s was wholly refreshing and now the circle has come around again – Dane is often cited as the Godfather of Grunge or the Great Uncle of Brit-Pop – his limited catalogue, just like that of The Beatles, is emerging as a strength as the runaway success of *Frank* (1998), the recent greatest hits repackaging, proves. Dane enjoys both longevity and integrity – a combination, rare in the rock industry, which could yet see him become the biggest of them all.

3

Beech Park, the present day

The water splashes off the proud white hood and laps against the window, coming in long slow rushes like waves on an easy beach. Brushes like hairy paint-rollers, vertical Dougal dogs, grunt into action, licking the fibreglass and chrome body, swallowing it. Soap runs down the glass. For a moment, foam and suds are everywhere, vision obscured. Then more water. Violently. Jets taming us from all directions. Clean, clean water. The car wash is nearly over.

Anyone watching would think us business men. Jonathan is regularly unconventional in contrasting jacket and tie, broadly cut, perhaps an advertising executive. He's got some sort of a souped up sports car with a twin this and turbo that and a top speed more than double the legal maximum. You'll know him as my regular bass player; he's actually my manager too.

I remove my hat to mop my brow. It's a warm morning and I am uncomfortable. For a moment, Jonathan's car beaming in the morning sun reminds me of Cal's old red Ford Escort and a dawn over Durham town.

From where we are standing, the car gleams, its chassis ready to pounce. But anyone looking closely, looking at the parts seen only by timid cats, would discover some secrets: caked on grease and dirt and features slightly off-centre. That's the trouble with looking closely at anything – perhaps that's why the modern world so lacks enthusiasm for it – but that is what I as an autobiographer am doomed to do.

Hand in my jacket pocket, I switch on and off the small cassette recorder that I have purchased to help me write this book. They're already saying it will be a best seller. My publishers and the music press, that is. So Jonathan tells me. I've stopped taking much notice of the music mags. In fact, I dislike them more now that I'm a 'true original' with 'integrity' than I did when I was 'derivative', 'unambitious' and 'smugly overweight'.

Jonathan says the record company want me to record another album. 'They're phoning twice a day,' he keeps saying. 'Before they go to lunch and four hours later when they get back.' I can't help. Not until I've got this book out of my system. Maybe never.

I want everything in the open so we are on our way to see Tony Beale, our Artists and Repertoire man at my record company Phonodisc to tell him what I'm planning. He'll be assuming we're going to tell him the new album's finally ready. I have no respect for Tony – he's an Oxbridge-educated chump – but I am nervous nonetheless about telling him anything different.

'I shouldn't bring it to London,' Jonathan begins as we shuffle along the Strand. He's talking about the car. With the windows down, we are at the optimum height to inhale the exhaust from the vehicle in front. 'You can't leave it anywhere. You put your life-savings in a meter and ten minutes later some bastard on piece-rate claps a wheel clamp on. Or you put it where they've sledgehammered the tops off the meters and come back to find the chassis on bricks. That's if you can find it at all. Don't know what's worse.' His hand hovers menacingly over the gear stick.

As we crawl past Old Compton Street a couple of guys wave.

'Your expectant fans, Frank,' says Jon, but I don't see it like that. To me, they're waving at him.

'I don't know why we didn't get the bus,' I say, fiddling about with the cassette recorder. It's voice-activated and cuts off the first word of every new sentence. I am contemplating recording the meeting with Tony. Lighting the blue touchpaper of my career and retiring might make a significant moment for my book.

'We didn't get the bus because...' Jonathan turns to peer at me over his Raybans. They have a curious medicinal green tint. 'Well, when was the last time you actually got a bus, Frank. I think they've been abolished.'

'There's one.'

'Of course, they have them up here. For the tourists. When is that arsehole going to move? Anyway the meeting's today not next week.'

Jonathan swings the car off the road into an underground car park. He operates the gear stick for the first time in half-an-hour. 'Should be an attendant here. It's expensive enough.'

I'm trying to relax. Remind myself that Tony is not what he was. He used to be sixpenny sharp, with fine judgement and a natural authority, making and breaking teenage hearts. Safety-pins and tie pins. Bollinger and bitter. Out of marketing meetings into The Vortex without missing a stride. But that was then.

And all these years later, I could bank with Coutts if I wanted to. Nobody would ask squirming questions or quibble over the number of noughts in my current account. But I cough and shuffle in the glossy leather passenger seat either wishing I had or feeling like I've already got a great mouthful of bubble gum. I still want to please. I know that Tony is not going to be happy and it sickens me. And it sickens me that it sickens me.

'I still think of you as my little Van Morrison, Frankie,' Tony will say as he always says at some point during our meetings, spitting the end of his cigar into the wastebasket like a pea from a shooter. 'You split the bollocking band, do one like a whatsit, Lord Lucan, and out *Astral Weeks*, *Astral Weeks*. Fucking brilliant. And again. Sod it. Like a fucking little Jack Horner. You keep pulling out the plums, Frankie boy. Keep pulling out those plums.'

But even the liberal plunder of his limited but graphic collection of curses is insufficient to take the cultured edge from his accent. He is, quite simply, an affected fucker, and despite his having overseen my career since the beginning, our only point of contact is when we shake hands.

Tony nearly spits out his preprandial gin when I tell him. Nearly. Would have done if he wasn't supposed to be on the wagon. I enjoy the moment. Freudian, I am. Not Sigmund but schaden. Tony is

27

getting old. He hasn't signed anyone decent for years. Still thinks a sample is something you provide for the doctor. If I dry up, what then? I can read it in the lines of his face. If he can't do the business with that difficult bastard whose pal topped himself...

'A book! Most fucking rock fans are illiterate,' he splutters. He fixes his eyes on mine. Slowly, he places the drink down on his leather-topped mahogany desk and looks at me as if I were a lump of excrement or a roadie.

'Actually, most of them are ABC1 white collar professionals,' chirps Jon.

'I'm all washed-up,' I say, churning on the clichés, Tony-esque. 'All played out.'

Tony changes by inches between our meetings: a couple more around the waist, a couple less at the temples and crown. Looking at his play-doh cheeks, I wonder if he *moves* by inches too. I'd like to be able to relate that his face turned red with anger but it was rosy red already – three parts alcohol, two parts cocaine and one part tropical sunshine. Tony flexes his nostrils. 'Shit. Fuck. Jesus.'

He inclines an unfocused gaze back towards me. 'Fucking illiterate,' he says, shaking his head like an ageing uncle at a loss with the ways of the world.

'There are no more songs, Tony. It's as simple as that.'

We were all young once and, if Jon and Cal and I had been hungry, Tony was ravenous. Now, heavier, tireder and desperate, he smiles. 'Frankie, Frankie, believe me: you should be sitting at a mixing desk not a word-processor. You're an artist not a fantasist.' I tighten my resolve not to speak. 'You make fantasies, Frankie. You are a fantasy. You're a. Shit. Bollocks.' He looks at Jon again. There's something in their eyes that's like parents with a wayward son.

'Tony,' I say after a pause. 'Don't get so hung up on product. This is the age of the multinational. Phonodisc own the publishing house anyway. You'll still get your profit-share.'

'Don't fuck with me Frankie as if this is just some bollocking financial kiss my arse relationship. We're talking...' Once again the rage evaporates to be replaced by a slow shake of the fleshy jowl. 'We're talking rock'n'roll here. The lifeblood of a generation. Fuck.'

I look into his eyes and he doesn't see me because that's it. The one who's all played out is Tony. After a moment of heavyweight silence, I pick up my hat and Jon and I leave, closing the door carefully as if on grief.

All the young punks got new boots and contracts, according to the Clash. We certainly did. A contract. An advance. Everyone within five years of your age and ten miles of your school claiming that they were in your class. It's a dream, until the second single bombs and you're back behind the counter at Dixons faster than you can say 'one-hit wonder'. And if you are successful, it doesn't really change. Things just get bigger. The same feudal principle remains: they own you and they can finish you. It's hard to take control unless being finished doesn't bother you.

The Go-Karts split up in disarray following Cal's death. Tony says that he hasn't touched amphetamines since. (This is probably true though he's touched, caressed, manhandled and mauled everything else.) Our first, our only, album *Rotten In Denmark* was still riding high in the charts and had gone gold.

The rest is the omniscient H. Five years later Frankie Dane and the Denmarks returned with *Stolen Moments*. Pleasantly surprised, the critics said. Thought he'd be nothing without Carter. We did it again with *Phoenix*. And sold even more albums. Now, as the tabloids might say, I am telling it all. I am sitting at my desk, I am sorting my papers and I am rewinding my cassette recorder. It is time for the truth.

First, some starters for ten. Frankie Dane. That's Francis Derek Dane. Francis was my mother's choice, Derek, my father's. He let her have her own way on that one. Nothing if not reasonable, my father. He told me that himself. 'Let her decide everything,' he would say. 'Except what's important. And let you decide what's important. That's the way.'

FD Dane it would have said had I been a cricketer. Born 6th June 1959 in south-east London. Education: Beech Park Grammar and the Open University. Club: Tottenham Hotspur FC.

My mother comes from a village in County Durham, her father a miner. He ought to have died before I was born, victim of a tragedy of folk song proportions but it wasn't like that. I am the spawn of the families who don't have stories. Where there is no heroism save existence and no passion greater than good sense. No glory days or vital hours. Few enough poignant moments. On our rare sorties north, my grandfather was always to be found sat in a tight little chair wheezing away, wasting away and always, to my grandmother's disappointment, letting his tea go cold. He may have been a big man once – his great arms hung over the wooden arms of the chair almost to the floor – but one Sunday he wasn't there any more and I didn't really notice until we were driving home.

My father grew up beneath the monochrome monoxide skies of Battersea (or South Chelsea as the estate agents now like to call it). His father worked in Covent Garden fruit market in an administrative capacity. I remember my Grandad's proud voice – me on his lap, his glass of stout in his hand. 'Porter this is, Frankie. Named after the porters in Covent Garden.'

'Are you a porter, Grandad?'

'No, son. I'm a book-keeper.' Too dull he was even to lug around potatoes.

My own father, a meat and two veg man but never one for fruit, didn't follow his father into the market. Until his recent retirement my dad drove for a living. Not black taxis but minicabs. Park Cabs was one of the first in London, apparently. Before that he drove lorries.

Both my grandparents with a smug Protestant symmetry that continues down the line produced one of each. My mum's brother Uncle Alan lives up north, my father's sister Aunty Anne just around the corner. As a child I used to wish it were the other way round. While I couldn't understand why when granted the freedom of the skies his pigeons should want to fly home so rapidly and repeatedly, at least Uncle Alan with his coot and his crisp country mornings offered something of interest. Aunty Anne just had her endless cups of coffee.

I was an only child, of course. My father, cheated by a handful of months of the chance to serve in combat, did his homefront bit for blighty with a diligence that never abated. He rationed even children and although I remember my mother asking me a couple of times if I would like 'someone to play with', no sister or brother materialised.

Today, I'm lucky enough to have two of everything. I have two homes – a semi in London and the apartment in Paris where we lived for a handful of years in the early eighties. Despite my dislike of motoring, I have two cars. And, I have, in the family tradition, two, as they say, lovely kids – Philip and Rebecca.

I also have a wife, Wendy, elder sister of Cal Carter. When I tell you that we have been married for nearly twenty years, the mathematical among you will calculate correctly that we took the plunge in the wake of Cal's death. Her first husband – a gentleman named Julian – could not handle being married to the sister of a pop star and he could handle being married to the sister of a dead pop star even less. She, like her father, works in publishing.

I tease Wendy that she got lumbered with the workhorse of the partnership when the creative one died. Certainly, that was the media's response once it drew breath long enough to reflect. 'Workhorse?' she says raising an already arched eyebrow still further. 'When are you going to do some work then?'

'When you can drive directly to the supermarket without getting lost,' I smile. 'I mean we come every fortnight.'

'Yeh, and they reroute the one-way system every week.'

I have been criticised because my songs are still about chip shops and vinegar kisses, Babycham and darts, broken hearts and rubber band engagement rings. 'Are we supposed to credit that a man with four platinum albums regularly adjourns to his local fish and chip emporium?' scoffed the reviewer in *The Independent*. Well, the answer, at the risk of making my family sound like The Brady Bunch, is yes. Or, at least, Wendy and the kids do. I usually stay at home and prepare a side salad with vinaigrette dressing. Wild man of rock. In general, we still live much as we did when Wendy was married to another and I was a civil servant with a battered guitar beneath his bed. The same part of town. A slightly bigger house.

You may have all my albums (and if you do, thanks very much) but I doubt you know what I look like – not any more anyway. There isn't an accurate photograph of me in circulation taken later than about 1983. I have a range of glasses, plain and tinted. And I have the hat collection from hell. Trilbies. Boaters. Panamas. Fedoras. Baseball caps. Balaclavas. Berets. Some of these I have been pictured in, some not, and ne'er the twain. Some of the locals know who I am, of course they do – the few who have been here as long as I have. Others, those who have asked directly, think that like my wife I work in publishing – proofreading or editing from home – but few ask. People don't. Suburbs, you see.

I haven't toured since the Go-Karts broke up. I reappear when a new album comes out and do the TV and the interviews, but I don't make a big deal out of my lifestyle or call myself a recluse. That's the way to guarantee that you get hounded. Nobody thinks my low-profile is a matter of policy. Indeed, I've never mentioned it at all until now. The truth, you see. That's what I want. After I've been on the box or done the pics for what they amusingly call the lifestyle mags, I shave the beard off and allow the apparently receding hairline to grow back again. I think that is the secret of my success: I make myself look less attractive for the media and who'd credit that?

Once, a make-up girl noticed the follicled pores on the top of my head, the dots of hair, and blabbed. This gave rise to the 'Dane Has Hair Transplant' story in the mid-eighties. It was quite the opposite of the truth but it kept my name alive between the two albums. One of the tabloids was ready to camp on my doorstep to monitor my visits to the trichologist but they never turned up. Jonathan says they found my address easily enough but the editor couldn't believe that with all my spondys I still lived in Beech Park. He assumed the info was out of date and sacked the researcher. Dull anonymity – it's the family trait.

Pedal Power Pop

by Ian Martyn-Baker
(from the New Rock Journal, *1978)*

Careering. They mean it, maaan. That's the Go-Karts. Go-getters, going places, all four. Places this scribe has never seen. We're in Goddard's Pie and Mash emporium in Greenwich near that big boat. Their choice, natch. Find it on the map and make it a shrine. These boys are gonna be BIG. Or should be. One day.

They're talking of meat and eels, gravy and liquor and some of the most infectious punk-pop this side of the safety-pin. Calum Carter, the little kid with the Telecaster, has hair longer than regulation but the hippie taunts don't harm him. He downs his cup of rosie. The chips aren't on these shoulders. 'If ripped T's are the new uniform we want nothing of it,' he says to communal nodding. 'Meet the new boss, same as the old boss,' the Go-Karts sing Peter Townsend to the accompaniment of Mr. Goddard's LSD cash register (sic). No new wave-old wave snobbery here.

Carter continues, 'It's part of what we're about.' He picks up a battered brown briefcase and puts it down on the table. 'This is where I keep the songs that will single-handedly bring down the establishment,' he says with an ironic chuckle. I dare to mention tongues and cheeks and don't get my pie and two mash upended on my head. It's a little refreshing.

Frankie Dane, Carter's songwriting partner, the one who plays the Townsend/Weller-esque Rickenbacker, is wearing a pin-striped jacket two sizes too small over his Too-Thick-for-University T. 'It was Cal's dad's,' he explains. (The jacket, natch) 'We're not in favour of that suburban conformity, any more than we're in favour of everyone wearing biker jackets and bondage strides or tightly knotted ties. Or flares for that matter.' Bassist Jon Waters has a pair of loon pants broader than Jimmy Page's ego and Carter himself sports a leather jacket. The point is well-made.

There's a quiet – and not so quiet when CC's in full flow – confidence about south-east London's brightest hope. No dedicated followers these. Individuals all. They even cover Presley. Three times. Tonight they'll be packing them in in Wardour Street. First-time headliners at the Marquee and they'll be opening with 'You Were Always On My Mind'. That's confidence.

'We usually do 'Promised Land' as an encore but tonight we might just do it second,' says drummer Charlie Ball. *[They did too – Ed]*

But these are no worshippers of the cabaret King neither. The Presley numbers get the same frenetic treatment as the originals, chainsaw guitars wrestling with the melodies.

Some people say you're too small to front a band, Cal. Is that the reason for the on-stage aggro with Jon here? 'We want to be known for playing good songs,' Carter says emphatically. 'Anybody worried about that is stupid,' says Dane, interrupting. 'The same people who say women can't be in groups and that you have to be able to play a diminished seventh augmented fifth twice removed to be a good guitar player.'

'No sweat,' smiles Carter, twisting his fingers into bizarre positions round the neck of a ketchup bottle.

They seem too happy with themselves to be as angry as they claim and somehow they don't quite sit (or stand or pogo) with their contemps. The Clash eating mash, The Jam saying what you wear doesn't matter (yikes!), The Pistols praising Presley? I don't think.

Phonodisc are said to be interested in the Go-Karts with the original 'Rotten In Denmark' earmarked as the single. This boy hopes that these boys get that little break they need but, as Calum Carter sings, nay roars, at the climax of their set, 'Do not adjust your scepticism. Do not adjust your mind-set. Do not adjust.' Can rock'n'roll adjust just enough to let the Go-Karts in?

4

After two weeks, I moved classes.

Mr. Parker was rearranging the tobacco dispenser at the back of his kiosk, a task to which he appeared to devote most of his non-serving time. He smiled his policeman's smile when he noticed me lurking. I didn't like to go too close. The edge of the counter extended a foot or so beyond the booth and when I was small I was forever cracking my skull on it, the blue paint flaking off into my hair.

'Is that the usual, young man?' he asked. Mr. Parker always wore a bow-tie.

I nodded, running my finger along the narrow strip of wood which was supposed to stop the newspapers falling on the floor. The nails were clogged with the fibres of inattentive sweaters.

'Mind you don't get a splinter.'

My pockets were full of foreign coins and football cards as usual. I sorted through them trying to assemble the right money. Mr. Parker sold a couple of newspapers to men in a hurry.

'You'll have noticed you've lost your resting place, I dare say,' he said as I pushed my little pile of coins across the counter.

I turned towards my window. I could guess from the shadowy shape pressed against the glass that somebody else was already sitting there and I had a fair idea who, too. Rapping on the pane with my knuckles as I passed, I strode casually out of the station.

Casually for Mr. Parker's benefit – he didn't strike me as the sort of man who approved of haste.

But it wasn't Cal looking down at me as I emerged onto the pavement. In my seat was his briefcase. He looked at me expectantly. I tossed him a ball of gum and popped another into my own mouth.

'You're coming in our class, you know,' he said.

'I know,' I said. It was the first I had heard of it.

'Mr. Jackson told us yesterday at home time.'

I nodded. Sometimes, most times, Cal sounded like a refugee from one of those Enid Blyton books which my mother brought home from the library and which my father discouraged me from reading. Mr. Jackson was Jackson or Jacko and only primary school kids talked about home time. Yet at the same time I admired Cal's unorthodox language, his unashamedly schoolboy language. I sweated and squirmed, struggling to ensure that nobody ever noticed me. Cal gave the impression of deliberately choosing words that would attract attention – as if his size were not enough.

Cal looked up at the seat and then at me without saying anything. I looked at the wrist where my watch would have been had I not forgotten it again. 'We'd best get to school,' I said, handing him his briefcase.

Cal and I walked up the hill. I gave him another bubble gum. 'What did Jacko say to you, exactly?' I asked.

'He just said we were having three boys from Mr. Blake's class and then he asked three boys from our class to stay behind afterwards for a quick word.' He raised his voice slightly as he said 'a quick word' and shook his head from side to side at the piteous inadequacy of adult euphemisms. 'They're being chucked out,' he explained.

'Who are the other two from Blakey's class,' I said, still fishing for some sort of confirmation. 'Apart from me, that is.' I didn't know if he was playing me along or not.

'He didn't say,' said Cal, swinging his satchel-cum-briefcase back and forth. He sniffed. 'But I know you're one. You're much smarter than those der brains in Mr. Blake's class.'

'Right,' I said. My hand, sticky in my blazer pocket, groped around for another ball of gum but there was only one left. I gave it to Cal and dropped the bag onto the pavement.

'Don't be a litterbug,' said Cal. He barely had to bend to retrieve the bag. 'That's what the bins are for. And it spreads diseases.'

I had to bite on my lip to stop myself from saying sorry.

Cal was right. That morning after assembly, Mr. Blake took me and a couple of other kids aside and told us we were being moved to another class. 'In Beech Park, we like to talk about moving sideways,' he said but he looked dead proud.

'Probably thinks it's something that he's done for you in the last two weeks,' Cal snorted when I told him at breaktime.

'Now, I know you lads won't let me down,' Blake said as he led us down the corridor to the more rarefied atmosphere of the annexe block. The three of us behind Blake, we walked through the main school, along its tiled floors and up its concrete stairways. It was a great privilege to be out of the classroom during lessons.

In the annexe block, the old school, it was cooler and darker as if curtains were closing out the morning sunlight. We moved to single file to climb the softly spiralling staircase to Jacko's room. I had never seen a spiral staircase before. It was a staircase that should have been in a museum.

I put my hand onto the gleaming bannister. I wasn't losing my balance but it was as if I needed to steady myself. The brown wood was gently gnarled, the grain flowing along its length disappearing in darker unpredictable whirlpools.

I sat next to Cal and by breaktime we were best mates. I felt happy – no, content – and Cal bought me a wholly-coated chocolate digestive biscuit, a plain one. The one with the red wrapper.

'Thanks for all the bubble gum,' he said.

We walked home together. He told me all about their teachers, their habits, the classwork, the homework, the other pupils. He didn't need to tell me about the subtly different way in which the teachers talked to us compared with how they talked to Mr. Blake's class because I had noticed that immediately. At the station, from where we were to go our separate ways, we paused, both looking up at the window ledge, my window seat.

'Are you getting up there, then?' he asked

I looked down at him. 'No, it's fine, you can.'

'Right,' he said, not moving. Cal's hands were in his pockets and in deep like a playground loner. It was as if he didn't want to meet my eyes.

'Here,' I said, 'let me.' I put my bag down and picked him up – he wasn't much heavier than the bag – and put him up on the ledge. He smiled broadly.

'Thanks, Frankie,' he said.

I stood with my back against the wall as Cal made himself comfortable in my usual seat. I couldn't see his face but I could tell by his ebullient chatter that he was enjoying himself, commenting on an urban landscape that was familiar to me but which he had never seen quite like that before. When I did turn to face him he was sitting very comfortably. I noticed this because I was becoming increasingly aware of my own discomfort when I sat up there. The window was not as cosy as it once had been. It was becoming cramped, forcing my back into unnatural positions. I had begun to worry that I would finish up like Auntie Anne, a walking set-square.

'Do you want to come to my house?' Cal asked.

Cal lived less than a quarter of a mile away from me, in the big houses next to the park that gave our suburb its name but, because the railway line was in the way and you had to go all the way up to the footbridge, it seemed much further. The house was bigger than the one I live in now and it impressed me then as if it were a palace. I knew that there were big houses on the other side of the track but until then 'big' was just a word. The roads – you couldn't call them streets – were wider and a different colour, pinky-brown with a gravel finish not like our black asphalt. You couldn't see half the houses because they stood at the end of their drives, obscured by hedges and thick white walls. Sometimes the chimneys were all you could see. They were red like great Lego bricks or tall and square as sentries. Approaching Cal's giant front door, their path like an unfinished road, I felt much as I had felt climbing the spiral staircase that morning.

'My mum will make orange juice,' he said. 'Well, it's not real orange juice, of course, it's a concentrate, a powder.'

'Right,' I said. Cal's mum. I hadn't realised there'd be a mum, hadn't realised there'd be people. I wondered if they'd be as big as the house. Proportionately. I couldn't imagine Cal with a mother. I couldn't imagine anything as my heart sank slowly in my throat like a depth charge.

I followed Cal up the steps to the front door. The steps seemed like cliffs. He pushed the heavy door open and his mother was standing there. I saw stockinged legs like the housekeeper in *Tom And Jerry* but instead of slippers, stilettos. My eyes turned away from my own feet and upwards. She was wearing a peach dress. I stumbled over the final step. 'Hello, Mrs. Carter,' I said, my outstretched hand clutching at the hem of her dress as I fell to the richly-carpeted floor.

'Mother,' said Cal, bestriding my prostrate form, 'this is Frankie that I've been telling you about. I don't think he's feeling very well. He wants to sit down.'

'Wouldn't a chair be more comfortable?' said Mrs. Carter, smiling at us both.

Cal took me up to his bedroom. He was looking at me in a curious way. 'I'll show you where I go when I'm not well,' he smiled. 'Or even when I am.'

Inside, tables and cabinets were everywhere covered with books, models, games and odds and ends like conkers and marbles. His Subbuteo teams were lined across a shelf as if they were meeting the Queen before the cup final. Posters obscured the wall paper - maps of the UK, the world and the stars in the northern hemisphere, diagrams of the human body and photographs of Apollo 8. But it wasn't a child's sense of order – even Aunty Anne would have had to concede that Cal's room was tidy – it was like a museum. Items were labelled with relevant information. *Found near Bognor*, it said on an unusually shaped piece of gnarled driftwood. *Nelson's flagship at Trafalgar when it was already 40 years old. Now at dry dock in Portsmouth*, it said on an Airfix model of The Victory.

'My mum says I'm a bit of a hoarder, he said following my awestruck gaze as it crept around the room.

He opened the door of a massive wardrobe. The largest piece of furniture in his bedroom by far, it was really tall and ran virtually the length of one wall. It was made from a dark wood ornately carved with gargoyle-like heads for door handles. Inside, the wardrobe contained not shirts and trousers, shoes and underwear but a beanbag, a tiny bedside table and sundry nicknacks. Cal had decked the interior out like a little room, a den. The back and sides were decorated with multicoloured printed fabrics and posters. He gestured towards the beanbag and I sat down. Then from beneath one of the drapes he produced a fishing stool which he put up and sat on himself. In the corner was a small cardboard box lined with polystyrene tiles. From it Cal removed two cans of Coca-Cola and handed me one. I'd never had a whole can of Coke to myself – I usually had to share with my father.

'Can you shut it?' I asked, fumbling with the can-opener, stabbing at the tin.

'Of course,' he said. Attached to the back of each door was a curtain tassle. Cal tugged on both and we were in darkness. There was the flash of a match and my host's face beaming at me. Candelabra were mounted all around as in a medieval castle. Cal lit each one in turn. The peace was tangible and terrible. I suddenly felt as if I was in a horror film, that I was actually breathing in the shadows around me, inhaling the grey of their shimmer. I thought I was inside a coffin. There was the smell of burning, the ghostly, flickering light. I was aware of Cal but no longer able to see him. The can was ice-cold in my hand.

As I tried to struggle to my feet the beanbag seemed like a live thing, catching my hand, pulling me back, swallowing my heels. And then I rolled over. The door flew open as I hit it and the next thing I knew, I was lying in Cal's bedroom at the foot of his bed.

'What's the matter?' he asked, towering over me once again. In his hand was the expired match, black and disintegrating. 'It's my camp. What's the matter, Frankie? Are you afraid of the dark?'

The can was still in my hand. I hadn't spilled a drop. 'No.' I sat up and took a long drink, my eyes fixed on the Coke. 'It was great,' I said, after a bit. 'I think it was the candles. Isn't that a bit dangerous? You know, fire.'

'Possibly,' said Cal. 'But then I am afraid of the dark so it's the lesser of two evils.' He touched his can to mine like a toast and started laughing. With both doors open, Cal's camp looked out of place and ridiculous. The candle light was as meagre in the daylight as the wardrobe's tiny furnishings.

'You're in good company, anyway,' said Cal. 'Jon didn't like the wardrobe much either.'

5

The family take shelter in a Georgian doorway. They are inappropriately dressed for the sudden sheets of rain. Packamacs and cagoules not seen since last summer and a small transparent brolly decorated with pastel pink and yellow flowers are scant protection when the streets flow like rivers.

Father swears as he steps in a puddle. Mother is fastening reluctant zips and sealing wayward studs. Son slides along the freshly polished step flowing blood red in the rain. We are family.

Wendy grabs at Philip, pulling him back beneath the shelter afforded by the pillared arch. The boy's irritation is replaced with curiosity as he notices the building's entryphone. He stabs at the bell with an eager finger.

'Beam me up, Scotty.'

Wendy catches my eye. The umbrella nearly catches hers. 'Careful sweetheart,' she says to Rebecca who is battling with the thing. She is smiling at me conspiratorially. 'What do Jeremy Thorpe and Captain Kirk have in common?' she asks quietly. This is my family. These are the moments. The perfectly ordinary moments that I once despised and now crave.

'What, Mum. Captain Kirk?'

On the other side of the road, a man liberally coated in black leather and with a green Mohican haircut tackles his own umbrella. He could be stripping down a rifle. Umbrella, black, raising the blood pressure, for the purpose of. The man's very presence on the streets of the capital would be sufficient to have my father screaming for the return of national service. The canvas inflates and expires like a battle-torn flag. His mohican droops.

'Can't you... Gordon give it to me,' says the waif of a woman half-jogging along beside him, her green leggings pumping away like frogs legs. Her long dark hair is pasted to her face and black leather jacket.

'It seems to be lifting,' says Wendy. She's not referring to their brolly.

I climb up onto the glossy black railings erected to prevent us trespassing on the block's concrete forecourt, my feet on the bottom rung. Over the park hovers a hazy hole of clear sky.

'Let's go,' I say.

'This is the voice of the Mysterons,' says Philip darkly into the entryphone.

'Pardon?' replies the entryphone. 'Is that you, Lord Mowbray?'

I nod towards the park and the kids shoot ahead, wrestling with their now constricting waterproofs. Philip casts a last look over his shoulder.

Wendy holds my hand as we pick our way along a puddle-pattered pavement. These are the moments. We are attending our local Country Fayre – a recent addition to the civic life of a borough that hasn't seen a farm since Doomsday. I wish I was wearing sensible shoes.

As we enter the park it becomes clear that we are just one of several parties of rain-ravaged stragglers tramping across the sodden grass, all heading towards an as yet uncertain central point. I can hear the sounds of the fairground. I can smell the flavours of a hundred fast food stands. I can see marquees, a gymkhana and three vintage traction engines. Damp pilgrims, we could indeed be going to a medieval fayre to sell our sheep, children and home-made mead. There's something medieval about us. Perhaps, there's something medieval about this whole business. I remember coming to a function this big in this park once before. I came back from France specially for it. The People's March for Jobs. There are no Socialist Worker Party banners this time. There's a range of drapes and throws hand woven in Mali instead, pots and figurines and waistcoats and little wooden plaques decorated with names like Charlotte, Rachel and Rebecca.

'There they are,' my daughter turns and shouts. 'Our school steel band.'

Wendy laughs. Our eyes meet. The mud squelches beneath our feet. 'This is all rather... '

'Yeh, ' I say. '1983 and all that.'

In 1983, Wendy and I returned home. It started with Jon sending us a postcard. It was blank except for a little red sticker in the corner. Where Will You Be On October 22? it asked. Then he called. Told us it was to be CND's biggest demonstration yet and he'd got me booked to play. One of the smart boys, Jon. How could I refuse? When I'd come back for the People's March I was alone. Stood staring at the stage willing reluctant tears down my face. We'd been to so many of these things together that Cal's absence was stark in a way that it never could be in Barbes or Pigalle. It made me realise I had to play. I had to get up on a stage by myself. Jon gave me the chance.

They say we were half a million strong that day and me, I was that tiny little figure on a distant stage with the out-of-tune guitar. I didn't know then, as I emerged onto the scaffold platform and rose above the crowd – the wind and the waving arms and the rolling ocean of faces taking my breath away – that this was the high water mark. A last hurrah. The super soaraway free-market funtastical eighties were upon us like rapists – the decade I really made it big.

Things have changed since the heady demo days when The Clash or Steel Pulse, Elvis Costello or the Go-Karts capped the politics with a punky reggae party for the radical. Things seem blunter now, lacking definition. We shrugged our shoulders when Thatcher won the 1979 election, took a deep drag and passed the joint on, but the future somehow seemed clearer. Now I can think about Jim Callaghan and almost get nostalgic. With our slight pictures of history, we took progress as read. 'Callaghan's cracking' Cal sang in 'Rotten In Denmark', little realising what would crawl out of the rifts and rents.

Look at Philip, in the queue for a hot dog already. Look at Rebecca, waving at her friends and singing along with their steel drum version of 'We Can Work It Out'. Steel drums are such happy instruments. Look around, this is a nice family occasion and I am lucky to be sharing it with mine. Lucky but those years nag like an wasp. The anarchists are accountants, the Marxists prefer Spencer, the girls in tactfully torn T-shirts and bright tight jeans run personnel departments. The greens are blue and the reds just a little rosy round the cheeks.

'Did they have beer guts in the seventies?' I ask, looking around. The beer tent is promising a three hour 'happy hour'.

Wendy smiles. 'Julian did but then he was a bit ahead of his time.'

I squeeze her hand – small in mine but not petite or in any way weak. I admire Wendy, respect her resilience as much as I love her. She breaks free, opening her money belt to drop a handful of coins into a bucket. The collector offers her a Save Our Woodland sticker in the same design as his white sweatshirt.

Ahead of us, the assembly are limbering down from the downpour. The sun is threatening. Jackets come off. Umbrellas retreat. There is the obligatory feedback from the PA system, a sound which reminds me with a tug of Cal. His easy politics contrasted so appealingly with my family's confusion of prejudices. Rebecca's music teacher is up on the stage now, leading the applause for the band, taking a modest shuffle of a bow. He's a big black guy – someone who obviously knows something about music and earns a pittance for it. How very different from the life of our own dear rock star. Wendy is back at my side. We tighten our grip on each other's hand. From the smattering of applause for Rebecca's classmates, a cheer erupts. Heads look up and roar as a familiar haircut strides onto the stage. It's a TV weather girl with a grin so broad you can see her flossed teeth from here.

'Not that old slapper,' says Rebecca.

'Can we go to the Cartoon Plus tent, Mum?' asks Philip.

So while our kids get their fix of animated American propaganda, we wander around the craft village. There's a CD stall. At first I can't find my own stuff but when I do I'm pleased to find that I still qualify for a separate plastic divider of my own with Frankie Dane printed on it. Surreptitiously I move a couple of copies of *Phoenix* to the front of the row. I buy some of the product by artists that Jonathan has mentioned to me. Wendy, clutching an offcut of material that will 'make a lovely curtain' laughs and remarks once again how I never play any of the albums that I already have. She says the money would be better off going to a good cause. I say that my sense of worth in myself and my life is a good cause. Wendy looks at me with her get-over-it look. But it's short – it's always short – and it transmutes into a smile. A moment later Philip reappears asking if he can have the new Lacto Bacto and the Psychodelic Yogurt Potz CD. Rebecca asks if Philip has any taste at all in his spotty juvenile head.

A beautiful day but it weighs upon me, its pleasantness too much to bear. These are wonderful moments, simple moments that I can never enjoy. They are even harder for me to record here than those from the past because as I write I think perhaps they're right, those conjurers of cliché. You have to move on. You can never go back. Alone with that littleness between the ears, I am terrified that they might be right.

6

By the time girls and examinations replaced football and football as our principal subjects of conversation, only Cal ever sat on the window ledge at the station. Only he could fit. I assume Cal welcomed these discursive developments. He never knew a great deal about football anyway, nor was he particularly interested in it.

At that time, standing around on street corners was not yet popular enough to be considered a sign of delinquency so every schoolday at four o'clock, Cal was to be found in his window seat. I was always there too, usually leaning against the wall of the station or squatting beside it, my chewing gum replaced by a cigarette. Not quite at Cal's feet but closer to him than anyone else. We were the self-styled smart boys, grammar school intellects with longer than regulation hair and there were five of us.

Terry Chambers managed to appear both gaunt and slightly overweight at the same time. His black plimsolls – the cheesy descendents of the ones that had served him so well in playground football – smelled like a sewer and he had a mind to match. Terry would shift his weight from leg to leg, swaying as he slandered each of us in turn, our sisters and our mothers with tales of all manner of sordid sexual activity.

Charlie Ball was about my height and had a receding hairline by the age of sixteen. For this reason, he would become the one who always went to the bar. His brow furrowed, his hand jerking automatically to brush back a nonexistent fringe, Charlie would try to keep a jumping bean of a cigarette behind his ear while calculating our collective debt on a bar mat. He rarely made a fuss about it and so was rarely paid.

Jonathan Waters always stood slightly apart from the rest of us, perhaps on the edge of the road, still juggling a tennis ball even as the mock O-levels came, went and gave way to the real thing. He fancied himself as an actor.

Cal was a midget, Charlie was bald and Terry was a pervert but basically I liked those guys. I wasn't so sure about Jonathan Waters. Had he not been one of us, one of the smart lads, I would have hated him. Jonathan, you see, had humiliated me.

It was during a drama lesson. My second week in the top class. Cal was off sick and as kids scurried across the hall for partners Jonathan, like me, seemed to be surrounded by an invisible forcefield rendering him unapproachable. Jon still had his prep school badge on one blazer pocket and the Beech Park Grammar badge on the other so he looked different, aloof, like a general or something, perhaps that was why. Or perhaps it was the fact that in drama lessons he took after his father, the leading light in the local amateur dramatic society. For one production, Anthony Waters had enjoyed eighteen credits in the programme (one of which was for 'human skull provided by'). Jon and I were left looking around despairingly before forming a reluctant pair.

We were told to mime – mime something that was important to us and to try to guess each other's. Jonathan mimed 'I'm going skiing at Christmas'. Overeager hands tearing beribboned wrapping paper; eyes beaming like a delighted child (or an axe-wielding maniac); ski-poles and a slalom wiggle of the backside; the sequences punctuated by bouts of pointing at himself. It wasn't difficult to guess what it was. It was difficult for me to guess why exactly it was important. I wasn't wholly sure I knew what it was. What did you do on a skiing holiday? Did you have to live in an igloo, for example?

'You're going skiing at Christmas,' I said, commencing my own mime. He looked a little disappointed.

I was miming 'Sitting On The Dock Of The Bay'. I'd heard it the night before on my transistor radio: a birthday present, red, six-inches square and tuned to Radio Luxembourg. I would listen in the dark, head under the bed clothes, tuning in, like thousands of kids across the country, to a different world.

I really loved 'Sitting On The Dock' because I knew my father would hate it. When he did hear it, he didn't disappoint. Called it bloody jungle music. Me, when I finally saw a picture of Otis Redding in the *New Rock Journal*, I thought his black face and white smile were the most exciting thing I'd seen. After his death, as is the way with these things, the record was a big hit. A classic now. Not then.

I was attempting to mime the sitting part which, in the absence of a dock to actually park my arse on, was a challenge.

'Crap. Crap. You enjoy having a crap,' Jonathan yelled excitedly. He was speaking deliberately loudly. The kids nearby looked over and, to be honest, I probably did look exactly like someone using a French lavatory. My pointing and raising of my palm to my forehead as I scoured the imaginary horizon only made matters worse. Half the class dissolved into laughter; the rest began doing Max Wall-esque impersonations of me.

The furore was sufficient to stir Mr. Crabbe from behind his crease-free copy of *The Daily Telegraph*. The simple folding of the newsprint, slowly like a starched sheet, silenced the laughter. A long angular digit beckoned me and Jonathan. Other kids backed off a pace almost pushing us in his direction.

'Now, what.' Mr. Crabbe paused, racking his brains. 'What is your name, boy?' he asked.

'Dane, sir.'

Crabbe nodded as if I had just told him the most tedious thing he had ever heard.

'Now, Dane,' he said, savouring my name like the new word it was. 'What is so much more interesting than the South African rugger tour?' He ostentatiously completed the act of the folding of the newspaper as he waited for my reply.

'Nothing, sir.'

He nodded again even more slowly and then rose from his seat. Mr. Crabbe had a beard like a goat and National Health glasses.

'A very amusing nothing nevertheless, boy. Waters?'

'Dane was pretending to go to the toilet, Mr. Crabbe.'

At this point, I could claim that my recall of the incident becomes happily hazy. These therapists on all those late-night phone-in programmes say we blank out the most unpleasant memories, bury them like dead dogs. I wonder if that's right. I wonder if we don't bury them like treasure, returning to them regularly as if they are an emotional nest-egg. Suffice to say, Mr. Crabbe made me perform the whole unhappy stunt in front of the whole mirth-struck class and that it was the talk of the first form for days afterwards.

Crabbe agreed that my mime was more suggestive of a man in the throes of terminal constipation than of sea breezes and gently lapping waves. He made me repeat the name Otis Redding several times over, slowly and at volume, before acknowledging that he had understood me. Then he repeated the name several times himself. Otis Redding. To me the name was exotic, charged with emotion and excitement. He made it sound like another word for shit.

Jonathan was never my favourite person after that. The only pleasure I derived from his hanging around with our crowd after school was from Terry Chambers' merciless baiting of him:

You wanking yet, Jonny? Did mummy tuck you in last night with a little kiss? On your little cock? How's your sister's hymen, Jonathan? You can't glue it back together you know.

I had the impression that Cal let this go on for a little longer with Jonathan than with the rest of us. It was not that Cal was exactly our leader or that he exercised any authority over Terry as such only that when Cal changed the subject, it tended to remain changed. He could produce items of interest from his leather briefcase like white rabbits: the manufacturer's prelaunch blurb for the Jaguar XJ6, a partially signed copy of the 1966 World Cup Final programme, an empty box that had once contained black silk stockings.

On this particular occasion, Jonathan was sitting in the gutter bouncing his tennis ball. It was May but for most of the day the sun had soared proudly as if it thought it were already August. Wilson. You could always still read the manufacturer's name on Jonathan's tennis balls. Wilson. Wilson. He bounced it with one hand then the other. Wilson. Wilson. His father had taken him to see the Harlem Globetrotters that weekend and typically everyone knew about it by registration on Monday morning.

Terry was reading extracts from *The News Of The World*. He read slowly not because we were savouring the detail but because that was the way he read. When I first went into the top class he was already there and the only kid I knew apart from Cal. I imagine Terry had been placed in that form because he could finish a maths paper in five minutes. Numbers he could crunch like a beetle beneath a boot but the problem was he did the same with letters. Crunched them. Reversed them. Put them in the wrong order. By the fifth form he was just about in the CSE stream. It was sheer force of personality, raw energy and hard work that enabled him to remain friends with those he had met in that first fortnight and sheer force of personality that impelled him to want to read to us on a regular basis. Poor Terry, by the time he was an adult he was worn out.

As he laboured, Cal winked at me and tossed me a cigarette.

'I owe him,' he explained to the others. He didn't.

Charlie was checking through his pockets for his own fags. Like me, he only ever bought packets of ten. His tie hung loosely around his neck, the tightly drawn knot level with the third button, the two ends tending in different directions. Charlie did up a button on his blazer. Although the sun was high there was an early evening breeze. Perhaps he was thinking about his walk home which was longer than for the rest of us. He lived past Cal, getting on for Camberwell.

'OK, Terry, that's enough about the shagging vicars,' he said, lighting up. 'What about the 16 year old schoolboys?'

'That's the point,' replied Terry, bitterly. 'They never get any.'

He looked up from his father's newspaper. His hair was lank and lifeless, but his eyes were like a hawk's.

'My dad fucked your mum on Sunday, Jon boy,' he began, singsong. 'Must have been while your old fella was taking you to Wember-ley.'

Jonathan bounced the ball, first with his left hand and then with his right. Wilson. Wilson.

'She was begging for it he reckoned. Desperate.'

Bounce, Wilson. Bounce, bounce.

'Your dad should give her a good seeing to.'

Bounce, bounce, bounce.

'Although perhaps not.' Terry looked around at the rest of us. 'She is a fucking crap shag after all.'

The tennis ball missed Terry's left ear as it went past but hit him on the back of the head as it rebounded from the station wall.

There was a pause then Terry laughed a snorting stunted laugh, a laugh through his nose. He looked at Jonathan who had turned away again. Terry picked up the ball and held it above his head, making as if to throw.

'Dance,' he said, 'dance,' as he had said many times before. The victim was supposed to hop around on the spot as if the ground beneath him were being peppered with lead. Terry was fond of these John Wayne games.

Jonathan simply sat. Terry threw the ball at him. Hard at his head. It missed and rattled against the old Victorian pillar box on the opposite side of the street – the one Terry always claimed said VD rather than VR. He reckoned it was for posting letters to the special clinic – 'very common in Victorian times, VD,' he used to claim. 'Fucking epidemic.'

The ball bounced and then rolled back down the hill towards us. We watched it come to rest on the grate of a drain. Jonathan got up and walked over to where Terry was standing. For a moment, he towered over him.

'Lanky cunt,' said Terry looking around the circle at Charlie, then at me, then at Cal. Jonathan removed Cal's briefcase from the window sill and swung it back crashing it first lengthwise into Terry's crotch and then sideways against his head.

'Thanks,' he muttered returning the case to Cal and starting up the hill. 'And Frank,' he said, turning to me. 'I'm sorry about that stuff with Crabbe.' I must have looked as blank as the others. He was looking straight at me, wide eyes brown. I don't think I'd really noticed what colour his eyes were before. 'That drama thing,' he explained. 'The Otis Redding...'

'Fuck. Fuck you,' shouted Terry as Jonathan receded into the distance. By then Jonathan and I had known each other for four years. The circumstances of our first dramatic encounter had never before been mentioned.

I was impressed. Not that he remembered it – God knows, I did and still do – nor even that he mentioned it – these things come out in the end – but that he mentioned it in front of the others. That was brave. Thinking back I think I was touched. It meant something anyway.

7

The thing about our apartment in Paris is that it's Wendy's. It's small and reached by a lift that is only really big enough for two people if they like each other a lot or if one of them is Cal Carter but Cal never saw it. He never got to use the petite ascenseur. Wendy bought it shortly after he died. Cash-buyer.

I encouraged her. Told her that if she wanted it she could have it. You see, the macabre thing is that Cal and I had written out our wills just six weeks before he died. We knew what was in each other's down to the last full-stop. We did it the first night of the abortive 'world tour' as we had come to call it. Jonathan's idea.

'Plane crashes, car crashes, poorly aimed vomit, it's all been done before, boys,' he explained. We were sitting in a dressing room that was actually big enough for all of us – band, roadies, a handful of fans, some bloke taking pictures – a sign that we had made it. I was reading the graffiti on the wall, not really listening to him, wondering whether the famous signatures I was looking at were authentic, wondering whether anyone would ever wonder that about mine. Marker pens of all colours and sizes, penknives and screwdrivers, biro and blood. Names, band names, obscenities and absurdities, lyrics and lies. I signed my name and then, in a different hand, Cal's. For good measure I added Jonathan's and Charlie's too.

'That stuff you put up your nose, Cal. These things happen. Best to be prepared.' He looked to me and then to Cal, the songwriting team. 'If anything happens to you boys, we don't want to spend the next five years haggling over the use of the name and who owns the demo tapes.'

Cal and I looked at each other and shrugged. When I looked back at the wall I couldn't remember where I had written our names. They had disappeared. I looked around for someone to pass me a drink or a joint. A man I'd never seen before tossed me a bottle of beer. It spun through the air.

'Well, Jonny,' Cal began, shaking his long hair from his eyes, 'we never chose you because of your bass-playing but...'

The two girls sitting at his feet giggled as he paused pregnantly.

'You're absolutely right,' I cut in.

Jonathan was sitting on an overturned drum box slapping his unamplified Fender Precision bass. This technique was becoming popular in funk and soul music but was a million miles from ours which was just as well. Jonathan slapped like a wet fish and Cal regularly told him so. Jonathan smiled and celebrated our consent with a finger-tripping run from Chic's 'Good Times'.

'Don't give up your day job,' said Cal, looking up from the set-list he was writing in thick blue felt. 'Oh, this is your day job.' Laughs again from mystery faces. Jon snorted and left the room. I was looking around for somebody to talk to – often Wendy was backstage but there was no sign. I started to write on the wall again – really writing this time. Lyrics for a song.

After the gig – three encores in a screaming sea of sweat, swagger and sex – it became obvious that Jonathan's suggestion was no sudden whim. We had been booked into one of those large, impersonal, could be anywhere hotels that are such a treat when you want to be anywhere but the stifling places you know. The bar was like an airport lounge. Cal compared the bedrooms to those in an American motel, a comparison only he was able to make. He noticed my shrug. 'You'll all see soon enough, boys. No sweat. When we do our States dates.'

Most of our dressing room entourage and several others beside had decamped to the bar. 'We slayed them,' said Charlie from beneath his hallmark sweat-stained baseball cap. Today, every theme park, every sports team, every brand of everything has its own baseball cap but then they were strictly Brooklyn. To cover his bald patch, Charlie wore one, a gift from Cal from Las Vegas, at our first gig and at every gig thereafter. His hairline turned him into a fashion pioneer. As we became more successful, he started wearing his caps backwards so that the photographers and TV cameras could see his face more easily.

Charlie rapped on the edge of the table with his drumsticks. Just a few months earlier he would have been concerned about who was watching and about whether he chipped the varnish. Now, on a post-performance high, he was taking notice of nobody. The girl sitting next to him began to accompany him, slapping her hands on her thighs.

'Listen,' said Jonathan. He adjusted his chair so that the three of us formed a discrete circle. Cal smiled at me. Jonathan caught the barman's eye with the merest movement of his palm. 'Have a look at these,' he said.

One of Jonathan's cronies stepped forward and handed him four identical forms. I recognised him as the man who had thrown me a beer. Jonathan seemed to acquire hangers-on like the rest of us acquired hangovers. But he didn't appear to regard them as limpets or leeches; rather he was friendly to them. 'Thanks,' he said.

The man was wearing a suit, which was unusual, and sipping occasionally from a Jack Daniels, which wasn't. No doubt the drink had been purchased on our tab. He stood and watched as the Go-Karts discussed their deaths and eventually our own drinks arrived.

'It doesn't have to be much,' Jonathan was saying. 'It just needs to be clear.' I was losing concentration. I needed someone else to tell me we were geniuses. That we had performed brilliantly. I fancied a fag, a full glass and fellatio. 'We stick together, our next contract could make us all very rich indeed. We owe it to ourselves to ensure that,' he coughed, 'the preliminary paperwork is in order.'

Jonathan was right. Our next contract, had we had one, would have made us very rich indeed. It was also understandable that he was concerned about maximising our income. As the songwriters, Cal and I got half each of the fixed six and a quarter percent copyright royalty as well as our quarter of the band's artists royalty. But although our contract was a good one all things considered according to Cal and Jon who seemed to know about these things, this artists royalty was still relatively small because, of course, we were, at the time of signing, unknown. It meant our income – mine and Cal's – was around three times that of Charlie and Jonathan.

One of the forms was already completed in Charlie's name and witnessed, as ours would be, by two unfamiliar signatures. It included a form of words concerning the band and its assets that Jonathan suggested we all incorporate into ours. Charlie's will then went on to leave all his private wealth to his mother.

'What you do with yours, of course, is entirely up to you,' said Jonathan as we read. 'However,' he continued, noticing the looks Cal and I were exchanging, 'you might want to think twice about leaving it to other band members as that could confuse the personal and professional aspects of the will.'

'Oh no,' said Cal, rising and downing his whiskey in one, 'we don't want to confuse the personal and professional aspects do we?' We both giggled.

'Jon, you know this isn't necessary.' Cal continued and he was walking towards the lift as Jonathan's pal produced fountain pens for us all.

By the time we had all finished writing and signing, Cal was making steady progress through what was, even by his standards, a substantial bag of amphetamine sulphate and the rest of us had summoned the last bottle of Jack Daniels from the cellar.

I told all this to Wendy as, bruised and battered in the aftermath of Cal's death, we meandered purposelessly up and down the narrow lanes of Ile Saint Louis, the smaller island in the Seine. We were searching for what our guide book assured us we would find there: 'a flavour of the old Paris'.

'Perhaps because I was drunk,' I told her, 'but I know every word of that will. You know how you get...,' I was rambling, looking at Wendy, getting excited, hopping from the cobbled street back onto the pavement, searching for the right word. 'You get focused on something when you're pissed. Can only see one thing. Well, I was seeing the wills open on the table and us sitting next to each other, me and Cal, and us writing, feint-lined paper and fountain pens and us, well... we were just schoolkids, Wendy. Just kids playing.'

Wendy had seemed to be only half listening but now she stopped and turned and looked at me. She took my hand.

'He left you the price of that flat and a lot more besides,' I said.

'What about that one then?' she said, pointing up at an apartment with its shutters painted to look like a window box forever in bloom. 'Or that one, or that one...'

Her hands were pointing here, there and somewhere else, animated. Her eyes were happy, or so I picture her now, dancing from side to side, her hair, the same gold as Cal's, flowing from beneath her hair band.

'We were so close. Cal and me. You were so close, Cal and you,' she said as we shared a bed that night. 'It's the right thing to do.' She kissed me on the nose. 'And a nice thing to do.'

That was our last night in the pension. The following day we bought and moved into the apartment, buying sheets and cafetières and coffee bowls and a bed as we went.

8
—

One day, the spring after I started at Beech Park, my father was late coming home from work. It was still unusual then.

Marching around the kitchen like someone in prison or a cartoon, my mother was muttering about pubs being popped into and dinners being spoiled. She turned the gas beneath the potatoes off and on again, off and on, igniting it with a tubular implement which she held like a gun. When his key turned in the lock, she froze as if the music had stopped. We heard the door open and the distant sounds of the street float in. As the door clicked shut again, her shoulders slumped as if they had disappeared from beneath her skin. She sat for the first time in over an hour, the chair, white with a red checked plastic seat, creaking beneath her weight. I hadn't seen her look like that before. For a moment I thought she was ill.

Looking at her, listening to him. I heard my father's footsteps – his heavy workboots on the thin narrow rug that ran the length of the hallway. The sound was more familiar to me than the sound of his voice. Although he was a minicab driver, my father never went to work without boots more suited to the market like his father or to the pit like my mother's – 'workboots, Frank,' he'd smile when I was very young, 'boots for work.' Their sound was haunting because the volume never seemed to change, the steps never seemed to get any closer. It was as if he were marking time. Then we both heard the tweet of a bird. My mother sat up with a start.

The kitchen door swung open and my dad came in carrying a small silver cage containing a green and yellow budgerigar. He put it down on the table and smiled at my mother in a fresh way. He seemed younger.

'Sorry, love, I had to. Janice was giving them.' He was breathless or speaking as if he were. He didn't sound like my father. 'She breeds them and um...' He smiled. 'I thought Frank might like one.' He turned and ruffled my hair, something else which was not a habit. Janice was the woman at the cab office who talked to all the drivers on the radio telling them about the next job. Around the home, my dad called her 'the fat controller' like in the railway books but I'd seen her and she wasn't that fat.

'Thanks, Dad,' I said without enthusiasm.

'Be careful he doesn't get out,' said my father. Then he kissed my mum.

A budgerigar is a far from ideal pet for a child – you can't really do very much with it, not like a dog or a cat. Even a hamster has more potential. For the initial weeks of its residency chez Dane, I occasionally fed it and changed its drinking water but by and large, its limited needs were met by my mother. She put an old tablecloth on the sideboard and set the cage on that. The budgie could see our little garden from there: father's tomato plants, mother's chrysanthemums and pansies, my football, the lawn like a green dishcloth. It seemed happy enough, tweeting away, irritating next door's cat, but it never uttered a discernible word.

'The green ones are the talkers,' announced my Aunty Anne when we told her.

'She should know,' said my father into his cup. Aunty Anne never heard him because she was busy telling me off for peeling the skin from my coffee. 'Don't handle your food, child,' she said.

Aunty Anne's coffee always had skin on it, folded like her face. Her breath was very close to you all the time, not just when she kissed you and her house smelled of hot milk and Sunday afternoons regardless of the day of the week. She had things with Victorian names that we didn't have at home, things like antimacassars and doilies, and the furniture was in dark regal colours: burgundy and purple. Sitting in the back seat on the drive home after our visits,

I'd regularly hear my father muttering about his elder sister's airs and graces but even as a small child I knew he was wrong. She didn't have any heirs at all. There was nobody for me to play with.

I put the coffee down delicately on the woven coaster and began shining my shoes with my handkerchief. My mother had long told me to polish my shoes until Aunty Anne could see herself in them. As a very young child, it had crossed my mind that this was because she was unable to use a wall-mounted mirror on account of her permanently stooped shape. Now I knew that it was to do with what my father called showing some respect and, if I didn't like her coffee I could at least have clean shoes. I was trying to be polite.

'Put that bloody handkerchief in your pocket,' said my father from the corner of his mouth, thin and downturned like the flourish of my cheap fountain pen. 'What do you think this is? A bloody boot room?'

'Derek,' hissed my mother. Aunty Anne never heard them. She was a bit deaf too.

After a few weeks, I tried to educate the bird. I thought that educating him would educate me. My memory was terrible. Everybody reminded me of that. I stood next to the cage looking down at him on his perch, a football annual in my hand.

'Brown, Baker, Henry, Blanchflower, Norman, Mackay, Jones, White, Smith, Allen, Dyson,' I whispered over and over like a mantra, my head less than a foot from his. After a day or two, I had learned the Spurs double-winning team off by heart but there was nothing from the budgie but the odd cheep. I tried something a little easier. 'John, Paul, George, Ringo.' Not a dickie bird.

I even tried singing softly to him but I didn't know the words. My father had a record player, a pile of 78s and six stereo LPs but none of them were by The Beatles.

'Jimmy Greaves, Jimmy Greaves,' I tried in desperation. After a few days, I was losing interest. So was my father.

'They may be the best bloody club side the world has ever seen but I don't...' And then he would stop, turn the page of his newspaper, call to my mother or simply sniff. He never finished the sentence. I decided that if I didn't stop soon, he might remember what he didn't, and I didn't fancy that. What I did learn from the whole thing was the value, to me anyway, of repetition. Later I would revise for my O-levels by talking to myself over and over like a madman or somebody training a bird.

So I let the budgie be until one slow Saturday a couple of weeks later when I was kicking around the house with nothing to do. I'd read my comics and my mum wanted me to tidy my room. Logically I should have gone out. There was a football match down at the marsh that we had arranged specially but for some reason I didn't feel like it. I was watching the budgie in his cage.

My mother called him Scratch because of his habit of scratching around on the newspaper at the bottom of his cage as if trying to dig a tunnel. My father and I didn't call him anything much. The bird jumped from one perch to the other and back again. He took a sip of water and jumped from one perch to the other and back again. Then he flapped his wings wildly, discharging loose feathers around the room and jumped from one perch to the other and back again. I realised how often my mother must vacuum the carpet. Scratch jumped from one perch to the other and back again.

I picked up the cage. The bird regarded me curiously, his head tilted to one side. Then I picked up the tablecloth and draped it over the cage. In the corner of my bedroom, I had an old folding coffee table with five years of comics on it. I put Scratch on the bed while I removed the comics to the floor. The table's pockmarked surface included a large ornate monk-like letter 'a' that I had engraved at the age of three. I covered it with the tablecloth and moved Scratch to his new home.

My mother was sceptical at first – she thought it was a ruse to get her to Hoover my room more often. In fact, it had the reverse effect. I happily took on the task myself and there was even less reason for her to come into my room. My mother liked this. My father welcomed it too. It both vindicated his choice of gift and meant that Scratch's constant cheeping was out of earshot.

I spent most of that summer playing dice-cricket. Round our way, the football season was 364 and a half days long (the close season being Christmas morning). As the nights got longer so simply did the matches. But I also enjoyed what my father called the summer game. I still played football at the marsh of course, but at the slightest sign of overcast or inclement conditions, weather which in my childhood seemed marginally more common in the summer than at other times of the year, I was indoors.

Football was fine. Football was fantastic but I was only one of, what, dozens. That year on Whitsun bank holiday evening, for example, as kids came back from weekends at the beach, in the country, or over their Aunty Anne's, we had reached 23-a-side. With dice-cricket, I alone picked the teams, placed the field, changed the bowlers, cheered the batsmen and took the glory. With football, the nearest thing was solo Subbuteo but, because you couldn't keep goal and shoot at the same time, every game ended up as a seven-all draw which was most unrealistic. Properly designed dice-cricket offered authentic scoring and strike rates.

Sometimes I would proceed with my play-to-a-finish match between the staff and pupils of Beech Park Grammar. It was a standard two innings affair but everyone played: thirty kids and thirty teachers. Like the original test matches, there was no time limit. In the first innings, FD Dane came in at number 17 and made a whirlwind century. More often, I played more conventional 'Five-day' test matches or even limited overs games between the teams of the moment. By that I don't mean Surrey or Kent but sides such as Frankie's All Stars, Former And Current England Players Whose Names Begin With B, The Spurs Double-Winning Team or Good-looking Girls Around Our Way (A Select XI).

During the day when father was at work and my mum was out, I would let Scratch out of his cage. At first, as his universe expanded exponentially, he just sat on his perch staring out of the open door. Then he edged nearer and peered around the pencil lead thin bars, head on his shoulder. His first flight was undertaken in panic and ended on the curtain rail where he remained for two hours: the ideal vantage point from which to witness the batting collapse of Good Footballers Who Don't Play For Tottenham: Geoff Hurst 12, Martin Peters 3, Bobby Charlton no score and so on. The innings was partially salvaged by a splendid tenth wicket partnership of 102 between Jimmy Greaves, 45, and Alan Gilzean, 57 not out (two Tottenham players having been permitted in the absence of eleven sufficiently qualified non-Tottenham players.)

But Scratch improved. As the summer rumbled on, he was making almost graceful flights between the curtain-rail and the top of the bookcase only occasionally troubling the scorer. He seemed to try to tunnel out of his cage less often and I toyed with changing his name to Swoop. I enjoyed his company, his chirping clamour whenever I exclaimed aloud or chuckled to myself as a wicket tumbled or a boundary was struck. When Cal was bowled first ball by Mrs. Garrison the art teacher coming on at the Radcliffe Road end, he positively squawked. Perhaps he even spoke.

That summer was a sad time for me: a nasty emotional awakening. It took me three weeks to figure out just what the problem was. Cal's family took him away to America for a month and I missed him. It was the first time I missed anyone.

9

Beech Park, the present day

I don't know if my mother ever received an actual diagnosis of Alzheimer's for my father. Neuroses, psychoses, does it matter what names we give to our madness? I wonder if she even noticed at first. The obsessiveness, the unfinished sentences, the meandering... nothing new there. He actually started to finish some sentences and to say some things that were interesting. Of course, it gets worse and after years of excusing and explaining, justifying, joking and plainly ignoring there comes that steely stark moment where perception and reality collide: the warm pool of urine on the museum floor, the once gleaming shoes now scuffed and damp and the husband who cannot understand why his trousers are wet.

'Come on, Derek,' I imagine her saying, leading him to a chair – 'come on' – and him, for once, coming.

Family Dane are at home. It is the first spring day, the sun uninterrupted in the sky, the daffodils just beginning. We are playing football, boys onto girls. I am attempting to recreate the golden goals I never scored in my youth. Our back lawn is like a soft carpet and Philip takes every opportunity to roll on it.

'Get up, you big girl's blouse,' says Wendy, kicking the ball towards the garden shed on which a goal has been painted in hesitant pink emulsion.

Rebecca stops, hands on her proto-hips, and turns on her teammate, 'why is a big girl's blouse such an insult,' she demands. 'Why not a big boy's shirt?'

'Big girl's blouse,' yells Philip, leaping to his fickle feet.

'Well?' Rebecca asks of her mother. Wendy takes the opportunity to sidefoot the ball home. 'Three-nil.'

Philip and I look at each other. 'Hey, that's not fair,' we say in outraged unison.

That's when my mother appears around the side of the house, the old wooden door swinging in her wake. She is breathless and urgent. In front of her, the ball bounces across the gravel path. Wide eyes follow its diminishing arcs, and for a moment I think she's about to join in. Wendy twigs.

'Where's Derek?' she asks.

My mother points vaguely back down the path.

Philip's muddy hands on the back of his shorts. My mother's random movements of her suddenly heavy head. Wendy's eyes. I run past them all, through the gate and out into the street. My father is walking slowly along the white lines in the middle of the road calling in a stilted disembodied voice my mother's name over and over. The car door, open, creaks in the wind, and slams shut with a fierce finality my father fails to notice. The driver's seat is forward now that Mum drives. As a kid I never realised that she could. For him, a symbol.

'Dad,' I shout, 'Dad.' He continues to walk away, continues to call my mother's name. I look right and left like a child crossing the road. 'Derek!' I say tentative at first and then again at the top of my voice. I like the taste. My father's senseless eyes look all around like a character in a film who believes he has heard the voice of God. 'Derek,' I shout again. He looks at me. 'Margaret?' He says.

I sense my family – wife, mother, daughter, son – behind me, scuffling and shuffling to their different halts. My father has turned and begins to walk towards us, his arms locked in front of him in an incomplete gesture of pleading. 'Poppet?' he begins, 'poppet?'

My mother coughs quietly and turns her heel in the gravel. 'It's what he used to call me,' she says. 'When we met.' Philip sniggers. Rebecca kicks him in the shin. I notice the damp darkness on my father's trousers.

We take him inside and I lead him upstairs. He raises not a word of objection when I take the belt from his piss-stained slacks and says 'thank you, son,' as I remove these damp and sticky encumbrances from around his creaking ankles. My father smells like a public lavatory but it appears not to bother him. Nothing does. He grins. I thread his belt through a pair of my old jeans. He is a grinning thing. I find him hard to look at. His face is of a naughty boy not reluctant to be dressed but not smart enough to help and his predicament passes him by like the years. I cannot make out what he is talking about at first. And not solely because I have not had a conversation with him for longer than I can remember.

'Beautiful, son. Wasn't it? Beautiful, like poetry in motion, it was, like poetry... beautiful. Mackay to Blanchflower.' Ah, he is on about the Spurs double-winning team. 'You remember. Five-nil they won. Glorious. Glory, glory. Sunderland, it was and Dyson scored twice.' I am doing up his flies, my flies. I was a toddler the season Spurs did the double and I know my father never took me to a game. The first match I can remember was in 1963, the season Jimmy Greaves scored 37 goals and we became the first British team to win a European trophy when we beat Athletico Madrid 5-1 in the Cup Winners Cup final. I didn't see that game either but I remember the breakfast table the following morning and the smile on my father's face as he spoke. That memory is vivid as a puddle of piss. 'Happy days, Frankie, happy days,' my father rambles.

'I knew there was something wrong,' my mother says, her hands clasping and releasing a steaming mug of coffee, clasping and releasing. 'When I said to him this morning, let's, let's go to the museum, he said that'll be nice. Didn't complain at all. "That'll be nice, love".' She looks at me. 'That was all he said.'

Wendy is ushering the children back into the garden. She throws the ball after them and, without the usual warnings regarding windows and the gardens of neighbours, closes the door. My father and I stand by the kitchen door – it's as if we are all giving my mother space. Proudly, he is wearing my old jeans. They are several sizes too large and the sort he would not be seen dead in yet here he is wearing them. Perhaps the situation in which he finds himself is worse than being dead.

Margaret Dane looks up at Derek Dane. They smile at each other but the smiles are fifty years apart. My mother shakes her head and sips slowly. 'Do you want a cup of tea, Dad?' asks Wendy.

We decide that they should stay with us for a few days. While my father festers in front of the television, my mother and I return to the family home where we walk through those familiar rooms selecting those necessary items. My mother packs an overnight bag, neither of us prepared to acknowledge that the stay is likely to be longer, much longer and possibly permanent. Tea as ever is the sustenance. My mother still hasn't switched to tea bags. The smell of fresh tea leaves is a smell of my childhood. As the steaming pot stands, my mother begins. 'We'll just let the flavour draw,' she says.

They'd been to the Horniman Museum and they'd both been inside. Surprising in itself. During my childhood, we visited the museum approximately once a month, my mother, father and I. Even though it was well within walking distance, he always drove us in the Morris Traveller. He walked around the gardens and answered mother's questions with me but he never went inside. 'You two go in, love,' he would say, 'I'll have a little seat here and read my paper.'

A little seat, a quick seat or a bloody seat, depending on his mood, but always the same seat. If the bench were already full, he would perch on the edge, by a single buttock if necessary. If it were raining, he would put the paper on his head rather than read it. (Both my parents considered umbrellas drew unnecessary public attention.) My mother tired of cajoling him and we always entered the museum alone.

'They have such marvellous collections here, Frankie. How could he not love the Peruvian whistling pots?' she said to me once in exasperation.

'I suppose it might help if they actually whistled,' I had said after a moment's thought.

We had our preferred routes which we followed separately and which both took as long as it took my father to read the old broadsheet *Sunday Express*. We rarely spoke and we certainly never discussed our collective instinct for the appropriate duration for the visit.

One exhibit which was on both our tours was the stuffed walrus that presided over the natural history section like an indulgent grandfather. It was here once in hushed tones that my mother made a rare joke. 'You know why your father never comes in, Frank,' she said, pointing a hesitant finger, 'he's afraid of being mistaken for that.'

I smiled a little as I felt I ought but back then that walrus, benign and stable, didn't remind me at all of my father who was actually quite slight and skinny. Perhaps my mother saw beyond the obvious: the shared moustache. This walrus did not have the cosy rolls of fat one would find on a live beast. It had been stuffed to the brink until it looked as if it might explode. Someone shot him, bagged him, made him a trophy, and neglected to tell the taxidermist what he looked like. That was forgotten in the happy round of lectures and salutes.

I am surprised that my father had gone into the museum at all and astonished that it was at his instigation. 'I went to leave him on the bench,' my mother says, 'but he said: "You don't get rid of me that easily."'

'It happened by the walrus. He was so close behind me as we went in. It was as if he had never seen it or me before. And he took my hand. It must be twenty five years since he held my hand but it didn't feel like him, not like his hand.' My mother looks at me. She is topping up my cup. 'It felt more like you Frankie, your hand. A little boy's hand. I didn't know what to say to him.' She stops, putting the pot down. 'That's what I found hardest to cope with. The accident when it happened came as a sort of a relief because I knew what to do then. Isn't that a terrible thing to say?' I shake my head, touch my mother's hand. 'It was a child pointing that alerted me, a child sniffing and pointing and shouting: "That man going wee wee, daddy".'

That night, after the kids and my parents have gone to bed, Wendy and I sit over a whiskey. There are so many things I wish I could say to my father and now the opportunity will never come. It no longer matters what words we exchange. From that point of view it is as if he is already dead but it is much worse than that: his blundering presence is a dribbling testimony to our failed relationship. I ache with all the things I have hoped that he would one day say to me and with all the things he did say that I will always want him to take back.

Then as I fill our glasses once again from the Jack Daniels bottle and my tears start, I realise that I have been here before in my life. I realise that perhaps most of all I am weeping for all the things I wish I'd said to Cal before he died. I look across to Wendy and wonder whether she feels the same. When our eyes meet, it is no longer necessary to ask.

10

By the end of the summer holidays, Scratch, known as Swoop, was banking and diving around the peaks of my bookcase and wardrobe like a multicoloured mountain eagle. On one hand, there was much to celebrate: the pupils had beaten the staff convincingly in the play-to-a-finish Test match, FD Dane chipping in a second century and three wickets including that of DIK 'Mister' Blake bowled first ball. On the other hand, the new term with its dull pullovers, itchy socks, grey shirts and rough trousers was just around the corner. School looming as it always did just as the weather was improving.

I played the dice unenthusiastically and was unable to derive any pleasure from the prospect of the one final sunbathed game of football on the marsh, the traditional climax to the summer holidays. Scratch's cheeping was beginning to irritate me and I looked out of the window constantly.

I was losing track of the game when the doorbell went. The sound of our doorbell could not be described as a ring. It was more like an expiring cuckoo clock as if the house were nervous of guests and ashamed to announce them. On the rare occasions a visitor activated it, Scratch would shake his little head and explore the room as if expecting to find another bird in distress.

Cal stood there naturally tanned and spoke as if he had never been away on holiday. 'Are you coming up the marsh?' he asked. He acted as if he called for me every day which he didn't. I tried to be as casual as he was.

'Suppose so,' I said.

Cal smiled. 'But not yet,' he said and raised his briefcase, level with his shoulder, my chest. It was open and, I could see, full with records, LPs and singles. 'Here,' he said giving me the case. I had never seen so many records, not proper ones with glossy sleeves and everything. They certainly dwarfed my father's collection.

Just as I was wondering whether they were a gift, Scratch flew over my shoulder and out of the front door. The white-emulsioned jambs framed Cal like the goalkeeper his build would never allow him to be. There was the familiar flailing of the arms as the object which he was attempting to save flew past him.

Our front garden was a slender affair barely one stone slab and a malnourished flower-bed wide, and with two flaps of his apprentice wings Scratch was away and over the road. Whether it was his enthusiasm or excitement or a gust of wind, I don't know, but in the blink of an eye the bird was as high as the clouds and fading as fast as the holidays. Cal and I were looking at each other. 'What was that?' he asked.

'My mother's budgie,' I replied.

'Oh,' he said. Our expressions were of two men with a shocking secret.

If he noticed the open cage on the table, he never said. I pushed the rule book, the scorecards and the chocolate biscuits, the paraphernalia of dice cricket, to one side and Cal and I sat on my bedroom floor and inspected and examined the records in a reverential silence. After a quarter of an hour or so, I said, 'We can go and play them on my Dad's radiogram if you like?'

It was customary to ask permission but I wasn't about to reveal that to Cal. As I held the needle over the run-in groove of the first disc I imagined Scratch winging his way across the London skyline, a free spirit. It was a single, a 45.

Within its sturdy wooden box, the radiogram offered four speeds: 16, 33, 45 and 78. I clicked the little plastic lever into position just in time. Otis soared into velvet action. I was knocked out by the power, I had only previously heard him on my portable radio. I watched the record label as it spun around: Sitting On The Dock Of

The Bay (Redding-Cropper); Otis Redding; Stax Records. I wanted to move as I imagined Otis might but I felt awkward, settled for a tap of the toe and a goose-like shuffle with the neck.

'I know you like this one,' said Cal offering me another disc. 'But I like this one'. It was an LP this time. It was Elvis Presley.

'The King,' said Cal, savouring the word. Of course, everybody calls Presley the King now but back then I'm not so sure. It's hard to remember. It's like trying to remember the first time you heard the expression 'OK' or 'Hi'. What I do know is that with us the expression stuck. 'The King,' I repeated.

Cal was dancing about the living room, clapping and shaking his hips. He couldn't dance for toffee but it didn't bother him. I tapped the other foot too but try as I might I just couldn't move on from a position that was basically standing with a few embellishments to fully fledged dancing. And so that is how Cal and I spent his first visit to my house. He took no interest in the things that had always embarrassed me about my parent's house – the painted furniture, the silly ornaments, the carpet, the wallpaper and the smell of bacon. He just danced to my dad's ancient gramophone.

When we went up to the marsh to play football I wouldn't let Terry Chambers pick me unless he picked Cal too.

11

Wendy's idea is to do some interviews.

A Sunday morning with a cafetière full of coffee and a house empty of kids. Philip is at a friend's. Rebecca is playing football in the garden and we can hear the ball bouncing off the garage wall. Newspapers strewn across the duvet and our feet peeking from beneath like pink soldiers. Wendy's toes flex and relax, rippling as fingers over a keyboard. My right arm stretches and stretches, groping for my coffee. I'm reading the sport section and reluctant to move. Wendy is watching. I know the smile that plays upon her lips and announces her cheekbones. She turns to face me, her chin cushioned in a palm, elbow forming a perfect soft white 'V' on the pillow. 'Lazy boy,' she smiles. A tender moment and then she is holding the milk jug above my face tipping it. The creamy meniscus threatens and then the milk rolls freshly down my nose, follows the lines of my face, finds the smirking edges of my mouth like Spanish wine. The Sunday supplement becomes soggy and I hit her with it.

'If you want to write this book so much why don't you invite Jonathan and Charlie over,' she says. 'You can chew over the old days.' She sips her coffee. 'Because let's face it, you're never going to remember more than a quarter of it.'

I watch her mouth and neck as she drinks and now I have to sit up. I reach for my own coffee and slowly lift it. 'Is that OK?' I ask, touching the china to my lips. I have been tentative – wondering whether she really approves of the project and its inevitable focus on Cal.

She nods. She says my memory is bad and she is right – I'll end up like my father – but the problem with my memory concerns not what is missing but what is packed tight present. My memory is clogged full of fragments sharp and random as broken glass. Is that what happens to old people? Their minds get cut up by a painful past? I'm reluctant to get right in there in case it hurts so I poke around the outside like a farmer with barren soil.

'You can have a tape-recorder going, take it all down. You've got one. That's how you musicians work isn't it?' Wendy peers at me from over her newspaper. 'Anyway, that's how the lazy ones work.'

'What do you mean?'

She's lying on her back looking up at the ceiling. 'Well, I've told you before. I can see why you were a team, you and Cal. Contrasting styles. Opposites attracting. That sort of thing. Cal was always strumming and scribbling. I never see you do a thing. You need others to bounce off.'

'I only release a record every blue moon, Wendy. What's that? Twelve songs, a thousand words tops, and how long does it take to write a song? 'She Loves You' – two hours, 'That's Entertainment' – ten minutes. 'Wonderful Moment' took less than an hour. I know because I was there.' I laugh and stroke her hair. 'It's amazing what you can get done when the wife's at the supermarket.'

'Lazy boy,' she repeats.

'I'll give them both a ring this afternoon,' I say, picking up the arts section.

'You know you saved me, don't you?' Wendy's words sound disembodied. I look over and those big eyes are dozy closed. 'And in a way, by doing what you both wanted,' (she's mumbling now) 'you saved him too.'

Jonathan and Charlie arrive at dusk to recall our once twilight lives. I provide the whiskey. Charlie tells us a story about his club, Strike Three, his hold on reality becoming more tenuous by the glassful. I don't really like these stories. They tend to concern girls who ought to be doing their homework not whatever they do in Charlie's clubs and I think of Rebecca; or boys with impeccable haircuts and fretboard technique and I think of the music I'm not recording; or drugs in gut-blasting quantities and I think of Cal.

It's not that Charlie has learnt nothing from our experiences – I'm sure he misses Cal too – but those were the lessons of a previous lifetime. The girl keeping him company tonight may have been born by the time Cal died but I doubt she had started school. He's what I guess you'd call an impresario these days. First there was Strike One on the Finchley Road then Strike Two round the back of the Elephant and then Strike Three off Dean Street. Happening places for the kids from the street with an eye for the main chance. By the time you read about one of Charlie's joints in the what's-on guides the clientèle that created its name have moved on. He's thinking about opening Strike Four he tells us. 'Won't that destroy the concept?' asks Jonathan.

Charlie's manic eyes swirl in his golf ball head. He fixes his inquisitor for an indistinct moment and then empties his glass. 'What concept?'

'Well, you know, strike one, strike two, like baseball ...' Jonathan trails off. Charlie and his girlfriend have begun exploring each other's tonsils. His partner's passion dislodges Charlie's baseball cap, her arm locking around his substantial neck. His hairline now is like a fondly remembered old schoolfriend and Charlie crops what's left tight. Cuts it as short as his relationships.

Jonathan, of course, I see regularly but I can't recall our last real conversation about Cal or that era. He doesn't honestly believe that this book idea is instead of another album and they're both sceptical, him and Charlie.

'We've come a long way since the Go-Karts, Frankie. You can't go back.'

'Who wants to,' says Charlie surfacing. 'Do kids today even know what a Go-Kart is, Frank? Do you, doll?'

She shakes her head obligingly. Her name's Claudia and I suspect she's a lot smarter than she requires Charlie to think.

'That's right. Still it's up to you, chum.' It's Jonathan again. 'I don't know where you'll find the time though. You ought to be writing that new album.'

'Yeah, well, just indulge me, OK.' I fiddle with the recording level on my tiny tape-recorder. 'Say something then.'

'My girl gives good head,' says Charlie with unaccustomed clarity.

'Charlie,' says Claudia. 'Oops, sorry, Mr. Dane.' A manicured hand cups her swollen mouth.

'Frankie,' I say.

'You realise that that tape-recorder makes you look like some sort of tabloid journalist peddling sleaze and salacious smut to the braindead?' Jonathan begins.

Charlie laughs. 'Perhaps you better put me down for a couple of copies after all, Frank.' He's sitting up straight now that the tape's running. 'Claudia, babe.' Claudia loosens her hold, retracts the cling. Wendy is out and Charlie has volunteered his girlfriend to baby-sit. It's hardly necessary since I'm here but I'm not sure Charlie realises this nor how old our kids are anyway. The only person who really needs a baby sitter now is my father. However, Rebecca is always happy to indulge the one she called, as a toddler, 'Daddy's dummer'. 'Another girlfriend, Uncle Charlie?' she asked when he arrived, taking him by the hand and patting it like a mother. 'You'll find the right one one day just you wait and see.' As with all the best sarcasm, you're never quite sure.

'The kids are upstairs,' I say to her, 'but they should be asleep. You just help yourself.'

The first floor is basically the kids' floor. They have their bedrooms and their own living room cum playroom. It's got a TV and I told Claudia to bring a video. She's got a duff-looking horror film I've never heard of which turns out to be partly financed by one of Charlie's companies.

Suddenly, with Claudia gone, it is silent. We're used to tapes running as we beat our drums or bounce around our bass or grind our guitars, but when it comes to talking... This is not a recording studio, this is my living room and the subject is the past.

'Well?' says Charlie.

'We could go downstairs,' I offer. The cellar has been converted into a 24-track recording studio. It's fully digital, both for recording and mix-down, with Midi, sampling, synths and all that modern stuff but Joe Meek or Brian Wilson would be equally at home as any contemporary producer. It's got two 1960s Vox AC30 amplifiers, one with both channels routed into one for maximum distortion, a Farfisa organ, two ancient reel to reel tape machines for genuine phasing and flanging, sundry 1970s effects pedals, a WEM Copicat analogue echo unit and all sorts of other little toys I've picked up on the way.

'Yes, in the studio we can synthesise our remarks?' says Jonathan with an edge. Charlie starts laughing again. Jonathan continues: 'You don't think this is exploitative, Frank, do you, exploiting Cal?' This sends Charlie on to another plane. His cackling takes the recording level, already in the red, off the end of the scale.

'You worried that he might tell the truth about the little bastard?'

Jonathan starts and then shakes his head, removes his glasses. 'Drink talking,' he tells me after a beat.

'Drink talking? Bollocks,' says Charlie, pouring himself another drink. 'He was a little shit.'

I'm fiddling clumsily with the tape recorder. I don't like what Charlie is saying but I feel I owe it to my book. For the record. Jonathan is topping up my glass and his. In the back garden, colours wrestle over the sun. It sets with a splatter: a tiny tantrum of red, and then soft shades of yellow scuttling across the sky. My trees, an oak and two beeches, silhouettes now, cast a pitch shadow across the lawn. The room is suddenly several tones darker. As Charlie rambles I light a candle. Jonathan walks across to the window and looks up and around and anywhere but into the room.

'I thought Cal was your friend, Charlie?' I probe like a journalist.

'He had an ego the size of a planet.'

'And don't say it didn't do you any favours,' says Jonathan slowly, not turning round.

Charlie's eyes are redder than the sky. 'Name one drummer better than me. Name one.'

'I don't think that's the point,' I say.

'That's the whole point. I never needed him. We never did. Come on, Frankie, you know how many people I've played with, how many sessions, albums – not just yours. Jesus, Frank, look at your own success if you need convincing. We were all there. We all did it. Cal's only superior talent was for dying young.'

Finally Jonathan turns round. 'No one's denying you were there Charlie. I mean, we could hardly have failed to notice the bloody racket you made. But would you have been there if not for Cal? If it hadn't been for him you'd be like that retard of a friend of yours, Terence: pumping petrol not schoolgirls.'

'Jealous.' Charlie pauses. 'Cal thought we owed it all to him from our first gig to our first number one. Bullshit. Come on, Jonathan. Is that elephantine memory of yours playing tricks on you? All those things he used to say about you and your bass-playing.'

'Don't you know that was all part of the act...' Jonathan trails off.

'Double-plus bullshit.' Charlie shakes his head. 'Funny. I never thought he was dumb enough to top himself though. What did Kurt Cobain's mum call it? The Idiot Club?'

'He didn't, did he. The inquest said so.' Jonathan shakes his head and walks from the room.

I pour Charlie and myself another drink each. Charlie starts laughing. 'It's a can of worms, Frank, history. Handle with care.' I nod. For a moment there is silence as we drink. Then Jon reappears. In his hands he's carrying the big wooden box that contains Philip's Subbuteo set.

'Sub-fucking-buteo,' says Charlie and he's a grinning schoolkid again.

We set it up on the floor and play all on to all with the third person reffing. I think this is called going with the flow. We argue about the rules, how long the halves should be and whether you can flick with the side of your finger. Candles surround the pitch as if this is some diabolic football tournament from hell. We're having fun. Charlie is drunk. He's playing his whiskey glass at centre half. I try once more. 'Do you remember Cal's World Cup Subbuteo?' Charlie gives me an old fashioned look and Jon a penalty.

Jon lines up the kick like a snooker player or a golfer with a putt. He's hoping that if he waits long enough Charlie will lose concentration or even consciousness. In the corner of Philip's box a familiar face catches my eye. It's only a couple of millimetres across but it's recognisably Cal. I pick the figure up and examine it, holding it by its semicircular base and plastic green tail-rod.

'Look at this,' I say.

It is one of a team of Subbuteo players in Tottenham Hotspur kit that I painted to look like my school friends. Cal's the goalkeeper, of course – I snapped the legs off a little to get the right height. I show Charlie and Jon their respective figures. I painted the hair, matched the eye-colour and added a few distinguishing features like Jon's yellow socks. The model of Simon Hawkins has a lump of plastic melted onto the stomach; Terry is playing in black plimsolls. They've never seen this team before. Nobody has because I thought it was stupid after I'd done it, sentimental. It must have been that long summer between the first and second year at Beech Park. I kept it though like we always do with sentimental things. To find it in Philip's box stirs a feeling inside me which isn't sentimental at all.

Jon sets the team up, swapping it for his own and, while Charlie is still wondering what's happening, slots home the penalty using the Subbuteo player modelled on himself.

We each take it in turns to play with Frankie's All Stars. And we each lose because the truncated plastic Cal is as much use between the goalposts as the real one was.

'Do you remember that time we lost 23-0 on the marsh?' Charlie asks me. 'Carter was keeper, of course.'

'Careful, Charlie,' says Jon. 'You don't want to go raking up the past now, do you?'

When it is late and the whiskey bottles are empty, my panicking father blunders into the living room. 'Frankie, Frankie.' The candles are still our only light. He is a frightened child awaking in the night. His pyjamas have ridden up his arms and legs. He stumbles, trips, clutches as if at straws and then falls with a deadweight down onto the floor crushing the Subbuteo figures and upsetting the candles. Claudia rushes in. At first she is concerned that the noise will disturb my real children.

'What the Dickens?' says Jon.

I take my father to the hospital. He's confused and in some pain. In casualty I am tempted as they punch my father's details into the computer to tell them who I am but the words just won't come out. We wait. The TV is broken and lines shoot across the screen like heartbeats. We see the triage nurse. We wait some more. It's late.

In the tiny hours, as I sit beside his bed until the sleeping pills work and promise the nurse I'll be back in the morning, I realise the truth. This has got to be my story, my recollection. I can't look to Charlie and Jon for this one. This time I'm by myself. Outside the hospital my car has been wheelclamped.

12

My first guitar was an old acoustic that had once belonged to Cal's father and which Cal had been messing about on ever since that first trip to America at the age of eleven. I inherited it when, for Cal's sixteenth birthday, Mr. Carter bought his son a Fender Telecaster. It cost more than £200, a sum that had my father gasping – he'd just spent less than that on doing up the master bedroom.

The Tele came from Ron's Music in Ilford market and it took us virtually all day to drive there. On the way back Cal spent most of the journey trying to tune the thing and mastered it just as we pulled into Beech Park.

I couldn't play a note then and Cal's monotonous twanging captivated me. It wasn't the sound, not of his playing nor of his father's occasional implorings to five minutes silence, but rather the appearance of both the guitar, jet black with gleaming chrome, and of Cal playing it. He appeared older, like a man with a purpose. There seemed more between us than a slice of shaped wood and six strings. I wanted some of it and as Cal's best efforts at that time were limited to strumming a few chords and picking out the simplest of tunes, I wasn't too far behind.

That summer we went to the marsh once, perhaps twice. I find it hard to believe now but the fact is that my heart wasn't in the football. I just wanted to play guitar. That was also the summer I packed away my cricket dice never to be seen again.

81

I spent the summer at Cal's house. The house seemed smaller than it had on that first fleeting farcical visit at the age of eleven. Now only enormous, it had umpteen bedrooms and rooms I'd never come across before in a house: a cloak room, a breakfast room, a shower room. The furnishings had cosy suburban names: flock wallpaper, sculptured pile-carpet, integrated central heating.

Cal's bedroom was still very different from mine. It looked more modern than it had on my first visit. Some of those old cabinets had gone – though the massive wardrobe was still there – but I could guess from the number of cupboards and boxes that Cal was still a hoarder albeit a more private one. While at home my posters looked incongruous on flowered wallpaper in a room furnished with old sideboards and coffee tables, Cal's came alive against a backdrop of geometric patterns and pastel squiggles and stuff from a place called MFI.

'MI5?' I said, touching the white sheen finish of his desk. In fact, posters were practically all our rooms had in common. He had Che Guevara and one with a black and white shot of a soldier, wilting at the moment of death. The caption said Why? I had one of Steve Perryman and the two from Pink Floyd's *Dark Side Of The Moon*.

I'd sit on the floor, back against the wall and he'd sit on the bed. He had a continental quilt – the sign of a lazy housekeeper Auntie Anne would have said had she known. He'd play the new Telecaster through a ten watt practice amp and I'd strum the battered acoustic. I got very attached to that guitar over those few weeks. It was a big, chunky affair, a country and western instrument, with a tortoiseshell scratch-plate. The varnish had long since gone from the tan body leaving the wood's grain softly exposed. The fretboard too was played raw and gently bevelled. If you could play that old thing you could play anything.

The Telecaster Deluxe was a new guitar, a new model. It had only been introduced in 1972, 'a rare innovation in a classic design,' the bloke in the shop had said. It had two pick-ups, a single-coil and a humbucker which made it very versatile apparently: the fatter, more rhythmic feel of the twin-coil humbucker and the searing treble of the thinner single-coil. This, he said, was 'located as near as possible to the bridge for maximum top'. We weren't quite sure what it was all about but there was a switch on the body where you could choose one pick-up or the other or both. Cal did this regularly, either by accident or design. By way of accompaniment, I strummed with vigour, frantic, loud and long, trying to keep up, trying to compete.

Our first song was David Bowie's 'Jean Genie' which we chose because, as an added bonus, it was also the riff to 'Blockbuster' by The Sweet. We performed it as a kind of hybrid. 'Aah, ah. Aah, ah,' I would go, impersonating the police siren. Cal would do his Bowie as Ziggy Stardust impression – an act made more difficult by the fact that we couldn't make out more than a handful of the words. We thought the Jean Genie lived in a flat and ate nutty slack. Cal would also play occasional notes as if threatening a guitar solo but mainly we strummed away in perfect disharmony, our two chords, E and A.

At first, we spent a lot of time watching *Top Of The Pops*, trying to pick up tips. Then Jonathan told us the programme was mimed. 'What do we do now?' I asked. 'Carry on,' Cal replied. 'Carry on picking up tips on performance.'

What we really needed to do was to see someone live. Not that there was much live music in Beech Park. There was only one 'venue', if you could call it that. So, one Friday night, we went down to The Roebuck public house where, according to a marker-penned notice in its frosted window, Dave Sidebottom Entertained. We coughed, smoothed back our hair, straightened our spines, stubbed out our fags and pushed the door marked 'public'.

The frosted windows were well-chosen: had you been able to see inside, you never would have gone in. There were three customers. Each had a cap and a pint and was dressed from head to toe in assorted shades of brown. There was a dartboard on which the numbers were virtually illegible and to which three chewed-up plastic darts clung. The pinball machine was blessed with a single flashing light and emitted the occasional high octave squeak in a tiny tinny attempt to entice players. Everything seemed to be coated with a gossamer thin coating of nicotine, including the barman.

'What'll it be lads?' he asked, wiping his hands on a bar towel.

At that moment, with those words in our ears, we realised that this was the local we ought to have been looking for. Cal, at the age of sixteen, was still every pantomime director's dream. A dwarf, perm any one of seven, Cal was your man. Tiny Tim? No problem. Babes In The Wood? At a push. And no chaperone required. He was still expecting a growth spurt. I'm sure he wasn't expecting to get served. I looked at him, characteristically tentative me but his eyes darted along the bar taps like a marmoset across a curtain rail.

'Two pints of special, please.'

By the time Mr. Sidebottom entertained we were well past following anything much, certainly not intricate fingering, which was just as well because Mr. Sidebottom didn't play a guitar anyway. He had a reedy, yellow organ of the type popular in school music departments. On this he accompanied himself in renderings of numbers made famous by Ray Conniff, Matt Munro and Val Doonican. He was rewarded with the intermittent applause of... well, me and Cal, in fact.

The three regulars had finished their conversation and were supping in hazy self-contained contentment while the handful of couples now spread around the room seemed more interested in their crisps, nuts, fags and each other than Mr. Sidebottom. He barely stopped between songs anyway and there was certainly no patter with the audience. Each number blended pretty much into the next: 'Jumbalaya', 'Solitaire', 'Loving You Has Made Me Bananas', all received the same jaunty treatment. Cal and I looked at each other and shrugged. 'It's all music,' said Cal. 'You can learn from them all, Bach to The Beatles.'

'Woof, woof, John. Woof, woof, Paul.' I said. 'Mine's a pint.'

After a while the seaside sound of Dave Sidebottom was little more than a familiar aural backdrop, reassuring like a rumbling central heating system. Then, after eight or ten numbers, it stopped. There was a moment of silence and then a fearsome explosion of pulsating colours and bells from the pinball machine. A tall rake-like man had got a replay and the machine was making a real song and a dance about it – lighting every light, ringing every bell and playing a succession of tunes like a speeding stylophone. A couple of other people joined him around the machine and everybody looked over. The guy grinned awkwardly.

When Dave Sidebottom started playing 'Pinball Wizard', he got his first response of the night. Eyes hopped around the pub, glances like moths, catching faces with a shadow of a grin. Slowly at first, unsure, and then louder and the whole pub was laughing, even the man at the machine who managed to lose all three replay balls in quick succession as a result. Dave Sidebottom enjoyed his moment and celebrated with a little ascending signature on the keyboard. 'Anyone got any requests?' he asked.

'Yeah,' said Cal. 'Play the guitar. That song should be played on the guitar.'

Dave Sidebottom's jovial manner changed. A plump man with a deceptive turn of speed, he got up and walked out of the pub.

'Hey, was it something that I said?'

'He'll be back' said the barman, 'I haven't paid him yet.'

The steady hum of chatter began to return. Rounds were bought and crisp bags opened. The pinball machine slumped back into its usual sombre stupor. By the time Mr. Sidebottom returned, Cal and I had given up on the music and I was once again paying a visit to the bar. Under the entertainer's arm was a battered old six-string that made mine/Cal's/Cal's dad's acoustic look like a Martin or an Ovation. A yellow sticker on the body, slashed to ribbons by so many plectrum strokes said Keep Music Live.

He was panting as if he had run back from the car. There was no guitar strap so he perched his bum on the edge of an unoccupied table, foot up on stool. He allowed the instrument to nestle against his stomach then stroked his beard thoughtfully. There was a pause and an E chord shape slowly picked to check the tuning. Then with a sharp chop across the strings he was into 'Blue Suede Shoes'. The money and the show and the go cats go, they were all there, the eponymous footwear replaced with a grinning reference to his 'old training shoes'.

Dave Sidebottom waved a threadbare tennis pump on the end of a tubby leg. His guitar style was simple but strident. He earned another clap and cheer. Later, as he put the kit away and we'd put another pint or two away, Cal went up to him. 'Do you know the blues scale, Dave?'

His ruddy face cracked a smile and he laughed from his stomach. 'Is the pope a catholic,' he said. 'Is Eric Clapton God?' We got a lock-

85

in that night and Dave showed us scale after scale, majors, minors, some I now know the names of – pentatonic, the mixolydian mode and the whole tone – and others he probably made up. By the time we left we were heady. 'Come back next week boys and I'll show you some blues licks,' he said.

13

Along with the rest of our crowd, I became an increasingly familiar guest at the Carters'. Cal's parents always seemed hospitable and pleased to see us. By the fifth year, it was, whenever it was too cold for standing outside the station, our regular haunt. Mr. and Mrs. Carter had leather armchairs and a matching sofa that you could lose yourself in. They were big and black and perfect for sprawling youths. Then there was the state of the art hi-fi, the Rise And Shine orange juice and the bookshelves which actually had books on them.

It was the spring before our O-levels and this particular evening, we seemed to have been lounging there for hours. I think the clocks must have gone forward because it was still light outside. There was palpable nervousness in the room with the impending examinations but we couldn't admit that. Only Terry was particularly talkative and he wasn't taking GCEs, only a few CSEs.

'Continual assessment,' he was saying, 'that's what it's all about, lads. And I'm not just talking about your tests here, no sir, I'm talking about life. I'm talking about your sex life.' This was sufficient to attract the attention of most of us. Only Jonathan was undisturbed. He and Terry were barely on grunting terms and Jon continued to examine the books on the teak shelves. 'Continual assessment, lads, not a one-off (and I don't mean a one off the wrist, Jonny). Like it's all very well to do it seven times in one night but not a lot of use if that's the only night. Know what I mean? You're going to have one very disappointed female for a start to say nothing of the damage to the male psyche. Much better to be a thrice a night man on a regular basis, don't you think? That's continual assessment, you see. Life's a marathon not a 100 yard dash with a couple of high hurdles.'

'Yes,' Charlie began slowly, 'but marathon runners hit a wall, don't they?'

'A wall, sure,' he raised a single finger. 'One wall, but I...'

'Know Your Own Personality', Jonathan interrupted, taking a book off the shelf and announcing its title. He treated the Carters' place like home. He'd known Cal since they were four. You could hear the familiarity in the way he spoke to Cal's parents.

'I don't think we want to know your personality, Jon-boy,' said Terry.

'It's Eysenck,' said Cal, 'Psychology.'

'Introversion and extraversion,' read Jon. 'Have you ever done something for which you feel truly guilty?' He looked around the room. 'Terry, perhaps we can start with you?'

'Know your own personality,' Terry scoffed. 'You might as well have a book, Discover Your Own Shoe Size or Find Your Own Dick Length.'

'If you don't know yourself by now, Jon,' shrugged Charlie, 'heaven help you.' He smiled simply.

'Come on, it'll be fun,' said Jonathan, 'you just write down whether you agree or disagree and then add up the scores.'

'Are you putting us on, limp-dick? What is this? Jackie magazine?'

'Do you ever have any problems sleeping?'

'No.'

'I bet you do. I bet you do.'

'No, I don't.'

'Yes, you do. All that testosterone's got to go somewhere.'

'This isn't a proper argument,' cut in Charlie. 'You're just contradicting everything he says.'

'No, I'm not,' said Terry.

'Yes, you are.'

'No, I'm not.'

'Aren't you prats interested in improving yourselves,' demanded Jonathan, slamming the book shut.

'Fuck off, you cunt,' laughed Terry. Then he tossed Jonathan the sweetest of sickly smiles. 'Sorry, sir, you want an argument? This is abuse. You want the room next door.' By now Charlie and Terry were creasing up. I looked across to Cal, buried in a beanbag, and he was laughing too. Misquoting Monty Python was on its way to becoming a teenage obsession to rival spot squeezing and masturbation.

'It's at the end of the corridor,' Charlie was choking, barely able to get the words out. The laughter was bouncing around the room. I nearly fell from my chair. Even Jonathan was smiling now. Each time it threatened to dissipate so a meeting of streaming eyes or the eruption of a rogue chuckle would ignite it again. We laughed as the minutes multiplied. When, at length the laughter expired and we slowly came to, we were all looking around the room at each other, looking for the next.

Despite the beanbag, Cal struggled to his feet and with his index finger indicated that we were to wait. He was out of the lounge for ages. The Carter's house was a large one but Cal was gone long enough to conduct the most intensive of searches of all of its many rooms. Jonathan had taken to reading out questions again and even Terry was occasionally answering them. Then we became aware of a knock-knocking on the lounge door. A puzzle.

'Come in,' I said after the fourth insistent rap.

Cal entered, his briefcase held aloft like a proud chancellor. He took some hesitant forward steps, obviously in role. 'I'd like to register a complaint,' he ventured. We started clapping and whooping like the audience on the *Live At The Hollywood Bowl* album.

'I bought this parrot not half an hour ago from this very boutique.' More claps and cheers. I rose to my feet.

'The Norwegian Blue, sir,' I said. 'Beautiful plumage.' They whistled and yelled.

Cal held the briefcase up, poking at it like a cage. 'I took the liberty of examining this bird,' he announced. 'And the only reason it was sitting on its perch at all was because it was nailed there.' Our audience were prompting us now when we weren't word-perfect.

'Had to, sir. Very excitable, the Norwegian Blue.' Dramatic pause.

'Beautiful plumage.'

'Get on with it,' shouted someone.

'This parrot is no more,' Cal clutched at a line, the script slipping away. 'Pushing up the daisies, it rests in peace in the garden eternal. A celestial sparrow. It is demised, defunct. It has ceased to be. It is...' and with this Cal whipped the briefcase over, 'an ex-parrot'. From the briefcase onto the carpet fell a dead budgerigar.

Terry, Charlie, Jonathan, they all visibly leapt and I, I am sure, leapt the most. Cal's pealing laughter drowned our collective intake of breath. He was hooting like a parade of parrots himself.

'Where the fuck did you get that?' said Terry, when he recovered. He prodded the bird with his toe and it rolled over onto its back.

'I found it in the garden and embalmed it with my chemistry set at the age of eleven,' said Cal. He shook his head. 'Your faces.' I noticed a label attached to the bird's leg which confirmed these facts.

If this were a novel, I'd tell you that it was Scratch, but of course I can't be sure and I want to tell you the truth. It could have been him. I can't claim Scratch had any distinguishing marks, no grey feathers or a bent beak (or if he did, I never noticed them). This bird was simply the right age and the right colour. The effect of its entrance was to render me speechless. For a split second I thought I might cry as if a friend had deliberately punctured my football but I was a sixteen year old youth with a silver medallion and blakeys in all my shoes so there was no danger of that. On my way out half an hour or so later I did pause for a moment. I sat on the garden wall behind a row of trees out of the way of the house but I wasn't sad, more melancholic.

A car pulled up. It was old and dirty but the engine sounded souped up like the Cortina that bloke who worked with Dad had. The door opened and a woman stepped out, brushing her hair with a giant brush. She looked like Cal's mum but she was younger. Cal's mother looked young but not that young. Had she been to a health farm? She was battling with the brush, tugging her hair, pulling it. It was long, thick and honey coloured. I'd never seen so much hair. Or such long eyelashes. Or such, well, legs. Her skirt flew a bit as she turned to wave at the car as it shot away. She blew a kiss. Unless you count grazed knees or bruised shins or other football injuries, I'd have to say I honestly hadn't taken much notice of legs before.

When you're a teenager, you know straight away when a girl is pretty because they make you feel a bit sick in your stomach when they smile at you.

'Hello,' she said and I thought for a moment my stomach was about to burst from my body. 'You must be one of Calum's little friends.' It was Cal's sister Wendy, of course. I'd seen her before on a number of occasions but this time she looked different. Then, as I looked up and smiled limply, I knew it wasn't that she looked so different, it was that I saw her different.

'You're Frankie, aren't you?' She stopped as if to talk and I was terrified.

'Yes, I'm feeling a bit sick actually.'

'I wondered what had happened to that cute smile.' She laughed to herself in a way that I didn't really get. 'I'd invite you to my 21st but the invitations have already been finalised.' As she walked away she ruffled my hair and then turned back. 'Do you want me to get Mum to give you a ride home?'

I leapt up. 'No, I'll be fine. Thanks.' I was walking away before I knew it. I looked back over my shoulder. She'd gone. The last time I'd seen Wendy hadn't been so long ago – perhaps a month. She'd been with that boy then come to think about it, I remembered the car. What had happened since?

When I closed my eyes I had a vision of that boy standing in front of me in a white shirt with twin crescents of lipsticks planted poutingly on the butterfly collar. As I walked home, the image wouldn't go away. I coughed. I had a feeling like my voice was breaking again. The collar flapped up and down and the lips tormented.

This is the promised land calling...

14

Wardour Street, 1976

When I went to my first proper gig, we were still largely in flares and smoking No. 6. Me, Cal, Terry and Charlie. Cal had a two tone blue and green cross-woven jacket which no tie could match. He hadn't tried and had settled for a black bootlace – not a bootlace tie but a bootlace from my size ten boots. Terry had a bandsman's jacket that could have come from the sleeve of Sergeant Pepper. On one shoulder sat an epaulette as large as his chip. On the other, the officer's pips had become detached and the embroidered strip of material flapped up and down as he hopped from foot to Dr. Marten-clad foot in his familiar nervy manner. 'Too hot to fucking shag,' he announced.

'I should co-co.' said Charlie automatically but the weather didn't seem to be bothering him. He was wearing a simple white cap-sleeve T-shirt and the sweatband he always wore for football. We were standing on the corner of Wardour Street wondering which pub to choose. The Intrepid Fox was a gay hang-out then – 'notorious' according to Terry. 'That's where we'll find Jonny boy, I'll give you a pound to a prick,' he said. He reckoned The Ship was where Jimi Hendrix used to go drinking. Charlie started his usual game of pointing out the location of the apparently legendary 2i's coffee bar where in 1956 Tommy Steele first introduced London to rock'n'roll guitar. To my certain knowledge this steamy-windowed café was the fifth alleged site. 'This is definitely it,' Charlie said. I told them The Flamingo Club at No. 33 had witnessed the impromptu first British performance of Simon and Garfunkel in 1964 but it didn't seem to carry quite so much weight. 'Berties' music,' said Terry. We were walking now, apprentice preening.

On the corner sat a wino accompanied by a brace of Double Diamond bottles and a smell. When he looked up at us he had to lift his whole slow head because his eyelids alone seemed too heavy. Such sights were not then part of London's street furniture. With a jacket and trousers from different suits and a too-tight waistcoat, he reminded me of an older Uncle Alan. Cal gave him some money.

There were posters everywhere for films I'd never heard of – X certificates mostly with explicit titles. We were in the broken heart of the British film industry but I wouldn't have known. The movies weren't for me – I couldn't sit still for an hour and a half. Terry reckoned his old man took him to *Last Tango In Paris* when he was thirteen but none of us believed him. '"Teenage Virgins In Need,"' he announced, reading, pointing at the poster. 'That's what we want, lads.'

'Needy's not enough. They'll need to be fucking desperate,' said Charlie, flicking at Terry's loose blue shoulder apparel.

As we crossed Brewer Street, cabbage leaves bounced and bustled across our path, congregating in the gutter with the newspapers and other litter. There were rotting carrots, cabbages and several handfuls of tomatoes. It was like this was the place where the dustmen emptied their vans. Other sharper swifter feet took it all in their stride. Terry kicked a light wooden fruit crate. From Berwick Street we could hear the clatters and shouts of the street market closing.

'Here it is,' said Charlie. The Marquee looked even grottier than in its pictures. Above the door, the name was stencilled in black sans-serif type, bold verticals and narrow horizontals. How could a shabby black and white shop-front be so exciting? There was a poster depicting an immaculately coiffeured youth with a big motorbike and a pistol to his temple. Eddie And The Hot Rods, it said.

Cal had been quiet. Now he strode up to the ticket box like a professional. It was just a hole in the poster plastered wall. There was a sliding glass window reminiscent of the one Aunty Anne had on her sideboard. The dust on this would have had her in a Mr. Sheen frenzy.

'Calum Carter plus three,' Cal said.

The woman looked at him with empty eyes. He leaned on the counter and lit a cigarette as she ran her painted fingernail down the guest list.

'There's no Colin Carter here.'

'Calum Carter.' He inhaled.

'There's no Carters at all.' She looked up and scowled. She'd been here before. The rest of us coughed, shifted our weight, made like we weren't with him. Cal slid his finger down the edge of the glass window like it was the blade of a flick-knife.

'Ed must have forgotten. Can you get him?'

'Do what?'

'Ed must have forgotten. Can you get him?' No fluster, simple repetition.

When the woman smiled she was sexy like Cruella Da Ville. 'A bit of advice. There isn't anyone called Eddie in Eddie And The Hot Rods. It's 75p each.'

He wasn't playing; he was ignoring her. 'Can you get Ed Hollis the boys' manager for me please? Tell him it's Cal.'

When she picked up the black bakelite phone on her desk and dialled, it rang and rang. Receiver lodged between her ear and shoulder, she counted a wodge of pound notes held together by a bulldog clip. Cal turned to the bouncers. He was becoming exasperated. 'Have either of you seen Ed?'

The bouncers were as tall as basketball players, as broad as American footballers. They dwarfed Cal as he questioned them. 'It's OK, doll. You're from the label intcha?' said one. Cal nodded like a patient teacher. The other one opened the door and we were in. I tried to walk as tall as Cal. The woman was unconvinced. Terry's epaulette flapped and bounced like a pepped-up puppet.

'It's Island innit, Mag. They employ anyone.' The bouncers laughed like boxers. 'Any size.'

Inside the Marquee was black as a catacomb with a heady smell – a cocktail of damp and cigarette smoke. Even the walls were sweating and we were happy to pay ten bob for our beer. 'Cocky cunt,' said

Terry, but really he was toasting Cal.

Perhaps there wasn't much room that night because they were recording the gig. There were leads and cable and roadies in black T-shirts everywhere. The T-shirts were too small and said things like Deep Purple and Emerson, Lake And Palmer. They were using a mobile recording unit, according to Terry. I didn't know what that was then but it was taking up half the floor. It was called The Moulin Rouge. Cal explained that this was French for red windmill which was even more confusing. We were examining it like men round a reluctant car engine.

As a result of the unit's presence, it was crowded down the front by the stage. 'Fucking swarming with punters,' Terry pronounced over the rim of his plastic pint glass. There were elbows and big backs everywhere making drinking hazardous. Cal knocked his down in one. 'Come on. Let's get closer.'

There was no pogoing or slam dancing. Not yet. Just lumbering Godzillas jerking their recalcitrant weight from sweat-stained sneaker to sweat-stained sneaker. Dunlop Green Flash. There were a few bondaged proto-punks who looked a bit scary and a bit silly at the same time. It was early. Punk rock – the English version, anyway – was still in nappies. Eddie and the Hot Rods played loud, fast and distorted but they still called themselves r'n'b. Maximum r'n'b they were like The Who when they played the Marquee.

Terry got into a fight with one of the sound crew that night – the mixing desk was in his way and Terry always needed to be given space – and you can actually hear it on the record.

The rest of us have been captured – imprisoned – on many recordings down the years but, so far as I know, this is Terry's one and only appearance. If you know when to listen and you've got loud enough and sensitive enough stereo equipment, you can hear him between '96 Tears' and 'Get Out Of Denver', just before the Hot Rods' singer Barrie Masters asks the crowd if they're all right. 'Fuck off, you ponce,' Terry's saying.

Charlie still likes it so much that he wanted to sample it for the last album. I say don't tamper with it. What's past is past.

15

We practised enthusiastically seven days out of seven. Sometimes I appeared with my guitar in time for breakfast. Running up and down the scales, finding new starting positions, faster and faster, all over the neck. As we did so we stumbled upon riff after familiar riff: 'Smoke On The Water', 'Satisfaction', 'Sunshine Of Your Love'. It was slowly becoming less mysterious and sometimes your fingers even seemed to know where they were going.

A couple of times when Cal was in the loo or getting more orange juice or raiding his father's wine rack, I picked up the Tele and put it through my paces. The action, the space between the strings and the fingerboard, was much lower and it made your fingers fly. The lighter strings fairly crackled beneath them. After the thick trunk of the acoustic, the neck was narrow and every stretch, every new shape, arrived that much more easily. The Telecaster made you feel like a guitarist and by turning up the gain knob on the amp you could make it buzz and pound. Once or twice when Mr. Carter was late going off to work I could hear raised male voices downstairs as I played – on those days Cal would return with even more goodies than usual including crisps and sweets.

One time I heard Mr. Carter bellowing, it must have been along the hall because there was a hint of an echo, 'But I don't understand,' he was saying. 'You can have anything you want, Calum.'

'Yeh,' Cal shouted back, 'so long as it's what you've already got.'

I just turned the amp up even louder so I couldn't hear. That time Cal came back with a bottle that he said was the best in the cellar – a vintage that had been laid down. As always when he returned, he was impressed by my progress.

'You want to play lead?' he asked, offering me the opened bottle of wine.

I shook my head.

'It's no problem,' he said. Picking up the old acoustic he started to use the cork like a bottleneck, sliding it up and down the strings. 'Who let the cat in?' he asked. It was the sort of thing my mum would say but when Cal said it, it didn't sound like a voice from ancient history. The wine tasted rich.

We were late getting to The Roebuck and Dave was well into his set. This time the guitar was already with him. He smiled as we walked across the floor and kicked into his version of Blue Suede Shoes. It was busier tonight: the regulars in ones and twos, some new couples and a group of girls in the corner of the lounge. I could see them from the other side of the bar. So could Cal if he peered round the beer pumps or stood on the support of the bar stool.

'Old enough?' I asked.

'Old enough for what? To be in a pub or to be on the end of your knob?'

We weren't standing in the playground now or outside the railway station with Terry and his pornographic repartee. I felt myself redden.

'I don't know,' Cal continued. 'You young folk are so osculatory orientated.'

'What?'

'To osculate – to kiss. I thought we came for a guitar lesson.'

We drank and listened and didn't say much and I tried to keep half an ear on the girls' conversation. It wasn't difficult. It was loud and of the type that would have appealed to Terry. It was even more exciting than barre chord fingering techniques. They were drinking Bacardi and coke and Vodka and orange and this and that, leaving lipstick on the rims of their glasses to match their cigarette ends. Voices were raised time and again, arms and hands and eyebrows. There were four of them.

Suddenly I felt a pain in my side which turned out to be Cal poking me in the ribs. I turned and he was rising, beckoning me. As I looked up and across the room, Dave nodded. It was clear that he had said something to us. It was clear that he intended us to join him on the 'stage'. Cal was ahead of me taking steps. Dave extended a chubby arm of welcome and Cal took the guitar. I looked at both of them – Cal, Dave, Cal again – and then at the custard keyboard, my eyes flitting from one to the other to the next, my brain cottoning on.

'What do I do?' I hissed from the corner of my mouth.

'Oh, don't you play,' said Dave as if amazed that there was anyone in the world unable to play the keyboard. He fished behind his music stand. 'Here,' he said, and gave me a tambourine.

And so it came to pass that Cal Carter and Frankie Dane gave their first public performance. Dring, dring, dring, dadada, dring, dring, dring, dadada. The opening chords of 'Blockbuster'. Cal stared at me. There was a steely look in his eyes for which expectation is not an adequate description. He stepped away from the microphone, inclining his head away from it and towards me. Dring, dring, dring, dadada, dring, dring, dring. He had no intention of singing anything. He was waiting for me. I started to play the tambourine and then, with a gulp, with a breath as big as a barrage balloon, I began to impersonate a police siren. 'Aah, ah. Aah, ah.'

I opened my eyes and looked around. We were getting away with it. They were amused. We were getting a laugh. I was getting a laugh. The girls joined in, caterwauling, 'ah, ah. Ah, ah.' And then Cal was singing. 'Does anyone know the way?' I did the high-pitched vocal in a witch's falsetto: 'we just haven't got a clue what to do' and got another laugh. I was enjoying myself. Steve Priest, eat your heart out.

We did great. I was impressed that Cal knew all the words and struck by his voice, the confidence in it. He was professional and competent while I was playful and amateurish. 'Thanks, lads,' said Dave. 'Give 'em a big hand, ladiesngennelmen'.

As we walked back to our stools at the bar, one of the girls flashed past me on the way to the toilet. 'You're funny,' she said just loudly enough for me to hear.

Cal snatched up his beer and downed the rest of it. 'What's up?' I asked.

'Hey' he said to the landlord, waving his glass expectantly and then he turned to me. 'What are you doing coming on like Eric Morecambe? Do you think we're a fucking comedy act.'

'We're not any sort of act, Cal.'

'Too right we're not.'

'Come on, I didn't even know we were going to do it. What was I supposed to do with a tambourine in my hand?' It hurt but I wasn't going to let Cal deflate me. 'Perhaps you'd have preferred a spoons solo?'

'You have to take it seriously, Frankie.'

The girl was coming back again. 'What do you do for an encore?' she asked.

'What do you do?' I said to her trail of scent, a little louder than I intended.

She turned round. Black skirt and bangles. Both of us a little impressed and a lot surprised by my cheek. 'That's for me to know,' she smiled and for a second, across the bar, across the tables and chairs, she let our eyes lock before spinning round again.

Cal was lighting up, inhaling slowly. 'This is all about your bubbling under teenage libido is it?' He was almost laughing at me. 'Frankie, that doesn't matter fuck you know.'

'It was fun.' I was shrugging. What could I say?

'You'd sabotage us. Make us both look prats on an outside chance of a long-shot shag with a long-nosed slapper. Fucking hellfire. It's not as if it's difficult.' He stopped. 'Look, have another drink.'

He ordered one from the hovering barman, for me but not himself, got up and marched towards the toilet.

By the time Dave came over at the end of the show a few numbers later, Cal still wasn't back so I learned about single string lead technique, about vibrato, slides, hammer ons and string bending alone. I concentrated hard because I didn't want to think about anything else. I felt suddenly sober. Dave was a good teacher, encouraging, his explanations peppered with references to particular songs and musicians. Sitting over in the corner of the bar, we played for half an hour or so and when I eventually lifted my eyes from the strings, the pub was empty. No Cal and barely anyone else. One of the girls came back into the pub. Not the one I'd been talking to but a plainer one, blonde with acne. She looked at me and then at the barman. 'You seen Jenny?'

I guessed Jenny must be the one I'd exchanged two sentences with. 'No, I haven't.'

'She's probably safely tucked up in bed by now, love, which is where you should be,' said the landlord.

'Yeah, you might be right there,' said the blonde. The same turn as Jenny on a similarly pointed heel.

'And where's your pal?' Dave remarked.

I shrugged. 'See you next week,' I said.

Outside, I looked up and down the street. I was half expecting to find him leaning against a lamppost smoking. Nothing. It crossed my mind that he could have got himself another pint and taken it into the beer garden. The gate opened with a creak. Cal and Jenny were on a bench in the beer garden. It was dark but there was a decent moon illuminating their whiteness like a taunt. Her torso. Her tits. The belt around his waist was undone. There were hands and hair and a slow sigh. In the grass, illuminated by the moonlight, a silver bangle. I watched Cal jerk into her for just as long as it took me to register what was happening. I think she saw me and Cal would have read the reaction of her body like a book. I walked home and the next morning I reported to his house for guitar practice as usual. We never said anything about it. We never needed to.

The day before we went back to school – that extra Monday they used to tack on sometimes – Cal thought that something special was called for. While he was rummaging around downstairs, I picked up the Telecaster. It was my first chance to try out the licks Dave Sidebottom had shown me. As usual, after the acoustic, my fingers felt fluid and free. It was possible to bend notes through two, three semitones. On my heavy old thing, I could barely manage one. I played every riff, scale and chord I could remember.

When Cal returned, I was feeling my way ponderously through a Chuck Berry lick. I'd spent three hours the previous night listening over and over again to the same thirty second passage. Picking up the needle and putting it back. Picking up the needle and putting it back. Searching for the timing and feel as much as the notes. Cal watched me. In his hand he appeared to be rolling a cigarette. 'You're becoming a proper little Jeff Beck, aren't you?'

'Hardly,' I said.

He sat down on the bed and picked up his Beck-ola album. He'd chosen his comparison pointedly – Beck not Clapton or Page. All three were in the sixties blues band The Yardbirds at some time or another. Beck was the best but also the least successful. Even if I practised forever, I could never play like Jeff Beck and I knew that even then. 'I was only playing it,' I muttered.

Cal was working with the LP balanced across his knees looking like my mother with a knitting pattern, his concentration equally intense. On top of the album was an open cigarette paper. He had in his hand a brown lump which he allowed the flame from his cigarette lighter to caress gently. It looked as if he was setting light to an Oxo cube. A thick sweet smell rose and filled the room. With his fingernail he chipped tiny charred pieces from the lump into his half-rolled cigarette where they sat up in the tobacco like freshly-grated pepper. He completed this chunky tube of temptation with the tiniest of movements of his tongue.

'What are you doing?' I asked but I knew the answer.

He lit the spliff without answering, inhaled, held his breath like a little brother with a tantrum and then released a great cloud of grey-blue smoke. We both coughed.

'Excellent,' he said. I expected him to pass the thing to me but instead he simply repeated the process, holding it all inside for longer this time, swallowing. Tears filled his eyes.

I held out my hand. His muscles, relaxed after the release, tightened again. 'You play the guitar,' he said and braced himself for another puff.

The spliff was on his lips as I snatched it away. 'Come on,' I said. I sat next to him, replicating in larger form his easy body position against the cushioned headboard. I was consciously copying him, taking the same king-sized toke and following it up with the same king-sized cough. My lungs were burning, the heat gently pulsing through my body and then hitting my brain with the sudden touch of an angel.

'I think the expression is 'far out',' said Cal.

We were laughing like kids. 'Where did you get this?' I asked.

He laughed again, raising an unsteady hand. I think he went to touch the side of his nose but succeeded only in poking himself in the eye. Everything was fine and we passed the joint back and forth – old men sharing a cigarette over the brazier, the silent giving and the taking. As we got better we could do it without coughing and then we could do it to each other: inhaling deeply and then exhaling direct into the other's mouth. That was a hit and a half.

On the floor, the record sleeve. On the record sleeve, the lighter, the Rizlas, the Old Holborn and a partly crumbled cube. Cal got up, moving in their general direction. The guitar sat proudly on his armchair. 'It's yours,' said Cal. 'You play. It's yours.'

'Why?'

'You have to feel the blues. You have to suffer. What's ever happened to us – middle-class white boys?' He looked at me. 'Well, me, what's happened to me? What we really need is a little bit of tragedy.'

I laughed again.

We smoked another two joints before my mother telephoned to see where the bloody hell I'd got to. The voice didn't sound like hers. My head danced, my feet dozed. The guitar wanted to wave goodbye. I ran my fingers across the top part of its neck in a tender parting gesture, the notes rolling and fading like ripples on a pond. 'I mean it,' said Cal. 'You play it. It's yours.'

I looked at him for a long heartbeat. 'Are you sure?'

He nodded.

'Okay,' I said, picking it up. 'I'll just store it up here then.' I climbed onto the chair, swaying a little, and placed the guitar on the top of the wardrobe behind Cal's suitcase. The suitcase was labelled: California, The Sunshine State. Just as I knew that I would never be Jeff Beck, I knew that there was no way Cal would ever reach that guitar. Even if he stood on two chairs.

'See you in school, then,' I said.

16

And then the examinations started. The smart lads were not a single unit any more. We were taking different subjects and were in and out of school at different times. The radiator in the vestibule by which we stood at break and lunch times was lonely now or in the company of different, younger children to whom it meant nothing. Generally we passed on the stairs or outside the tuck shop exchanging words of encouragement, moans of suicidal despair and crisps and cigarettes. Rarely were we all in the same examination hall.

In fact, I saw more of Charlie than of Cal. Although Cal and I were taking several common subjects, Charlie and I were both taking Art and there were umpteen Art exams. Unlike other exams you could talk during them. We were well into the fourth hour before I paid any attention to what Charlie was actually painting.

For my pictures, I had taken advantage of our frequent museum visits to produce a series of charcoal studies of the walrus. I was working the best up into finished watercolours. Charlie must have also been busy at home. He was working on a massive canvas in acrylics and was over half way through his second tube of matt black when I turned away from my own pale delicacy with its sultry pastel shades and gentle washes, and looked over his shoulder. The texture of his work, by contrast with mine, was thick and imposing. He was layering the paint on with a plastic knife producing uneven circles and harsh horizontals.

'I like abstract,' I said.

'It's not abstract,' he replied, keeping his eyes on the spreading blade. 'It's a drum kit.'

'A drum kit?'

'Sure is.'

'Do you play?'

'Sure do.'

'I didn't know.'

'Do you think I'd tell you piss-taking bastards?'

'No, I suppose not.' I said. I turned back to my own work, inclining my head first one way and then the other, trying to look at it like someone looking at a piece of art.

'What's that, Frankie? A whale in a duck pond?'

The only person who was around every day was Terry. He had hardly any exams but seemed to prefer hanging around at school to hanging around at home. He was often waiting as we emerged into the daylight, checking on our progress and laughing at Jonathan's hay fever and sure enough he was there when the art exam finished.

'Want a fag, lads?'

'Thank you, Terence.'

'You look like you've been doing the fucking decorating, Charlie.' Charlie's hands, shirt and idly knotted tie were covered in black. He could have been my father after creosoting the fence.

'He's painting his drum kit.' I explained.

'Well he certainly can't play the fucker.'

'Fuck off,' said Charlie, trying to trip Terry up as he skipped a yard or two ahead of us down the path.

'Have you heard him?' I asked.

'Too fucking right I have. Fucking earthquake or what.' Terry laughed. 'Fuck me.'

'Terry?' Charlie began. 'Do you know any verbs other than fuck?'

'Bog off,' said Terry, grabbing Charlie's carrier bag and dancing off with it. We were walking across the playing fields towards the great arch. The gates were open.

Charlie went to chase after Terry and then paused and shouted back to me over his shoulder. 'Come back to mine and see them if you want,' he said. 'My drums.' Then he was off, pursuing Terry across the middle of the cricket square. My eyes followed and then, lighting upon a group of five or six first-years playing football, were distracted. I would have liked to have joined in but of course it was not possible. That was a boy I used to be.

In the corner of the playing field, a games master was bullying an adolescent high-jumper into Fosbury flopping. 'Of course you won't break your back landing in the sandpit, boy. What do you think I am, some kind of a sadist?' Around us rose the imposing red and grey flemish bond of the school wall; ahead of me: an opening.

Terry and Charlie were virtually at the great arch, shouting, swearing and I remember at that moment thinking that we could have a band. We had a drummer and we could have a band. Charlie was calling to me to catch up and, with a self-conscious glance over my shoulder, I broke into a gentle trot. I had just one examination left, the sun was still high above the great arch, huge as a saucer, and we had a drummer and could have a band.

I was catching up when suddenly Terry dropped the bag. He cast it to the ground as if it were contaminated, his sinewy body moving with speed and purpose. With the other hand he grabbed the sleeve of Charlie's blazer and pulled him down on to the grass causing the pair of them to sink to their knees.

'What?' demanded Charlie.

Still hanging on with the other arm, Terry presented his palm. It was black, coated in paint rich and viscous as oil. The handle of the carrier bag was covered in the stuff. Charlie was laughing and then I was too, coming to a muddy halt, towering above them as they swayed back and forth on their knees like religious fanatics, children of the earth or something. Terry was trying to finger-paint on Charlie's face; Charlie was ducking and diving and trying to break away. They were both laughing.

'Well, you wanted it,' said Charlie, between breaths. He pushed his slighter friend away once or twice and then he gave in and let Terry paint his face.

'What are you two? Six and a half?' I said but they weren't paying any attention to me. With swirls and stars and fierce frown lines they came to resemble the choir from that end of term favourite at

Beech Park, *The Lord Of The Flies*. Terry painted Charlie and Charlie did it back to Terry. They looked like girls playing with make-up.

But it wasn't just what they were doing that reminded me of girls. They had an easy companionship that was indifferent to the usual flinches and tensions of masculine physical contact. As they put the finishing touches to their war-paint, I watched the eleven year olds play football.

Charlie lived up past Cal's. 'Will that come off?' I asked as we were walking down the road and they looked at me as if I was the last of the Mohicans.

I never saw much of Cal at all during the three or four weeks of the exams, partly because he seemed to be taking virtually every subject. I also sensed that to see him could have been potentially fatal for me. I knew that I needed to revise even if he didn't. That afternoon round Charlie's was about the only time I went out and that didn't last long. Five minutes was sufficient for Charlie to demonstrate that at that stage he knew about as much about playing the drums as he did about painting them.

'I've only had them a few days to tell the truth,' he said.

'You don't say,' said Terry.

'Actually, they're a present for passing my O-levels.'

'Passing them? You haven't fucking finished them yet.'

'Yeah, well...'

In the event, both Charlie and I failed Art but for quite different reasons, he for using too much paint, me for using too little. We got our O-level results through the post, of course (I opened mine in the toilet) but failures were summoned to a personal interview with the relevant subject teacher. Quite a queue formed outside the office of Mrs. Garrison the art teacher.

She peered at me over the top of her black-rimmed, crescent-shaped spectacles. Two matching wisps of grey hair accentuated her taut temples while the hairgrip charged with containing the brooding black balance of what everybody knew to be a wig shook menacingly as she spoke.

'Water colour does not mean that one paints exclusively with water, Dane.' The words left her lips like recalcitrant peas. 'It is necessary to employ a certain amount of paint in order to render one's work visible.' She showed me a sheet of damp paper which she said was one of my submissions. There was a faint blur of brown which I identified for her as the walrus. As she slowly shook her head, her pupils held me like wire. I looked down, embarrassed, shy and feeling stupid, and noticed that she was writing a letter to Charlie's parents. It included a bill for thirteen classroom size tubes of matt black paint.

Cal passed all his exams and got As in pretty much everything. But, surprisingly enough, I did second best with nearly as many passes – in fact, I also passed everything I sat except Art – and nearly as many As. All four of us – Cal, Jon, Charlie, me – were comfortably into the sixth form and eligible to do A-levels. Terry got his three CSEs, one, some technical subject, at grade one.

We all finally met at Cal's end of exams party. It wasn't a party in the numerical sense – only the five of us were present – but it was certainly a celebration. Cal had the key to the wine cellar with his father's blessing while Terry, having tapped his old man for a post-exam present, turned up with a crate of Long-Life. It was fairly typical of one of our teenage events, more keenly fueled with alcohol than most with Jon, rather to my surprise, proving as adept a roller of joints as Cal. With the other three locked in some debate over the correct way to use a condom or how best to pull a non-English speaking bird or the benefits of water-based lubricants, Cal gestured for me to follow him.

The old country and western guitar was lying on his duvet, a plectrum stored between the strings. Guitar books, song-sheets and records littered the room upsetting its usual dense museum-like serenity.

'Well, get yours then,' he said.

I was confused. I took a step forward and went to pick up the ancient acoustic but he stopped me with a hand on my forearm. 'No, that's mine,' he said. 'Yours.' He pointed to the wardrobe.

I pulled up a chair and climbed on it. On top of the wardrobe was the Fender Telecaster just as I had left it. I ran my finger along the scratchplate disturbing the accumulated dust. I looked down at Cal who was smaller than ever.

'Get it down,' he instructed.

'Haven't you played it?' I asked.

'No. It's yours.'

Cal tossed me a T-shirt with which I cleaned the guitar's neck and body. He watched me as I dusted it, my movements slow and tender like caresses. I was unable to believe that it was mine yet he clearly hadn't touched it. The lead was still plugged in as I had left it, twisted around the strap. Cal waited patiently as I tuned each string, picking notes for me on the acoustic as required.

'Have you really not played it?' I repeated.

'No, you're the best. You play lead.'

He watched for a moment as I played my usual licks. I was slow, rusty having been away from it for over a month. I made mistakes. As he watched he held the acoustic around its neck like an expired chicken.

'I'm a bit out of practice,' I said, repeating a creaking note-bend.

'Yes, he said and then proceeded to do things on the flabby acoustic that I couldn't even do on the lithe electric: no more clumsy strumming, no more wayward fingers, no more fumbled fretwork. Cal had been a hesitant beginner and I had surpassed him rapidly. He had not failed to notice how and now, as his fingers flew around that old six-string, the roles were reversed again. I held out the now gleaming black Fender and our eyes met like reluctant neighbours. He put the other guitar down carefully and accepted my offer. I plugged the other end of the lead into the amp. Listening to him play the electric was, I can admit now, a treat: six weeks on the older instrument had given his hands strength and precision, his technique fluidity and style.

When I picked up the acoustic, I'm not sure I even felt upset or hurt. We sounded so good, you see. As if there might be something there.

'We've got a drummer,' I said. 'Charlie's got a drum kit.'

'I know,' said Cal.

The Sultan of Shakespeare

*Ten years on, Frankie Dane treats Miranda Paxton to a slice of the
south London he once shared with his fellow Go-Kart, the late Cal
Carter.*

(from one of the Sunday broadsheets, 1989)

Designer jacket, loose-fitting flannels, a hat, of course, sunglasses
and a few days' growth. Frankie Dane doffs his fedora and smiles.
The thinking man of punk is back and looking rather donnish.

We're sitting in The Duke in Deptford and he's relaxed and oddly
at home. The docks have gone but this is still a working-class
drinking den. Dane's chatting before the pints are on the table. He
tells me there are rumours that the area's one south-east London
landmark – an art-deco cinema at the top of the market, a listed
building – is to be sold to a chain of hotel developers.

It's a travesty, he opines, but his is no Johnny-come-lately
celebrity concern. Dane comes from round here. The Go-Karts
conducted their first interview in the pie and mash shop down the
road. 'We have to take responsibility. That's the lesson of the last
ten years.' Dane is very open and not at all as one might imagine
given he has a public profile lower than Lord Lucan's. 'You can't put
your head in the sand.' He describes the pastel green cinema as a
fading emerald, one of the area's last links with its past.

'I don't say glorious,' says Dane, 'There's nothing good about
back-to-backs, outdoor bogs and ringworm.' But history is on his
mind, of course. It is almost ten years to the day since the death of
his close friend and songwriting partner Cal Carter from a drugs
overdose. Does he dwell on the past?

Dane laughs and deflects the question. 'Not at all, but did you
know that in the late sixteenth century this pub was once the local
of playwright Christopher Marlowe.'

Did you come here with Cal?

'You know there are some people, academics, who think he
wrote Shakespeare's plays.'

Who? Cal Carter?

'They say Marlowe was never killed in a bar-room brawl at all but escaped to France and wrote on. Shakespeare was his nom de plume. Legend has it that the fight started after a quarrel over the bill and that's the bit I don't find convincing. Have you ever actually seen that happen? A fight over the bill – that's so soap opera. At the same time he was wanted by the Queen's Privy Council on charges that were never disclosed, and after his apparent death was condemned for his atheism and blasphemy. Motive enough to do a runner?' He pauses. 'But why Shakespeare? That was as much a stupid name then as it would be now. Unless, it was symbolic, the pen being mightier than the sword and so on...' he trails off. 'Others say this is rubbish and that actually Francis Bacon wrote all Shakespeare's plays.'

I get the message. Dane looks well and so he should – his one solo album to date, *Stolen Moments*, has sold more than anything the Go-Karts ever did – but inside the scars must still be there. In the meantime, he's doing an Open University degree and is obviously keen to tell me about it.

'The thing is,' he says, 'does it matter? Who cares who wrote them? All I care about is whether they touch the soul. Whether they stand up as art. There's this middle-class obsession with authors as individuals. I don't want to decontextualise but you can deconstruct so much you're left with nothing but some sort of literary determinism. What surely counts is the plays, not who wrote them. The key question is are they any good?'

Dane is one of the few contemporary pop stars who can use a word like art and get away with it. And, of course, the Shakespearean references are nothing new. The Go-Karts debut single, arguably punk rock's first number one, was the anthemic 'Rotten In Denmark'. Dane chuckles when I remind him, but right now he's keen to show me more of south-east London – he has a zeal for his home that most reserve for Greek islands or ski resorts. Nor is there anything patronising about his enthusiasm. He says his one regret is that his fame and his subsequent choice of lifestyle, the pop star without a public image, prevent him from participating in his community to the full, and I believe him. Dane is genuine. Many of the new wave's icons are tarnished now: Joe Strummer, Paul Weller, John Lydon have all lost direction or to use the common parlance 'sold out' but you don't hear anyone saying that about Dane.

We're in my car. Dane doesn't drive. 'I leave that to my wife and my manager,' he explains. In the mouths of some that would sound pretentious, arrogant even; in Dane's it just sounds as if he's not a very good driver. Suddenly in the middle of Greenwich, he slams his paperback – I wonder if it's a copy of Dr. Faustus rather than the new Frankie Dane songbook – onto the dashboard like a driving examiner.

'That,' he says, indicating a hostelry called The White Horse, 'is a piece of pop history. That is the pub Mark Knopfler ducked into to shelter from the rain. Inside, he found a trad jazz band playing to a pubful of teenagers who were completely ignoring them. The dichotomy inspired him to go home and write "Sultans Of Swing".'

'Sultans of Swing', Dire Straits' first single, went to number 8 in March 1979 and Mark Knopfler and the band went on to become one of the biggest bands of all time. Is it true?

'I don't know. But it's a good story.'

I sense another opportunity. Is Dane jealous of Knopfler's success? If Cal had not died perhaps The Go-Karts would have become as big as Dire Straits?

'I'm not jealous. I can't play like Mark for a start. And I think Cal's music does live on. I certainly wouldn't want to be in the public eye like Mark is. If Cal hadn't died, yeah, maybe we would have become like Straits or U2 but I'm not sure I'd be very happy.' Then Dane looks at his watch and he's keen to get off. There's a curious mixture of easy-going openness, when he's giving his opinions, and a fierce closedness when it comes to his private life. That, he explains simply, is why he so rarely does anything. He hasn't toured since the Go-Karts – just a couple of benefit gigs – and only one album in all those years. My remark about Lord Lucan was no joke. Our cuttings library actually yields more information on his recent life than on Frankie Dane's.

'It's all about family. I don't want them dragged into it,' he explains but it's rather enigmatic. Dragged into what? Dane, with his books and his local causes and history and his one blockbuster album every five years seems to have an idyllic lifestyle. 'Yeah, but I wouldn't have if I did too many of these, would I?' he says, referring to his distaste for interviews. Why did he agree this time?

'For Cal. I don't want to talk about him but I wouldn't want you lot thinking I'd forgotten.'

Dane has a second solo album out shortly too. 'It's not really solo,' he says, self-deprecatingly. 'Most of the old band are in The Denmarks as well as a few people who can actually play a bit.' In the meantime you might be able to find him in a Deptford or Greenwich bar looking for inspiration for his new single but even if you do recognise him, don't expect to be invited back for coffee.

17

I knew that on paper I had good enough exam results to do A-levels. Apart from Cal only a handful of boys had done better than me and they were all very boring people. Indeed, for that short, sweet shaft of summer after the results came out and before we went back to school, I felt proud – savoured the feeling of being even taller, the feeling of the air going right into your lungs. Even my father was not able to puncture it, although to be fair to him I don't think he was trying.

The new school year began with a personal interview with the headmaster. We were waiting in our common room with its easy chairs and tea urn – rejects from the more refinedly furnished staff-room.

'Got a fag?' Terry asked Charlie, stirring a seventh teaspoon of sugar into his putty coloured coffee. The three of us exchanged cigarettes – trying each other's brands while protesting an intimate knowledge of all of them. 'Those Sobranie Black Russians,' Charlie was saying, 'well classy fags.'

'Foreign shit,' said Terry. 'Dunhill, mate.'

I sucked on my Silk Cut – shifting uncomfortably in my chair. 'This cushion's got a fucking spring sticking out of it,' I observed tightly.

'Jonny boy,' called Terry, 'Frankie's found a nice seat for you.'

Each sixth former had been allocated a locker. These were housed in a single wood construction that ran the length of one of the common room walls and resembled, to my way of thinking, nothing more than a great pigeon coot – the executive version of what Uncle Alan had in his shed. Cal had been allocated a top row locker and was completely unable to reach it. 'Come on,' he was saying to anyone who would listen, 'swap. Come on. Top row's best. Jesus, what's the matter with you? You won't get expelled for changing your locker!'

My locker was in the middle row and I knew, when the time was right, that I would swap with Cal. However, I wasn't about to do it now what with him scurrying around all over the place drawing attention to himself like he had a label on his head.

'Look, I'm too short to reach it. I'm a fucking midget. It comes from having a heavy brain you know – stunts the growth.' Still nobody was paying much attention. His voice was growing louder all the time. 'And also because all my growth is in the underwear department – my skin quotient is used up – exploited to the full – by my twelve inch cock.' He was both bellowing and belly-laughing now: dancing from side to side, like Mr. Magoo, and pulling people by the sleeve. 'Twelve inches when flaccid that is, when it's fucking flaccid. That's limp to you, boys and girls.'

He was getting through. Even the surliest, snottiest students were laughing. The atmosphere had changed and we were kids again. Simon Hawkins, who had the only bottom-row locker which still had a door, began enthusiastically kicking it in. 'Someone else will do it sooner or later if I don't,' he explained excitedly, 'I may as well get the pleasure.' We watched. After three blows from Simon's size nine's, the door was hanging by a single hinge. Simon wrenched it off and stepped back proudly. 'Look out, the head's back,' shouted Terry, his terrorist's timing still impeccable.

Simon Hawkins leapt diagonally backwards and up – a distance of about six feet. He was no longer the junior zeppelin he had been as an eleven year old but he was still a substantial lump of youth. He fell awkwardly over a low-level table and as he hit the floor screamed too loudly for comfort. In his hand he still held the locker door.

'Thanks, Simon,' Cal said and began putting his stuff in Hawkins's locker. 'And someone call the ambulance, will you, because no one's ankle is supposed to be that shape.' Even as Cal was stealing his locker, Simon Hawkins, through gritted being-a-man-about-it teeth, appeared to be thanking him.

The interviews were in alphabetical order so I was after Terry. When he and I later passed on the stairs we could hear an ambulance coming up the school drive. He was lighting another cigarette, I was looking around for somewhere to stub mine out.

'Fucking old cunt,' Terry began, smoothing his hair. 'They don't want me here, do they?'

'Don't they?' I managed to reply. And that was when I noticed. I'd been aware for a while that there was something different about Terry – certainly since that time I'd gone to see Charlie's drums. Now – standing on the stairs, Terry on the stair below me – I saw it. Somewhere down the years he had stopped growing.

When we had first started at Beech Park, Terry had been one of the tallest in the year – dominant in playground football and condemned, with me, to three years in Mr. Blake's 'big kids with no talent' rugby set. Now I stood a clear head and shoulders above him. It was possible that even Cal was taller than him now. When had he stopped developing?

'Senile old fucker – told me this wasn't a kindergarten. Some bollocks about the pursuit of academic excellence. He said he'd give me a reference and a start down at the garage.' For a moment Terry's eyes lost their jagged sparkle. 'What's he fucking think I am – poxy petrol. Jesus, the cunt. I'll show him – I don't need his shitting reference.' With that he took my still burning cigarette from my hand and stubbed it out right in the middle of the stairs. Then he did the same with his own, lighting a fresh one even before it was out. There was a slight smell of burning – varnish and then wood. Terry inhaled.

'You better hurry up, Frankie, mate,' he said, moving up the stairs. 'I'm gonna burn this fucking dump down.' I watched him go. At the top of the stairs he muttered, 'as if I need a reference for that fucking garage.'

I took a deep breath and eased the dog-ends into the corner of the stair with my foot. Then I rubbed my shoe against the back of my calf – grey fag ash on grey trousers – trying to get a shine in it.

Below me, the heavy oak door swung open and the head appeared in the doorway. 'Next,' he boomed like a sadistic dentist. His eyes skipped up the stairs two at a time and locked on mine. 'Ah Dane,' he said, turning on his military heels and disappearing back into the office. He said it the way he always said it, the way most people seemed to say it: as if he was spitting between the gap in his front teeth. My own feet fumbled beneath me and I almost fell down the stairs and through the door behind him.

Somehow he'd already managed to seat himself behind his desk and once again those eyes rose to peer at me from over the top of his spectacle rims. He was stroking his fountain pen. The leather writing surface in the centre of the desk upon which he rested his forearms was uncluttered; a file with my name on it lay untouched to one side. 'So, Dane, you wish to do A-levels,' he said as if it was the most ridiculous thing he'd ever heard.

'I thought I...'

'Did you now? Did you?' He was slowly turning the pen in his fingers as if it were a majorette's baton and he was practising a complicated manoeuvre.

'I just thought... With my ordinary grades...'

'Of course you can do A-levels.' Some unfamiliar activity in the mouth region suggested he was trying a smile. 'If you can't I'm buggered if I can think of anyone who can.' It broadened, almost to a chuckle.

He guessed I was taken aback and he was right. I'm not sure if it was the smiling or the remarks concerning buggering or simply the contents of what he said but taken aback is what I was. He gestured for me to sit down.

In front of his desk was a large green leather armchair with thick wooden arms. I expected it to make a farting noise like CJ's in that sitcom about the bloke who fakes his own suicide. Reggie Perrin. It didn't.

'Dane,' he said. 'The only thing daft about you is your absurd lack of self-confidence. I don't say this often but I am delighted to have you as a pupil in my sixth form and will give you my blessing for whichever subjects you care to select. And,' this time he definitely smiled, 'I am more than happy to repeat this information to you daily until such time as it finally sinks in.' Somehow, as he was

118

speaking, he had pulled the folder towards himself and opened it. His pen was poised. Clearly he had work to do.

'Right, thank you, sir,' my dry throat managed at the second time of asking. I rose. 'I'll, er, remember that.' I took my leave with a strange loping movement that propelled me and my body towards the door while my eyes remained fixed on the head and his ready pen. The door handle was elusive. The headmaster was still smiling.

'Dane,' he said, eventually, pointing at my open file with the nib of his pen. 'Which subjects would you like to study?'

That evening Cal had a driving lesson and I was walking home alone. Despite what the head had said I felt uneasy. Perhaps it was because it disrupted my world picture but I don't think so. I kept thinking about Terry. The summer had definitely gone. The air seemed heavy and a brown pallor hung over Beech Park like a smell. Cars lined the streets as they had begun to line our conversations. The staccato of stops and starts and shunting gears, the whisper of noxious vapour like a bad memory, it reminded me of home.

In my bag I had more new exercise books than I had used in my entire school career hitherto. For English they gave you an exercise book for every book you studied – as if they expected you to write a book about the book. Through my holdall I could feel their dumbly demanding presence – ruled narrow feint with margin. Something was nagging and the following morning Jon and Cal were waiting, all chat and easy laughter with each other, when I walked into the common room.

The common room was already billeted with a series of discrete camps of the type children construct with bedroom furniture. Most had a hazy roof of cigarette smoke. Alone in the middle of the room were the two almost facing chairs at which Cal and Jonathan were seated. The two coffee cups and single ashtray at their feet sat up like little islets in an ocean of wooden flooring. The three of us surveyed the room like landlords inspecting chipboard conversions.

'Well what do you think?' asked Jonathan.

'It's a fucking mess,' I said and I meant it. In my mind I could hear my mother in her wifely mode assessing the furniture. It might not have been new but there wasn't a scratch on it. Look at it now. Ought to be ashamed...

'No,' said Jon. 'This.' He was referring to the bass guitar he had perched on his knee like a nephew.

'It looks great,' I said, prepared. 'Let's hear it.'

It was black like Cal's guitar and also a Fender. Fender Precision. I smiled. Never, it seemed, had an instrument been so inappropriately named. Jon's fingers limped retardedly around the fretboard as he attempted a funereal version of 'Money' by Pink Floyd.

'Cal just showed me,' he explained, barely even sheepish. There was a faint ripple of applause from behind one heap of old gold foam cushions, a groaned cheer from behind another and unrestrained laughter from a third.

Jonathan had clearly never played in his life and already he was performing to a larger audience than I ever had. He was absolutely awful and it didn't appear to bother him. He simply smiled back. I've never been inside the door of one but it seems to me that in prep schools they give you something priceless, something that otherwise you can spend a lifetime searching for. It's self-belief. It's balls. In our primary school they gave us a bottle of milk (one third of a pint) and a three-inch opaque grey drinking straw. At Cal and Jonathan's school they served a cocktail of confidence which pupils slurped up through great red and white striped straws , dexterous, intelligent and at least a yard long like the Humphreys in that TV ad.

Jonathan's general crappiness was compounded by the fact that his father had - naturally - bought him a long scale bass - the professional size, the most expensive size. It had a neck about half as long again as a regular six string guitar with a bright sheen finish that even the common room's yellowing beams of frigid fluorescence could find. With the September sun already screaming in through the dust coated windows, I found it difficult, as the light caught the guitar, to look either of them in the face.

Jonathan had slim elegant fingers which with his light, still bony build made him a natural for most of the female leads in the school play. On the bass's broad, fresh fingerboard and across its straight stark frets, they tripped and stuttered like stilettos on a polished dance floor.

'There's a little practice needed of course,' he said.

'Of course,' I said.

'Hear, fucking, hear,' said an armchair.

Cal said, 'Look, I need to get something Frankie. I've left it at home.' He gestured towards the door. 'Do you wanna...?'

I nodded.

'So, Mr. Pastoris,' someone said as I followed Cal out of the door, 'when is the Jonny and Calum brazen showband's first jig to be, then?'

'It will probably be around Christmas,' Jon said without a flutter in his voice.

'What have you forgotten?' I asked Cal.

'Only the most important thing,' he said, clapping me on the back like a sports coach and shoving me down the stairs. 'An instrument pour toi. We have to be a four-piece. All the best bands are four piece. The Beatles, the Who, Floyd, Zep...'

'Paper Lace,' I said.

'Exactly Lieutenant Pigeon, Kenny, the Rubettes...'

We strode from the sixth form block onto an autumn morning with dew on the grass, a nip in the air and the sun hanging low in the sky. The term block was something of a misnomer – it was actually an old house. We believed it was still standing by virtue of some planner's oversight and, in order to disguise the error, had been incorporated into the school grounds. At that time, it looked like one of the slum dwellings they'd knocked down in the next street from me so as to build the Bevan Estate.

'They're getting close,' my mother had said when the bulldozers moved in. 'Too bloody close,' replied my father, temporarily putting down his paper and adjourning to the bay window. Now the sixth form block has a preservation order on it.

What must have once been the garden path up to the house led behind the main body of the school and out into the playground.

'Where we going?' I asked as Cal turned across the school field towards the arts centre.

'I've had a word with Blakey. He says you can borrow one.'

'What?'

'Blake says you can borrow a school guitar.'

'Right. What is it?' Most of the school guitars I'd seen were worse than Cal's dad's.

'One of those ones from Woolworth's I'm afraid but it plays and you can share my amp. We'll find someone to make you a fuzz box for their electronics project – that'll sort it out.'

'Right.' When it came to sorting it out, Cal was right up there with them.

Mr. Blake was tinkling away at the piano when we walked in: a jolly jungle of notes. I didn't recognise the piece which was a pleasant surprise. I had assumed, on the basis of five years of school assemblies, that Blakey's repertoire was limited to 'Kumbaya', 'To Be a Pilgrim' and a sprinkling of the less offensive carols.

'Ah, Frankie. Calum,' he said, in his chummy way, as if we were old mates and equals. He was OK, Mr. Blake. Unimaginative in his choice of hymns perhaps but a decent bloke – what my father would have called hard but fair. I'd only been in his class for those two weeks at the start of the first year but he still always said hello when we passed in the corridor and asked how I was getting on. In fact, once I'd left his class he treated me more like an uncle might than a teacher: something I'd been particularly grateful for during those first few months when secondary school seems like a Gestapo camp. Blake had a reputation as a strict bastard and my easy familiarity with him impressed my classmates.

'So,' he continued, sitting back and closing the lid. 'Calum tells me you're becoming a bit of Django Reinhardt?'

What was that? Rhyming slang for Old Fart? I looked at Cal. Blakey laughed. He was negotiating the room now – moving maracas and shakers, tidying the chime bars. 'A bit before your time I suppose, Django Reinhardt – jazz guitarist. It's all Jimi Hendrix and Jimmy Page now isn't it?'

'That sort of thing, sir, yes,' I said.

'Well, it's not much but you're welcome to it as long as you're at the school,' Blake said. He was rummaging in a cupboard. Piles of sheet-music tumbled out and then a wodge of pink examination papers tied up with string. He emerged with a red guitar, a bit dusty but, if the condition of the scratch-plate was anything to go by, not much used. It looked like the sort of thing that Pete Townsend used to smash on stage.

Blake ran his thumb along the fingerboard. 'Of course, it needs playing in a bit.'

'I'm sure that won't be any problem,' Cal said.

I was finding chords and strumming as we walked. It wasn't easy as the guitar didn't have a strap and my tie kept getting in the way.

I gave up, resorting simply to carrying the instrument. 'So we're doing a gig at Christmas?'

'Jon would like to.'

'Why not,' I said, my hand beneath the curve in the instrument's body, the neck pointing forwards and down like the beak of an ostrich searching for a little soft sand.

I sensed Cal turn his head and look at me. 'We'll write some songs,' he said after a moment.

The bell was ringing now – the peal that punctuated our day – and suddenly, the headmaster, looking more like Batman than ever in what appeared to be a new, longer and even wider academic gown, overtook us. I wanted to talk to him, cleared my throat to, but he had gone.

18

The first practice of the still nameless band was scheduled for Sunday morning in Cal's garage. He and I were to spend Saturday writing songs. On Friday night I turned down Jon's offer of a lift to Scamps, our nearest nightclub where Terry and his new crowd – 'gainfully employed, mate' – were to celebrate his first pay packet. Instead I sat up in my bedroom writing lyrics.

I remember this seemed a symbolic, if not surprising, thing to be doing – not going to Terry's first do as an adult. Don't forget I'd known Terry the child longer than I'd known the others – we'd been at the same prefab primary school – but now I was choosing a different direction for my life, stating it and fixing it. Different people. A different type of people. I was opting for a future with the prep school boys, Cal and Jonathan.

Jonathan wasn't going either. He was just offering lifts, enjoying being a car-owner. He particularly hated Scamps with its cheap neon flash and syn drum disco, wall to wall with plastic glasses and plastic smiles. I think he expected to get beaten up every time he walked in there. With his accent and irritatingly polite self-assurance he probably wasn't wrong. He was to spend the evening with Cal improving his still fragile bass technique. As for Charlie the drummer, well, he was practising too in a manner of speaking, practising hitting things – drums, beer, the dance-floor at Scamps, strutting soul boys.

I attempted a few lines on a kind of coming of age theme but they read like one of my discursive essays: lacking sparkle. Rock lyrics seemed to me to be about 'breaking away' from things, leaving them all behind on 'highways', or about injustices and exploitations. I racked my brains. Discounting those at the hands of my parents, the biggest injustice I could come up with had been perpetrated by Mr. Duncan, the PE teacher, who deemed that my inability to produce a wet towel proved that I had not had a shower after games, and, in gross violation of local authority policy, clubbed me around the ear. (The truth was that Cal, who was in the shrimps rugby group and hence in the next door changing room, had borrowed my still-wringing towel having forgotten his.)

Mr. Duncan was never particularly interested in the truth anyway, regarding order and press-ups as more important. Terry reported how in Geography (the star-jumping sadist's second subject) dough-head Duncan had insisted that the Bahamas was not a country but French for Barbados. When Terry produced the atlas to prove the contrary he was sent to stand outside the classroom for the remainder of the lesson.

They say Elvis Costello used to keep a little black book with the names of all those who had offended him – an aide-memoire to retribution. I suppose that's the sort of thing you need to do when you come from Liverpool. But I don't need a book. I can remember Duncan's name.

I tried my hands at lyrics about breaking away from Beech Park – Gonna leave this dusty suburb and hit the road, that sort of thing – but they didn't really work. I kept spinning off into cliché at the first bend. That's how I started writing lyrics about the ordinary things, my ordinary life.

Everybody thinks 'Wonderful Moment' is about Wendy but it wasn't. I wrote it that night and it was about Brenda Bagley, a cohort of Terry's sister, whom I'd snogged briefly before expiring amongst the Party Fours at Cal's birthday party the previous weekend. She had a face like a dangerous dog and a personality to match so I suppose there was a bit of poetic licence there but basically that was as it was. There's a passion, a hunger in your soul when you're seventeen that's called desperation if it's still there at twenty five. It wasn't very wonderful (although it did only last a moment) but Brenda Bagley, wherever you are and whoever you're under, I salute you.

'Rotten In Denmark', later the title track of our first album and responsible for more of the bullshit about the Go-Karts than any other song, was also written that night. With my mother making her cocoa downstairs and my father's television roaring, all canned laughter and packaged punches.

The headline on that *New Rock Journal* front cover, the issue that was changing hands for thirty quid just after Cal died, 'Punk For The Thinking Man (or doll – natch, politicos)', was based on those three magic words. Rotten In Denmark. Sure Cal and I were able to milk it – Hamlet was on the A-level syllabus – but it was never intended. Not by us. The song 'Rotten In Denmark' has nothing to do with Shakespeare. It was inspired by the 14 point headline to a small item in the corner of an inside page of that Thursday's *NRJ* about how Johnny Rotten, in the wake of the latest Punk versus Teds scuffle, was supposedly going to Copenhagen.

What we always liked about the song was that anybody could have written it. Simple chords, simple images. 'Market fascist – Nobel prize.' Up a fifth. 'The Adverts' Gary Gilmour's eyes.' Up another fifth – it's pop by numbers. 'The King is gone, Johnny Rotten In Denmark.' Back to the tonic. 'Where Paris chic is outside drains.' Here we go again. 'And Steven Biko dies in chains.' The chorus took five minutes to write. 'Rotten In Denmark – walk that mile and let me know'. Downstairs, the News At Ten chimed its own headlines and Andrew Gardner took up the news beat.

Admittedly the intro riff is a little more complicated but only a little. It's just that fourth chord – the F#, the supertonic (chosen because we liked the name) – that makes it remotely interesting. Anybody could have written it. There's been a lot of speculation about what the song is about and who exactly are all the people mentioned – a debate that has been complicated by uncertainty over whether it was Cal or me or both of us who actually wrote it. I'd love it to rage – I love this being Dane/Carter's 'You're So Vain', musos and anoraks squabbling over its meaning – but the truth I promised and at least this bit is easy to tell.

I wrote it. Apart from Cal, of course, only Wendy knew that before now. Even Charlie and Jon didn't know. The Dane/Carter compact was tightly closed to all but the two of us. Wendy came up to me after the first proper Go-Karts gig, placed her hand on the body of the guitar which was still hanging around my neck, and asked me 'I know you're not supposed to say but 'Rotten In Denmark' – just tell me that who wrote that one?' She still used to hide behind blusher and eyeliner then. 'I promise I won't tell.' Her manicured hand. My cheap guitar with its Fender strap. Despite the rips and tears in my T-shirt and jeans, I had sweat pouring down my face. She dabbed it off with a powder puff. I told her.

On the Saturday, Cal and I put the finishing touches to the two songs I'd been working on, did something similar with one of his and then wrote one together. Then we worked out 'Promised Land'. We were determined to do something by Elvis Presley and 'Promised Land' was both Cal's favourite and easy to play.

We worked together easily and comfortably: one of us strumming and singing on the acoustic, the other messing about on the electric. Cal had also written lots of lyrics – he kept them all in that old leather briefcase, the one he'd had as an eleven year old – so we had plenty of material. In the afternoon we recorded our five song set on a cassette player – twice so we had one each, watched the football results and *Doctor Who* and speculated upon just how famous we were going to be.

'Of course, you want to be able to walk down the street unmolested,' Cal said over his pint when we were sitting at the bar in The Roebuck – our glasses sharing a black and gold Double Diamond bar towel.

'Well, not totally unmolested.' I said.

Cal shook his head. 'Look Mr. Lennon, my sister is not available for your Yoko-ing purposes. To put it bluntly, she's out of the frame for you, sunshine. You were, in the words of the song, born too late. She is already, even as we speak, being fitted for her nuptial gown.'

'She's getting married?'

'Aye, lad. In a wedding dress of the most virginal white. Another dream made real by Mr. Alexander Carter.'

Although I would have surely swopped mine for his, I was strangely reassured by the disparaging way in which Cal would often refer to his father. I smiled. That Wendy was getting married came as no surprise. And hardly hurt. I knew my Eddie Cochran, I knew she went with only guys that were out of my class.

'Three to one on – someone from your father's work,' I said. 'Evens – another publishing company; three to one against – some other smart arse city slicker; and 500 to one, Terry Chambers.'

Cal laughed. 'You could make a good book,' he said.

I finished my beer.

'I'm just letting you know,' he said, squeezing my knee like Auntie Anne did when I was in short trousers. 'Now, what do you want?'

The bar man was loitering. It was Saturday night but The Roebuck was no busier than on a wet Wednesday. 'Yes, lads?' he asked. Cal ordered.

The lack of customers was obviously bugging the landlord too. 'I'm thinking of having these bands in on Saturday,' he began. 'Pub rock, the brewery call it. What do you think?'

'Good idea,' we said, sharing a thought.

I looked around the bar: the usual crowd. There was also a table of bikers who appeared to have just crawled off the set of *The Wild One*. 'They look like they'd enjoy it,' I offered.

'You reckon?' said the landlord. 'They look like they need a good wash. Two pints, son, that's 72 thanks,' he said to Cal. Cal pushed a pile of coins across the pockmarked counter.

The landlord looked like a man requiring reassurance. 'Bands are a good idea,' I said.

Cal was nursing his glass, waiting for my attention. 'Are we going to do that thing, then?' he asked.

'What thing?'

'The Lennon and McCartney thing. Every song we write regardless of who does it: me, you, both of us. Every song has the same songwriting credit. Every song says Dane/Carter.'

'And we always split the royalties?'

'Of course. Like Lennon and McCartney.'

Sunday was infuriating and exhilarating in equal parts. When Cal and I presented our five songs, Jonathan was overwhelmed and Charlie open-mouthed.

'We're going to do five different songs,' said our bass player, aghast. 'Five songs today.' He made it sound like the musical equivalent of swimming the Channel or climbing K2.

'You want me to play Elvis fucking Presley,' demanded Charlie when words finally came. 'The guy's a bloody dinosaur. And I don't just mean physically. We'll be doing fucking Frank Sinatra next.'

'We thought Nancy,' said Cal.

'Jesus Christ.'

'Has he had any hits?' asked Jon facetiously. 'Apart from with the Miracles that is.'

'Course not, Jon,' said Cal. 'The devil's got all the best tunes.'

'Charlie,' I said. 'Listen to it. It's not 'My Boy' or 'Moody Blue'. It's rock and roll. It's got lots of really loud drumming in it.'

Cal produced a tape and played our version which, of course, didn't have any drumming on it at all but it seemed to work. Before the demo was through Charlie had applied the backbeat and was rolling around his tight-skinned drum kit with a sadist's savagery. 'Nice one, man,' he yelled.

'Charlie,' I said, waving my arms to catch his attention behind the beechwood blur of his drum sticks. 'Would you mind shutting up until we've plugged in our guitars?'

Cal had promised us that despite the fact his father wouldn't be seen dead doing DIY the garage had four power points, making one for me (if and when I got my own amplifier), one for him, one for Jon and one for the vocals. As we plugged in and tuned up Jon practised. 'Promised Land' had cheered him up too.

'It's just that twelve bar walking bass thing you showed me yesterday, right?' he asked Cal.

Cal nodded. For the vocals we were using Mr. Carter's old hi-fi. When Cal had told me this I had imagined some great heavy radiogram like my dad's but this was actually only about a year old – almost state of the art. It had two enormous speakers and a very professional looking microphone which we attached to the overhead light fitting and allowed to hang down for singing into. A dispute ensued as to how far it should be allowed to hang.

Cal pulled it down to his height.

'I can't reach that,' I said, raising it.

'Well, I can't reach that,' said Cal. We looked at each other and around the room – little grins beginning.

'Couldn't you stand on a box?' asked Jonathan.

'I am not standing on a fucking box,' said Cal Carter.

In the end we compromised by putting the mic halfway between the two of us. This was probably the best of all possible worlds because as a result the vocals were inaudible.

It didn't matter at first anyway as we ran through 'Promised Land' a couple of times without any singing.

'You getting the hang of this then Jon?' asked Charlie, after the second time.

Jonathan nodded.

'I have to ask because I can't hear a fucking note you're playing.'

'Charlie,' Cal began, 'No one can hear a fucking note that anyone is playing because your drums are so loud that the sonic boom from this garage can be measured on the Richter Scale. Every time you hit the fucking snare I feel like I've been shot. Look, they sound great and I'm sure they'll be brilliant live but in this little garage...'

Charlie was cursing under his breath as he loosened the snare drum. 'What'll I do about the others?' he asked, a little smugly.

'Try these,' said Cal and from a tea chest in the corner of the garage he began to pull old blankets and sheets. We helped Charlie to tie them over his tom-toms and bass drum and, where possible, to stuff them inside. They were mostly pink and decorated with flowers. I wondered as I placed one over the floor-tom and smoothed it down whether it had once been on Wendy's bed.

'Can we get on with it then?' requested Jon.

'Not quite,' said Cal. 'Charlie does have a point about your dearth in the audibility department.'

'But the amp's at max volume. I can't turn it up any more without the cabinet rattling,' replied Jon, demonstrating his problem.

'Is that so?' said Cal, striding menacingly towards it. He inspected Jon's brand new but perhaps rather small bass amplifier for a second or two and then kicked the back in. Two sharp kicks and the rear of the speaker cone was visible through the shattered wood. Cal pulled away the loose fragments. 'Try that,' he said.

'What the heck.'

When the amp's position was adjusted so that it was the correct distance from the solid wall of the garage, the volume of Jon's bass was increased about a third. At times the whole garage seemed to shake. 'You cannae change the laws of physics, Jon,' said Cal, 'and you've got to admit it sounds better.' Jonathan sulked and muttered his way through another rendition of 'Promised Land' – audible in every sense.

'Okay, boys, let's hear some singing,' said Charlie as the final cymbal crash died away.

Cal and I looked at each other. We hadn't actually got round to working out who was going to sing what.

'Do you want to give it a go?' he asked me. My guitar part was easier.

'OK,' I said. 'Have you got the words?'

In the corner of the garage I had already noticed a brand new sports bag – one of those massive ones that were fashionable. Apart from a few spare guitar leads it was virtually empty but it was Cal thinking ahead. From deep inside the bag he took out the old briefcase and from the briefcase he took two sheaves of paper.

'I got the old man to photocopy the lyrics,' he said and gave me a set. The paper was shiny like photocopies were then.

'These are probably easier to read,' he said, giving me his own copy of 'Promised Land'. I looked around for somewhere to put my set but I didn't even have a guitar case.

'You may as well have this too,' Cal said giving me the old briefcase. 'I've got the bag now.'

There was something about being given that briefcase, my first briefcase – an adult symbol if ever there was one, that reinforced the feeling I had had about not going to Terry's party – the feeling of opting, the feeling that I'd decided what my adult life would be and that now it was starting. I put the photocopies in the case. There were lyrics and chord sheets and licks noted in tablature. I liked the briefcase even more now that it was old. It was rough and grainy like a face.

I took Cal's handwritten lyric sheet and attached it to the microphone lead with a bit of sellotape. Then we played 'Promised Land' again and I sang.

Don't Talk To Me About The Next Big Thing
The Go-Karts, The Roxy
by Ian Martyn-Baker
(from the New Rock Journal, *1978)*

You want a band who are wild with a capital P.A.R.T.Y? You got it.
Midway through the first number the diminutive lead guitarist hurls
his outsized instrument to the floor, marches across to the bass
player's amp and cranks it up. 'You may be shit but you may as well
be audible,' he bellows at a volume that transcends both his size and
The Roxy's poxy PA system. It's what you might call an inauspicious
start but with it hangs the heavy irony beloved of the paperback
writers that Cal Carter (for it is he) and his loping, lanky, less
digitally dextrous partner Frankie Dane yearn to be. And they yearn
with a vengeance. On tonight's electrifying evidence, the Go-Karts
can run anyone off the tracks.

And they run through their tracks with a punch if not a precision,
a vigour if not a virtuosity (dread mot), that suggests the debut
album will be a veritable stonker. The buzz seems to have reached
the tiny minds of those executive dinosaurs with a rare pace that
would appeal to any Karter. The message that these boys are hotter
than a Harley on heat has resulted in the collective removing of
fingers by the record companies and, if the suits around the bar are
any sign, something of an auction ensues. All power to your pedals,
Cal.

It's bassist Jon Waters who's on the receiving end of Carter's
vitriol but if anything it fuels his performance. He responds with a
curt two-fingered gesture and an open grin. The Go-Karts may be
shelling the castles of reaction but they're cute about it too. The
Roxy has ne'er seen so many lasses. And not all in leather or
bondage gear or bodices, ripped and torn. No, some of these ladies
look good enough to take home to mother. Carter, at barely five six,
appears to break the first rule of masculine attraction but nobody
here seems bothered. He's a little ball of teenage lust – the bastard.

If occasionally Waters stutters rather than strums, drummer
Charlie Ball more than makes up for it – crisply efficient, he's got

rolls as long and loud as Keith Moon when the moment's right. Over the top, the dual, or is that duel?, rhythms of Carter and Dane roll and crash, peak and soar. Their voices, low and high, rich and reedy, are equally complementary. Sometimes it sounds as if rock'n'roll was only ever meant to be this way. Sometimes. And then Dane breaks a string or Waters treads on his lead. There's something refreshingly human about their deity.

In 'Wonderful Moment', there's the briefest of brief bass breaks and Jon drops his plectrum – no finger-picking here. Ball's been twice round the kit with tread to spare before anyone but Carter notices. However, his anger is awesome: 'Jon, the one meagre moment when you matter and you fuck up.' Waters holds it together until the end of the song – his thumb, a blubber of a pick, slobbering over the strings – and then, as Carter is pattering, chattering, he picks up the leader's truncated microphone stand and shoves the base through Carter's amplifier.

The little leader is inaudible but his body language is a scream and so ends one of the gigs of the decade. It's lasted barely twenty minutes – and I don't give the band a lot longer – but in years to come so many people will claim they were here tonight that you'll think they must have been playing Wembley. Which is where they'll be in six months time if they last. Come on, record companies get on your bikes: the world deserves at least one album before the Go-Karts spin off, crash and burn.

19

It wasn't all plain sailing from that first practice because, and you won't read this in any other rock biog but it's true about most bands, we were bloody awful.

Charlie could play but, as Cal said, Charlie had spent too long playing with himself. He paid not the slightest bit of attention to what anyone else was doing. We could have been Gregorian chanting for all Charlie cared. Cal used to change the lyrics, frequently singing of how Charlie had carnal relations with animals, with his parents, with Terry or with whatever came into his head. Charlie never heard a word of it.

Jonathan, as you have probably gathered, couldn't play. He still had regular lessons with Cal but at practices he tended to gradually ease down the volume control on his amplifier until only a dumb animal with incredibly sensitive hearing at extremely low frequencies could possibly have heard him. 'But only a dumb animal would want to,' said Charlie when we confronted him with the problem.

At that stage Cal was probably the only one who was good enough to have been in a professional band. Wendy later confirmed that none of his family knew I had put the Fender Telecaster out of his reach on top of the wardrobe. 'It would have necessitated asking for help, you see,' she said. Getting an electric that was my own, albeit on loan from school, perked me up. So did simply being in the band. I started practising again. Not so much to catch up with Cal – he'd got far too good – but just to be good enough. At rehearsals we would swap guitars regularly anyway – getting the two sounds right and then switching depending on who was playing lead or rhythm. Anyway, I liked to think my contribution was as much in the songwriting as in the performing.

To this day, I have never had a songwriting session like that first Friday night. That night when within three hours I wrote two Go-Kart classics. Slowly, we came up with more material. We aimed for a song a week. If we hadn't written one, we arranged a cover version.

We practised most weekends – usually on Saturday morning (so that we could watch football in the afternoon) or Sunday afternoon (so that we could play for The Roebuck's woeful football team or recover from hangovers or both in the morning). We also practised in a more acoustic fashion in Mr. Blake's music room at lunchtimes.

And thus were our sixth form years much the same as everybody else's then and, if we are honest, now. Whatever else changes in the flux of the human experience, the appetites and interests of older teenagers remain as stubbornly conservative as a bridge club. People ask me if I worry about what Philip will get up to. It's not worth worrying about. It is going to happen. It's as sure as the Ace of Spades. We went out (regularly); we drank (excessively); we slept with girls (infrequently and rarely successfully) and we followed fashions (slavishly).

Once they started having bands on at The Roebuck we went down there most weekends – usually Friday because on Friday nights, the fashion Cal and I followed was for smoking dope. Generally, after a spliff or two in the garage or some other unoccupied wing of the Carter mansion, we were stoned by the time we arrived at the pub. On the night of my seventeenth birthday we'd started early and had an extra one for the road. Cal was feeling talkative.

Terry had his gladrags on but his military bandsman's jacket and tightly drawn tie looked tired and old now like cheesecloth shirts. I doubt he'd had a bath. He smelt of petrol. Charlie, returning from one of his visits to the bar, offered to light his friend's cigarettes for him to minimise the danger presented to him by a naked flame. 'She's over there again, Cal,' Terry said, ignoring him. He had a fag on the go already.

We were still pleased to see Terry – he at least had money – but I think Cal was beginning to get fed up with his regular opening gambit. Terry jerked his head forward like a woodpecker and then did it again in case Cal hadn't noticed. Cal was drinking. Charlie and Terry had got there early to get the best table, the one in the booth opposite the stage. In a clumsy piece of symmetry it, like the stage, was raised about a foot from the wooden floor and afforded a view across most of the pub.

At another table, Jenny was chatting to a familiar gaggle of girls. Fingers flouncing through hair, a kiss of fuggy air, a swill of Screwdriver. We'd seen them in here quite a few times since. We had learned that they came from Bromley which was arguably even duller than Beech Park and because the drinks were cheaper, they popped into The Roebuck as a fueling stop before going on to a club.

Cal brought his empty pint jug down on the table like a gavel. 'OK, Terence, what do you want to know?'

He'd never risen to the bait before. Of course, I'd told the others what had happened between Cal and Jennifer in the beer garden – he would have expected no less – but whenever the subject was raised he sidestepped it like the winger the Beech Park PE department had always hoped he'd grow into: off on another path before anyone had drawn a breath of anticipation. It was no big deal, he'd always imply. Terry was so taken aback he had no idea just what he did want to know. He opted for a moment or two of clarification.

'So you'd never met her before?'

'No.'

'And you sang 'Blockbuster'?'

Charlie laughed – he'd heard our 'Blockbuster'.

'That's right,' said Cal.

'And you just went over and asked her if she wanted to come outside?'

'Yes. So what do you want to know?' Cal repeated.

'Well, to put it simply, chum, how the fuck you did it?'

Cal smiled. 'Well, to put it simply. Young Frank here was so distracted by the female form and all its felicitations that he performed like a left tit.' He clapped me on the shoulder. 'And so in order to support my contention that the birds and the bees are a delightful accompaniment to life rather than its whole point of no return, I pursued the said female and,' he shrugged his shoulders and laughed, 'made my point.'

'Yes but how?' asked Charlie. Terry was bouncing on his stool.

'Did you not attend Miss Shag-nasty's biology classes, Charlie?'

'You know what I mean.'

'I just asked her.' He said picking up his glass. 'I just asked. Now, does anyone want another pint?'

With that he was away. Charlie looked at me expectantly.

'I don't know,' I said.

'But the guy is tiny. This is the only fucking pub in the world where they don't ask him his age so how the in the name of buggeration does he get a shag?'

'Size isn't everything,' said Terry, sadly.

'Well, have you lost *your* Brian?' Charlie demanded of him. Brian Ferry – cherry. (In The Roebuck they still served snowballs with a glacé Brian.)

'Not exactly though there is this bird who comes in for Paraffin and a gallon of three star...'

'Quite. Nor's Frank and nor have I and,' Charlie looked up and smiled, 'nor I imagine has he.' I turned around and saw Jonathan push his way through the pub – his sports jacket older than his years. He was all angular – elbows and knees and chin, juggling his car keys and chatting to Cal as the smaller, stockier figure walked towards us with a tray of drinks. Cal's hands only permitted him to carry two pints at a time which, now we were five, would have meant three trips to the bar. Definitely less cool than carrying the tray which he now plonked down in the middle of the table. Jon was still fiddling with his keys like a Catholic with beads. 'Evening, chaps,' he said, picking up his pint but not sitting down. Cal too remained standing. Terry was looking at him pleadingly – he hadn't attended Mrs. O'Shaunessy's biology lessons.

'Look,' said Cal, he took a sip of his beer and placed the glass on his beer mat. 'This is how it is: knowledge begets confidence begets charisma. End of story.' He sat down. 'You been practising Jon?'

'It may be the end of the story, Cal,' interrupted Charlie, 'but what about the beginning of it. The little epigram is all very well but where did you beget the knowledge?

'It's simply part of one's general education,' said Cal, primly. 'Perhaps you should regard your continuing virginity as more a reflection of the quality of your education than of yourselves as people.'

'Ok, then,' said Terry, 'educate us.'

And this, over the ensuing few pints and a less than inspired set by a group called the Love Pump Monsters, was exactly what Cal did: most popular sexual positions for males; most popular sexual positions for females; how to reconcile the two amicably; how to stimulate the clitoris ('Stimulate it? Terry can't spell it,' said Jonathan); how to use a condom (They're for poofs,' opined Terry). It was raucous stuff. Amazement, laughter and horror in equal measure. Our heads hovered only inches apart like a gang of scheming criminals. How to practise oral sex; how to do it for real; the difference between a vaginal and a clitoral orgasm ('What about the fucking penal orgasm?' asked Terry); how to increase your staying power (What would I want to do that for?' Charlie this time with a laugh.); finding the G-spot... 'Where's that?' asked a female voice from out of the ether. We were bellowing now to make ourselves heard above the tired, uninspired but deafeningly voluminous heavy metal riffing of the Monsters.

'It's an absolute myth, darling,' the voice continued. 'Devised by the publishers of glossy women's magazines.' We all sat up sharpish as if a seance had been successful.

'Fucking hell,' squeaked Terry. Women over forty in peach coloured two piece suits and wearing perfume that didn't smell like the eel-counter at MacFisheries were rare in The Roebuck.

'Hello, Mum,' said Cal.

'Calum, your father and I are off now.' She had just a hint of lipstick. 'We hope to be back early next week. If you and your friends are tedious enough to insist on having a party, please be good enough to invite your sister.' She smiled. 'And tidy up afterwards. Jonathan?'

Jonathan rose and accepted the offered arm. 'I'm running Mr.

and Mrs. Carter to the airport,' he explained.

'I'm so sorry to drag you away, Jon dear,' laughed Mrs. Carter. 'Now you'll miss foreplay.'

I guess Cal had what my own mother would have called modern parents. As his mum and Jonathan descended the steps to the main body of the pub, Cal proffered the rest of us his empty glass. 'Lucky I haven't passed my driving test yet really.'

I stood up – it was my round. 'Better make this the last,' said Cal, looking at his watch. 'We've got a party to organise.'

I noticed that Terry had disappeared. 'He's probably gone for a wank,' said Charlie.

But Terry hadn't gone for a wank. Jonathan told us later that he'd seen him sitting on the bench outside. Terry Chambers was making notes.

That night we did have a party and, no, Cal didn't invite Wendy. I'm glad about that because even with my new found knowledge I don't think I would have fancied my chances with her. I'd seen her twenty first birthday party from Cal's bedroom window with the Fender Telecaster strapped round my neck. It had been a garden party. A very adult affair with canapés and vol-au-vents and not a lot of lager. There were Cal's parents and buckets of other people who looked like them wearing dinner suits and frocks. I watched Wendy share a glass of champagne with a man who used Brylcreem and turned my amp up loud. Not my kind of party.

As it was, Jenny Barclay was perfectly happy to sleep with me just as she had been perfectly happy to sleep with Cal previously. She seemed grateful almost because Cal, you see, was no longer interested. Jenny's friend, the spotty blonde one who had come to look for her that evening, had lost her spots, put on a stone in weight and looked fantastic. It was she, dressed in something tight, black and almost big enough to be a dress, who Cal invited to the party not Jen. Her name was Linda Sadler and Cal went out with her for a couple of years afterwards.

While Charlie went home to raid his father's drinks cabinet, Cal and I walked back up the hill to Cal's house, starting on the only bottle of take-out whiskey the landlord was prepared to let us have. Jack Daniels. The group of girls arrived later – swollen on the way by a few more females faces and a brace of boyfriends. One tried to look like John Travolta. The other was more Maurice Gibb. Cal slipped into the role of host, putting on the language and behaviour of his mother like a coat.

'Glad you could come,' he said, kissing cheeks and shaking hands. He helped Linda with her coat. Jenny was still wearing hers. It was a black satin tour jacket. Aspirational but a bit flash for me.

'Hi,' I said to her. 'How are you?'

'Frank,' said Cal, handing me a couple of parkas and a donkey jacket, 'Do you and Jen want to take the coats upstairs.'

The Carter's stairs were broad enough to climb two abreast. This we did but in silence and looking straight ahead. I pushed open a couple of partly ajar doors – one I knew was Cal's room. I wasn't quite sure where upstairs Cal had in mind.

'Is this the master bedroom here?' said Jennifer, as we turned the hall corridor. The heavy pine door, stripped and finished, was shut but not locked. Inside the room smelled of Mrs. Carter's perfume. It was much the biggest bedroom I'd ever been in with two of everything: dressing-tables, full-length mirrors, wardrobes and even two double beds. I dropped the pile of coats onto one of them.

Jenny ran her finger down one of the three ties hung over the top of the furthest of the mirrors. 'Silk,' she said. Then she took her own coat off and tossed it on top of the others. 'Do you think they have orgies in here?' she asked indicating the acres of bed spread.

I grinned gibbonly. 'I shouldn't think so, not knowing old Mr. Carter,' I said. Not that I did know old Mr. Carter. I sounded like someone else, like the besuited buffoon in black and white comedies or Kenneth Connor in the *Carry-Ons*, shuffling from one foot to the other.

'Do you want to see if they're comfortable?' I asked, taking a step forward. Now I sounded like a different someone else: a booming kind of person with robotic moving habits.

Jennifer sat on the coat-free bed and I joined her. Something in her suddenly girly manner told me that I had taken the initiative. I wanted to be honest, wanted it to be clear where we were going so I helped her off with her red jumper – a bit impatiently, rather like a mother with a child who is slow to undress. She wasn't quite what my father might have called a sweater girl. Sitting there in her bra, she looked a little as if she may have been expecting a preliminary kiss. I leaned over and touched her neck, allowing my fingers to fall down her flesh and follow the curve of her body. Then cupping a breast, I did kiss her. Gently as I could manage. I was frantically trying to swallow the bubble of panic in my throat but I kept getting her tongue instead.

We had tumbled back now. She was lying on the bed with my hand between her and the burgundy satin counterpane. We were still kissing. Time was running out. I didn't want our lips locked for twenty motionless minutes like thirteen year olds and I was up against a technical problem. Cal's lecture had rather skimped on the preliminaries and undoing bra straps had been taken as read. It wasn't easy to move my hand anyway. We were still kissing but I could sense her tongue tiring. I flexed my fingers: half caress, half catch-seeking probe.

'It's here, babe,' she said, coming up for air. With an easy movement, Jenny unclipped her bra from between her breasts – the cups falling away like wrapping paper.

I could feel my jeans getting tight. As my hands caressed her tits, her hand fell to my crotch, the other struggling with my belt. I became aware of another imminent problem – the presence of my Dr. Marten boots. These took the best part of five minutes to remove at the best of times. In a frazzling first-time frenzy, God knows how long it would take.

Fortunately Jennifer didn't seem over concerned about the niceties – footwear and so on. I'd heard that socks in bed were a no-no but, for Jen, at least, DMs didn't appear to be a major concern. She still had her own wedge heels on. She'd got my trousers and pants down to my knees and was tugging at the zip on her skirt. I had my hand on the crotch of her knickers but I couldn't really feel much – particularly through the layer of nylon. This stimulation stuff was a lot more complex in practice than Cal had made it sound in theory. What would the clitoris feel like – the bulls-eye on a dartboard?

Suddenly, I could feel a weight against my head as if the ceiling were coming in. It was Jen's hand. She was pushing my head down between her legs. I looked up like a scuba diver. The skirt had come undone and she had somehow wriggled out of it. With the other hand she was snatching at her knickers. I could feel the underside of my cock grating up and down on what appeared to be a surprisingly coarse choice of carpet for a bedroom.

Now with full visuals in place, it was easier to get a handle on what Cal had been talking about. I tried to be gentle with my tongue, tender, but Jen kept pushing me in. Judging by her noise, things were going well. I was wondering what colour vaginal juices were and laughing (nearly choking) in case they tasted like coca-cola or Aunty Anne's coffee. At seventeen even thoughts such as these cannot dampen your erection.

'That's gorgeous, Frankie,' panted Jen. She was pulling me up by the hair now.

Despite the best efforts of the carpet my cock was still hard, albeit red raw. I saw the wink of her belly button as I came up and the soft mounds of breast. I fell on top of her and just slid inside. There was none of the fiddling about by both parties that I later discovered was so characteristic of this business. None of that adult version of the getting the right shape in the right hole game. She sighed and so did I. It felt so small inside, like a child's tiny finger swallowed and tender. It was my seventeenth birthday and I'd just lost my virginity.

Later, when, in Wendy, I finally met a woman to whom I was close enough to talk about these things, I discovered that some of what Cal had told us was less than accurate. 'Part of that fantastical, mysterious conspiracy that unites pornographers and pimps with publishers of women's magazines and romantic fiction is the idea that somewhere with someone in some place in some position it can and will be perfect,' she said. In truth, I think Calum Carter had the same approach to the location of the clitoris as Captain Scott had to the south pole – it's around here somewhere, I'll find it if it damn well kills me and when I do I'll stick a flag in. Perhaps, Cal's epigram needs rewriting a little. It's not knowledge that begets confidence, it's belief. Conviction.

'It's like pin the tail on the donkey for most men,' Wendy said.

'And a fair few women,' I replied.

That would have been about 1980, I guess. We were lying in bed, where we had been for the best part of three days, contentedly eating ice cream. It was Wendy's Paris flat – très joli, trois pièces, 50m² – the one that's currently on the market for 180 million francs.

'It wasn't all rubbish though, right?' I said dropping a dollop of M. Berthillion's cassis flavour ice-cream on Wendy's navel. 'Cal's lovemaking lecture?'

'No, it wasn't,' she gasped, rolling over – the scoop of lemon sorbet in her hand was dangerously poised. 'Just rather heavily embroidered.'

The ice cream I'd cruelly deposited slid down her tummy and soaked into the crumpled white bed-sheets like blood. 'Hey, I was eating that,' I said.

'You know he got it all from a prostitute,' said Wendy, motionless for a heartbeat. Then she dropped a scoop size boule of lemon sorbet onto my cock from a height of three feet.

'I know,' I uttered like a scream.

20

Beech Park Crematorium, the present day

On this the sunniest and brightest of autumn days, I try to comprehend the absence of light. The blackness that is in these ties and tones of voice, in and beneath these eyes, in these tins of soot for a soul. I think of it and I don't like it. This is where we all go – a fact which no intellectual contortion, not even Calum Carter's finest, can cheat.

There are the flowers, slightly more than I expect and there are the cars, slightly fewer. I am standing by the crematorium door as the mourners arrive. It too is black and its design Gothic but it's not even as old as the body in the coffin. Those churchly features that are present in this soulless place appear to have been chosen from some ecclesiastical catalogue. The brickwork reminds me of the Bevan Estate – something produced on the hoof, on the cusp, just after the planner's enthusiasm ran out and just before the money did the same. Arranged on the grass are the flowers for this and today's other funerals and nearby are the urns, still vacant.

There's none of the fuss of a cemetery, nothing so dirty as dirt and the unregulated elements and the sad, stooping stones marking another patch of neglect. Nothing so stark. Here you disappear in a puff of smoke like a rabbit. The curtains close and it's 'more whisky, vicar?' time. For a moment I yearn for something more flamboyant than this cheap magician's fancy. Like the Taoists with their ancestor worship – no problems with words unspoken there – or even those pretty, pictured plots like they have in Père Lechaise, for God's sake. There's Wendy smiling at Jim Morrison's graffiti splattered tomb: 'You can't really do that with an urn of ashes, can you?' she said, her arm through mine. 'Not unless you call in the engravers.' It was that first time in Paris but much later – just before we came back. 1982?

I don't have my sunglasses on this time and it's useful. Squinting into this sunlight produces a suitable display of emotion. As the mourners pass from the daylight into the black hole in which our service of remembrance will be held, the occasional palm pats my back or grips my hand. There's the odd damp, dull peck on the cheek. I keep looking straight ahead.

I'm not thinking of the man lying in that box. I'm thinking inevitably of an earlier funeral. While the tears, at least, were genuine that day, so much else about Cal's funeral seems as unreal as a dream – all bizarre mismatches. For so many of the congregation it was just another event like the Reading Festival or the Living Marxism conference: the punk rockers, musicians and wannabes, the hangers on. This time all of the faces are familiar to some degree. There are no gate-crashers or death groupies.

At Cal's funeral one guy dressed in hippie pelts and beads and a threadbare kaftan was striding around the graveyard with a skull and a Steve Hillage album proclaiming that punk rock was an offence against the pagan spirits and that this was the result. He called Cal's death Thor's revenge. Three skinheads, each in green harringtons with a Go-Karts patch on the upper arm, left him bleeding behind a marble sarcophagus. It was this incident which prompted the Metropolitan Police's first visit.

At the time I would have preferred it if the skinheads had saved their energy for Tony Beale. He was skipping around the church and graveyard like an excitable child at a party talking to anyone who would listen. 'Don't worry,' he was saying in a stage whisper 'there'll be a single out next week.' I took him to one side, suggested that the time perhaps wasn't right. Tony Beale laughed. 'You punk rockers and your little middle-class sensibilities,' he said. 'And there was me thinking you wanted to change the world.'

145

'And me thinking you just want to sell records.' I could barely focus on him. I was tired. My eyes felt like they'd been punched close.

'It'll be all right, Frankie,' Tony croaked, trying a smile. 'You'll survive. The company will stick by you. You know how much we believe in your talent.'

'Tony, now is not the time.' I felt Wendy's presence at my shoulder. 'Someone you owe a lot to is lying in that hole in the ground. I think you should show some respect.'

Tony looked from Wendy to me and back again, slowly registering our unity. 'I owe *him* a lot?' he scoffed. 'Suck my seven inches, boys and girls. I think it's the other way round.'

As he went to walk past us, Wendy's shaking hand leapt out and shoved him over a low-standing moss-ridden headstone. He crashed onto his back, his head landing in the dried crumbling stalks of what had once been a bouquet of flowers. He tried to slam his hands onto the grass to break his fall but he was too slow, too drunk. The cracked old vase that had contained the flowers toppled over on top of him.

'Sorry,' said Wendy simply.

'You fucking bitch. Look at my suit. I'll...' He was red with rage, quaking so much he was unable to find his feet.

'Don't tell me, Tony,' said Wendy. 'You'll see to it that Cal never works in this town again.'

I started laughing. So did Wendy, her arm hugging my waist. So did Tony. Then, just as swiftly, he started crying. A kind of whimper like a struck dog. 'Poor bastard,' he said. I helped him to his feet and Tony Beale tried to brush the mud off himself.

And with that I'm back with my father. I think of his hugs. He hugged me seven times after diagnosis. Real bear hugs not manly standoffs with a concern for social niceties. Holding on to me for dear life. But he wasn't in his right mind, then was he? He hugged me seven times after his diagnosis and that made a total of eight times altogether. I think of his hugs and I try to find something inside but already my father is floating away like grey smoke.

Wendy appears. She's been with my mother. 'She's in surprisingly good spirits,' she says.

'What's so surprising about it?' I reply.

Philip and Rebecca are handing out an order of service. They have on their Sunday best: white shirts and teeth. Philip's hair has been introduced to a comb. I watch my daughter as she assists Auntie Anne. She helps without hurrying, talks and smiles without losing the necessary solemnity. My daughter is blossoming.

'Do you think we can still call her Rebecca?' I ask.

Wendy looks puzzled.

'Well, Rebecca's awkward, isn't she. In the Hitchcock film.' I explain. 'Plain.'

Alexander and Faye Carter pull up in her Lexus. Wendy moves towards the car. 'You're thinking of the nameless narrator,' my wife says over her shoulder. 'And she only appears to be.'

I watch as Alex emerges from the low slung upholstery, projects himself vertically, stretches for those extra inches. If only. Then I reckon he might fancy himself as a Laurence Olivier in *Rebecca*. He's got that erectness and breeding, that steady voice and countenance, that moustache. A smile hovers like a sneeze. The women might fancy him as Larry too. They're of that generation. I can't see Mrs. C as a Rebecca or a nameless narrator. She's certainly not a second wife type. She wouldn't be second anything. But then she's not the suicidal type either and nor was her son.

They're walking across the asphalt towards me. I owe them a lot, the Carters, from the early days. I know that. Yet I also know the sense in which Cal in the separation of death is relieved of them. Know it and now feel it. Mr. Carter has a similar deceptively large presence to Cal – he's taller, of course, but he's still a short man. 'Frank, my boy,' he says, firm hand emerging from his crombie. At his side, Siamese close, she's got a fur for every occasion, Mrs. C., this one's black and as thick around the throat as a cancer. When she smiles I see much of Wendy in twenty years time and I remember how I stumbled over the Carter's front step.

'Thanks for coming,' I say. 'Dad would have wanted it.' The words tumble in an adult manner. There's nothing the naked eye could detect but I am lying. I haven't a clue what my father would have wanted. If pushed I would have to confess that, on the balance of evidence, he probably wouldn't have wanted those 'bloody snobs from up the hill' at his funeral. But does it matter? He's past caring. Funerals are for the living.

And now I'm thinking about my own funeral. I've thought about it a lot since Cal's. My will, my codicil to the one we drew up in the Go-Karts, lays down quite clearly what I want to happen: music, songs, speeches, Subbuteo tournament. But none of it will happen I realise if the living don't want it to. The Carters have passed inside and Wendy is squeezing my hand. I am standing on the step and that realisation nearly blows me over. Once you are inside that box, you take it all with you: your grudges, your anger, your hopes and dreams, your secrets.

I turn to Philip and call him son for the first time. Then I take him by the hand though he's too old for it. 'Won't be long,' I say to Wendy.

They both look confused. There is an expanse of lawn where the ashes of the once living and loved are scattered between an avenue of trees. Pigeons feed. After the concrete the earth feels soft beneath my shoes. I feel as if I could slip into it easily. Six feet down, no problem. I am still leading Philip.

We stop in the middle of the field. 'How's school?' I ask.

'It's OK.'

His hands, one pushing back his hair, the other threatening a fist, give a different answer. To avoid towering over him I get down on my haunches but that doesn't really work either. Now he's much taller than me. Wendy will want to brush his hair again.

'You know you don't have to stay there if you don't want to.'

'What do you mean?' He's looking down on me. I notice that both our shoes are muddy.

'I mean if you want to go to the College you can. If you want. We'll pay.'

Philip looks at me and there's the vulnerability of the truth in his eyes. He knows I can let him down. 'What about the waiting list?'

'That's... That's been taken care of. Your mum...' I laugh nervously. 'She put you down when you were an egg, mate.' I don't know if the turbulence in my throat is because of my distaste for this subject or something closer to home. I cough, trying to clear it. 'Look, you know some people there already don't you, Jimmy and Mark?'

'Jamie and Marcus.' Philip turns away. 'It's... well, Dad, I know you don't approve and maybe I don't either, but I know it'll help. I don't want a free ride and if you don't want a free ride you've got to maximise your opportunities.' My son sounds more mature than I could ever imagine. 'Thanks to your generation, Dad, it's every man for himself.'

'Do you...?'

'Yeah, I do. I'm not as smart as Mum or Rebecca. And I, I haven't got a talent like you. I need that leg up.'

'Then it's yours.'

We don't quite know now how to react. My hand hovers as if to extend itself to shake but I know that's not right. Then Philip hits me on the shoulder. A play punch. It's not hard but I wobble on my heels.

'Don't say you're not smart.' I say, knowing it's what I've said about myself for most of my life. 'You're saying how you feel. You're being honest and believe me, that's a real talent.'

Philip gives a self-deprecatory shrug and a grin.

'There's a catch though, Philip. I've got to do something difficult now, myself. I've got to say something at your Grandad's funeral. Look.' I show him the pieces of paper. I've typed it up: every word. 'Do you think you'd like? Do you want to help?'

Philip smiles and nods. We walk back towards the crematorium holding my speech between us, deciding who is going to read what bit. Chatting like two actors enjoying the power and vulnerability of the method.

'Come on, the vicar's waiting,' says Wendy trying to sound as if she's not shouting. 'There's another one in twenty minutes.'

As we enter the building, I put my hand on Philip's shoulder. Just as we are about to speak something comes back to me from Cal's funeral. Something amusing. I am standing in front of the congregation at my father's funeral and I want to laugh. Amidst all the extravagances around Cal's burial, the showbiz shit, I remember my old blue linen holdall, the one my dad kept his tools in. I had filled it up with all sorts of stuff that had meant something to me and Cal down the years. When they lowered him down I lobbed it, still unzipped, into the grave on top of the coffin and as the mourners tossed on dirt and flowers, my future wife, standing vertical and still beside me, black, mournful, was whispering from the corner of her mouth, 'Frank, was that a dead budgerigar in the bag?'

At my father's funeral I stand at the front biting my lip like a child.

The Effortless Ascent

Extracts from the galley proofs of the Go-Karts: The Warm-Up Laps which was originally scheduled for publication on our return from America. Somehow Cal got hold of a copy and he and I added our own inane comments and silly doodles. Following Cal's death it was hastily rewritten with what Jonathan called a 'Stalinist regard for accuracy' and published on the day after Cal's funeral as Cal Carter: The Crash Landing Of A Pop Star.

They call it paying your dues. Most bands have been through it but then the Go-Karts are not most bands. The Go-Karts' third gig was at the Marquee Club, London's top club venue. Other groups to have graced its stage include The Rolling Stones, The Who, Pink Floyd, Led Zeppelin and The Jam.

'It was actually our fourth gig if you count The Roebuck eighteen months earlier,' says Frankie Dane, ever a stickler for accuracy. The Roebuck, fact fans, is the local pub in Beech Park, south-east London, from where the boys hail.

The first two gigs (or the second and third if you prefer) were as support act at the now defunct Roxy, for which they received more press coverage than the headline group and then at the Fulham Greyhound after which they were signed to Phonodisc.

Cal Carter who with Frankie writes all the group's songs grabbed the headlines at The Roxy for throwing a tantrum at bass guitar player Jon Waters during an explosive twenty minute set. 'But we're great friends really,' says Cal. Fans will be relieved to hear it. Such antics coupled with the band's distinctive sound inevitably led to the Go-Karts being labelled a punk rock band. However, for the discerning listener, there was much more as Tony Beale, the man who pipped all of Britain's other record labels from EMI to Polydor to sign them for Phonodisc, recalls.

'There is a timeless quality about the Go-Karts' music. I don't have any worries about it going out of fashion. Once the new wave balloon bursts we'll be left with the three, perhaps four, bands of true class. The Go-Karts will be one of them.'

'At first there is no doubt that we benefited from being called punks,' says Frankie, 'because it meant the punks all gave us a listen and a lot of them liked us but equally we're not into spiritual straitjackets.'

'We're not really into any sorts of straitjackets, in fact,' says Cal. 'Except Charlie, of course. He's quite fond of them.'

Charlie Ball is the Go-Karts drummer and a man with a head for fashion. He took to the stage for the band's first date in an American baseball cap and he's been wearing them ever since. 'I started wearing them back to front when people started taking our photos – the peaks used to cover my eyes half the time and you couldn't see it was me,' says Charlie, modesty ablaze. There's a practical reason too. 'They soak up the sweat better that way too.'

The franchise on baseball caps is now one of the group's most successful. Their copyrighted design is a familiar sight at their concerts but don't try to count them, there are many too many.

That first Roxy gig was witnessed by the *New Rock Journal*'s Ian Martyn-Baker. 'It was just chance that I was there – you're always on the lookout, hoping to break the next big thing, especially when you're a young freelance trying to get a foot in the door. I'd gone to see the headliners because they were creating a bit of a stir on the circuit. In the event they were a bunch of no-hopers called appropriately enough The Unknown but by then, of course, it didn't matter. I'd seen the Go-Karts. It was clear that they were something special. At first the kids spat on them like they did with most of the punk acts but then they stopped and listened. The music was so powerful.' *[Marginal note in Cal's handwriting: absolute bollocks]*

Tony Beale takes up the story. 'We'd heard there were going to be other labels at The Greyhound gig so we tried to put the scam on them. We put it round that we'd already signed them for a six figure advance. Very big money. More than EMI, A&M or Virgin had paid for the Sex Pistols. It had the opposite effect. Suddenly everybody wanted to be at The Greyhound – labels who hadn't been interested before. The rumour was that even Brietkopf and Hértel were there and they're classical publishers!' *[Marginal note in Cal's handwriting: absolute bollocks squared]*

'We signed for Phonodisc because they guaranteed our artistic freedom,' Cal says. 'We choose what we record and when and what we release. Some labels seem more interested in coloured vinyl, twelve-inch remixes and other gimmicks. At Phonodisc it's music first and marketing second.' *[Marginal note in Cal's handwriting: absolute bollocks cubed]*

Within a week or two of signing and before they'd released a record, the Go-Karts were being featured on the front covers of the music papers. In all they've been on fourteen front covers in less than a year. It's a record few bands could match but that, of course, is the case with all the Go-Karts' records in every sense of the word. In late summer 1978, the debut single 'Rotten In Denmark' came out and within three weeks it was at number one.

This propelled the Go-Karts out of the London-based new wave scene and into the nation's mainstream pop consciousness.

'We started getting fan mail,' Charlie says. 'Mainly Cal. But even Jon got one. I didn't get many but then I can't read.' He's only joking, girls. You can still write to Charlie and all the Go-Karts at the address on page two. Jon, Cal and Frankie share a flat in south-east London so the boys are sure to pass your letter around! 'It means you don't have to walk very far to share an idea or a can of beer or to go to a party,' is Cal's explanation of the living arrangements.

The band embarked on a tour of the UK playing bigger venues than ever before and filling them comfortably even in less prestigious towns. The Top Rank in Reading, for example, said they could have sold every ticket three times over. 'The manager at Reading told us it was madder than during Beatlemania and we were delighted, couldn't believe it,' says Frankie. 'Then we discovered that The Beatles had never played Reading.' Yes, folks, it's yet another example of the Go-Karts eclipsing the fab four. *[Marginal note in Cal's handwriting: absolute bollocks to the power of absolute bollocks]*

21

We'd been to the Marquee again. Our place down the front. The rolling, leaping crowd which was already swelling and salivating like a many-headed beast surged into spasm as the band took the stage and began to play. Our legs were hard against the edge of the stage. My jeans were tearing, weals developing in my thighs.

Cal, that much shorter, went to shout out but nothing came. I could almost see the air being squeezed from him. A hand flailed. One moment his chest seemed to be disappearing and then just as swiftly it was back – waistcoated, T-shirted, rising above the stage. Then his legs too. His little denim coated legs. Cal was growing before my wide eyes yet I was still towering over him. I looked around, twisting my neck further than it wanted to go. We were climbing like soft-pack cigarettes, magically rising up onto the stage. A roadie beckoned us into the wings. A couple of others, a hippie and his henna-haired girlfriend, scurried in behind us – the roadie pointed to a vantage point behind the speaker stack. The crowd had literally lifted us. The surge of excitement.

We were exhilarated by it all – the sprinting beat, the burn of the guitars, the leaping, twisting, crashing chaos of the dancing, the heat and the sweat and the emptiness just behind the eyes. The simplicity of it all. Something inside my soul was singing.

After the gig we sat on the edge of the stage, wasted, and waiting for the club to thin out before we left. Our clothes were glued to us with so many pints of sweat and Cal emptied a plastic glass full of lager over his head. 'Beer's good for your hair,' he panted.

Between gasps, I grunted, 'But the stuff they sell here's water.'

The laugh caught in Cal's throat. A hippie and a punk were struggling towards the door, each leaning on the other. A skinhead couple, smoking, drinking and looking mean, held the door open for them. Someone made a joke and there was more laughter.

I battled with my own cigarettes, removing the battered packet from my trouser pocket. To Cal, I vaguely offered its bent, soggy contents. Then I tried every other pocket on my person looking for a match. Eventually Cal waved a rather pathetic little arm at the skinhead and he came over with a lighter. The smoke bounced around my lungs like a first joint. We were slowly coming down.

Outside, we walked in meandering monochrome down Wardour Street, slowly, somehow disembodied like two malnourished Martians. There must have been other people passing, but I recall an empty street like an early morning: a black is black and white is white sort of world of stark kerbs, sudden leering pot-holes and the odd patch of cobble.

A couple of the tube entrances at Leicester Square already had the iron gates across. We were in last-train territory with the itinerant drunks and London's handful of beggars. We saw the same ones every time. There was an old woman with her grey life in two torn carriers – one from Harrods, the other from Tesco. I always gave her a copper or two because she looked like she'd had a hard time. And the man with a perfectly fitting tweed Saville Row suit that was cut off just below the kneecaps like a pair of jeans. Varicose veins belched from beneath it and struggled down to his battered brown brogues. We called him Bermuda Shorts. Cal always used to give him money because he looked like he'd had an expensive time.

Tonight we were more generous than usual, emptying our change into their respective receptacles – an empty Max-Pax cup and an upturned flat-cap made by George Malyard, SW11. The yellow tiled floor of the ticket hall stretched away like a dance-floor. There was no ticket collector just piles of pink and yellow tickets spewed randomly about his box. Only the down escalator was still working.

'I've got no ticket,' I said to Cal as we began our descent. In my jeans pocket the return portion of my ticket had simply rotted away – the victim of my sweaty exertions. All that was left of it was a smeggy lump which I flicked from the moving handrail. It stuck to a poster with a picture of a corkscrew and a slogan about avoiding the rush-hour.

The platform was deserted and we were beginning to wonder if the last train had already gone when it appeared: red with grey doors, one of the newer ones. We were chattering now, recalling highlights; Cal was enjoying his near-death experience, recasting it as evidence of immortality. 'I knew I wouldn't suffocate,' he said. 'You can't die within three yards of a Fender Telecaster. It's a well-known fact.'

There was nobody in our carriage but there had been. National Front stickers were running down the side of each sliding door – 'Ain't No Black In The Union Jack', said one. 'End Immigration, Start Repatriation', said another.

Cal spat at one but he had hardly any phlegm. He started trying to peel it away but the paper was tough, thick and thoroughly stuck-down. 'Do they use a special fascist glue or what?' His nails were scratching at the edges.

'You're wasting your time,' I said, lighting a cigarette.

Cal looked up. 'We're not in the smoking carriage, Frank.' He said, scraping again at the red, white and blue labels still more vigorously. 'We're in the racism carriage.'

Suddenly Cal fell back. I thought the sticker had come away in his hands. Then I saw that his hand had come away in the sticker. Cal's hands and wrists were turning blood red, drops of the stuff falling to the wooden floor and spreading with the grain. At Cal Carter's feet I saw a razor blade and the top of at least one of his fingers. Blood was bobbing out like a leak. Cal wasn't saying anything. He was staring at where the tips of his fingers had been.

I pulled a sweat sodden handkerchief from my pocket and moved towards him. It seemed like slow motion. There was already a thick crimson puddle on the floor. He was standing stock-still, the right hand holding the bleeding left one up by the wrist. I wrapped the handkerchief around his fingers and pulled it as tight as I could. The damp white cotton turned red immediately but then no more and the throbbing flow stopped.

'It fucking hurts, Frankie,' Cal said, his eyes looking up into my own.

The tube was slowing for the next station.

'Come on,' I said, leading him towards the door. 'You need a hospital.'

A slim snaking stream of blood was running down one side of the door staining the remaining stickers. I ran my finger over the raised surface of one of them and felt the hidden blade.

We stumbled back out into the night, crossing Hungerford bridge like fugitives. Charing Cross Hospital I thought at first and then, with the clarity of adrenaline, dismissed it. Charing Cross Hospital was in Hammersmith. I took Cal's hand, his good one. I was practically pulling him. He seemed dazed. 'I don't want to go home,' he kept saying. 'Not home.'

We went to St. Thomas's where I don't think the nurse believed us. It did sound a tall story the scrambled way we were telling it. She thought we'd been fighting. 'Why don't you pick on someone your own size,' she said to me. There were a couple of drunks singing 'why are we waiting' as she led him off.

'Have you had a tetanus, love?' she asked Cal.

'Yes, he has,' I shouted, sitting down to wait on an orange plastic bum-shaped seat which was welded to the floor.

While Cal was gone two blokes who really had been fighting rolled in, blood all over their sports jackets and turtle necks. One of them had a bandage around his head and a jam jar in his hand which he claimed contained his ear. They went to sit down by the temporarily vacant admissions desk.

'You Van Gogh then, sonny?' one of the drunks called over, conversationally.

Bandage Head looked up and walked like a cowboy towards him, as if seeing them for the first time. 'Yeah,' he said, nodding his head slowly. 'And you're fucking Admiral Lord Nelson.' He punched the drunk in the eye.

The drunk tried to scramble to his feet.

'Don't get up, Grandad or I'll rip your fucking arm off too.' As Bandage Head plodded back, both he and his pal descended into deep, dark, raucous laughter.

By one thirty, Cal and I were back on the street. Losing the tips of two fingers was obviously small beer by central London standards because there was no mention of a lift home. There was little traffic and certainly no sign of a bus.

'We could phone your old man,' I said.

'Yeah, he'll probably send a car.'

I laughed.

'I'm not joking,' said Cal. 'I know he's done it before. For Wendy.'

I shrugged. 'Well, that's great then.'

'I don't want that,' said Cal. As an old Ford Anglia limped passed, Cal stuck his bandaged hand out in a pitiful attempt to hitchhike. Pulling his jacket up around his shoulders, he looked smaller than ever. In my damp jeans and T-shirts, I was beginning to feel cold. Ahead was a phone-box.

'I'll phone my dad's firm,' I said.

The phone box smelled of piss as usual. I was wondering what the chances were of it working when the dialling tone clicked in. I had the numbers in my head and two pence in my hand. I dialled. The Fat Controller ummed and ahhed about not being a West End service especially at this Godforsaken hour. When I told her I was Derek Dane's son, she reluctantly agreed to get me a car.

'You sure you're Derek's lad?' she hissed.

'Course I am. Who'd want to make that up?'

'And we don't want your friend bleeding over the upholstery either.'

'We'll wait on the bridge,' I said.

We leaned over Westminster Bridge, tossing dog-ends into the Thames. As the lights from the hospital played on the ripples, you could just make out the water. It looked like tar. Cleopatra's Needle, the Royal Festival Hall, Parliament and Big Ben, the Post Office Tower, St. Paul's, Tower Bridge and the Tower of London. We ate up the view, Cal pointing places out to me. I still love those views – the London bridges in the small hours.

'They've finished the National Theatre,' said Cal.

'Right,' I said but I hadn't a clue what he was on about. I hadn't heard of the National Theatre then though I'm a patron now. Cal never did get to visit it.

A couple of black cabs swept imperiously across the bridge. I'd only ever tried to catch a black cab once – it was after another gig when I'd lost whoever I'd been with and it wasn't an experience I wanted to repeat. 'Beech Park, pal,' snorted the driver. 'Never heard of it.'

I suppose if I had given it a moment's thought I could have guessed which Park Cabs driver we were going to get. In fact, in hindsight I'm sure I could hear my father's Morris Traveller rumbling along all the way from the Elephant and Castle. The vehicle ground to a halt about twenty yards away from us at the start of the bridge and for a moment or two there was a standoff before Cal realised that the flashing headlights were intended for us. 'That's our cab,' he said, striding towards it.

'That's my dad,' I whispered.

I can't say that my father was pleased to see us. He opened the back door without looking and he didn't ask about Cal's fingers though he must have noticed the bandage. I went to get in the front as I always did when Mum wasn't travelling with us but he leaned across and locked the door. 'Paying passengers in the back,' he said, still not looking at me.

As he did a U-turn and set off back past Waterloo Station, I gave my father a potted account of the evening. He stopped at the lights to let a couple of chuckling railwaymen cross the road and turned round briefly to see Cal's arm. 'Let me know if you need the hospital again because I don't want you waking your family when you get in,' he said. That was his only comment all the way home.

When I woke next morning and went down for breakfast my dad had already gone. He'd decided to do an early shift. On the table he'd left me the bill for an early morning run to Waterloo.

Cal was late for school but when he did arrive he didn't seem appalled. 'He's treating you like an adult,' he said, simply. 'We'll go halves.'

'Why don't you tell your dad?' I suggested. 'He'll pay it.'

'Exactly. That's why we won't tell him. Where do you think I've been this morning? He's got a friend who's a surgeon. Not just any old doctor but a surgeon who specialises in fucking fingers.'

'What happened?'

'He just put a couple more stitches in. It'll heal.' Cal said. 'Eventually.'

He showed me his hand. The tips of his first and index finger were topped off with Band Aids. That lunchtime the dual rhythm guitar style that characterised the Go-Karts was born. We dropped all the guitar solos because Cal couldn't play them and churned out the chords together. Cal called it a wall of sound like Phil Spector; Charlie christened it chainsaw rock. Jon said it was a bit loud but even he had to admit we sounded better.

'You know,' said Cal Carter, his plastered hand looking grossly large compared to the rest of his body. 'We might have got something here.' There are stories, aren't there, of Johnny Rotten miming to 'School's Out' for Malcolm McLaren, of Joe Strummer meeting Mick Jones and forsaking rhythm and blues, of Siouxsie, another Bromley girl, reciting the Lord's Prayer over the riff from 'Smoke On The Water', but, as far we were concerned at least, that lunchtime in Mr. Blake's music room was when punk rock was born.

22

The Bromley contingent and their Friday night fashions were getting weirder and wilder. In the corner of the Roebuck a group of perhaps six or seven including Jenny and Linda were dressed in what looked like customised scuba-diving equipment. It was known as bondage gear. They spent more time in the pub these days. They had to. Dressed like that you couldn't get into any of the clubs round our way. You had to go up west for that.

In town, especially round the Kings Road, you saw the odd gang of punk rockers: leather, chains, kilts, flaps of fake leopard skin over their bums, what looked like kitbag straps holding their knees together, and, of course, we saw them at gigs. It was still a rarity in Beech Park and Jenny's crowd loved that. For me it devalued it all a bit, I preferred it to be something special, something you only saw on a night out. The idea that these were people like us who lived in dull suburbs with bingo and overweight mothers seemed sad. However, within their pseudo sadomasochistic, fetishistic parameters – whips and dog collars were both popular – there was always something nouveau. Another night, another costume or accroutrement. They bought a lot of their gear at shops with names like Let It Rock, Sex and Seditionaries. Only several years later when I met Malcolm McLaren did I discover that these were actually all the same place regularly revamped and renamed. No wonder we could never find any of them.

Beneath black panda-like eye make up and matching lipstick, there was Jenny. Sitting on the edge of the group, her bottom perched on the edge of a seat on which three others were already sitting. With the exception of a pink kipper tie and a tiara, her entire outfit was black plastic including her shoes. As my eyes ran down her body, any lust I may have still had for her evaporated.

'Wouldn't it be nice to play at least once in public before we go our own separate ways?' bleated Jon. He was talking about A-levels. Or more particularly about what would happen after them. This gambit triggered the usual vagueness and indifference. Nobody wanted to think that far ahead.

Although he hadn't even an O-level in the subject, Charlie had this notion about going to Art School. 'Naturally I mean Art in its broadest sense,' he would say.

'Yes but do they, Charlie?' Jon would reply.

Jon and I had done the UCCA thing and it was now just a question of grades. I had no great enthusiasm for any of the universities I'd visited for open days or interviews. I believed like you do when you're seventeen and senseless that it was people made places so be they ancient stone or redbrick or plate glass, as Cal had called Sussex, they were all the same to me. Campus or town setting, couldn't care less. Cal would be going to Oxford, you see; he'd already passed the entrance exam. I needed three As if I was going to get into Oxford. Fat chance.

We'd discussed playing The Roebuck umpteen times – the landlord had even asked us to – but Cal, perhaps recalling that first performance, always vetoed it. He always said we weren't ready – that perfectionist in him. Now the opportunity seemed to be ebbing away from us. Cal wasn't paying much attention. He was drinking and smoking and watching the band. They were a typical pub-rock outfit: a couple of hippies, an ageing bluesman and a sixteen year-old behind the drum-kit. There was a rule that the one with longest hair sang. Cal wasn't even doing them the compliment of tapping his feet.

'I mean to say,' Jon continued, 'we're far superior to this lot.'

'That's right,' said Charlie.

'Maybe,' Cal nodded. 'You're right, of course, but what's the point of doing it unless we're going to do it properly. And there's no future if everybody's going off to University?'

Jon shrugged. 'Cal, it's two wholly different things. We're talking about life and careers on one and we're talking about a bit of fun on the other.'

Cal got up. 'You might be,' he said.

As Cal walked over towards Linda, Jon looked at me, shaking his head. 'Cal is not going to give up Oxford for our stupid little band, is he? We can't even play properly.'

Charlie leaned forward. Now it was his turn to shake his head. 'No, Jon. You can't even play properly.'

I laughed and got up to buy a round. The landlord was watching me as I strode towards the bar and had started pulling the first pint as I arrived. 'Usual?' he asked. Introducing live bands had lifted The Roebuck's fortunes a little but not a lot. The landlord's voice still sounded like two sheets of glass paper rubbing together. 'Quiet.' I observed in a high-pitched tone that I hoped suggested surprise.

Presumably Cal was fixing up Saturday night with Linda – they'd been going out for best part of a year. She looked less ridiculous than the others, I must admit. Still dressed like she knew a bit about make-up. Wore the odd skirt. Jesus, I sound like I'm a hundred and seven. Cal didn't seem to mind, anyway. They joshed with each other like friends, 'a match as rare as their rich and golden hair,' Jon had scoffed. I could hear Cal's easy laughter as they exchanged some dodgy joke. The difference was that Linda was still herself. Her personality wasn't lost beneath that gear. Jenny's, by contrast, was buried.

We'd had a couple more nights, Jenny and I, but for her it seemed as if once of anything was enough. The Wednesday after Cal's party we did it with her on top in the middle of the park. This position and the pain of a thistle in my left buttock enabled me to delay ejaculation almost indefinitely. On the Saturday we did it doggy-style in her bedroom while her mum was down the shops. 'And you'd better be quicker about it this time,' she'd said. 'She's only gone to the Spar.'

These encounters exhausted both our repetoires and the relationship. Of course, I felt that turbulence in my tummy when I first heard that she'd slept with all four of the Bromley boys, that sickness that says you're alive, but I couldn't care less now. It was up to her and there was no point being angry. After all, I hadn't done it doggy since. In fact, I hadn't done much of anything. The pints stood there on the bar like sentries, guarding my three pound notes and a tiny pile of change. I took a big gulp.

As I was taking Jon and Charlie their beers, I noticed that Cal was no longer chatting with Linda. The band were taking a break and Cal was talking to the singer – a simian individual with hair down to his nipples, a tatty leather biker's jacket and Jack Daniels T-shirt. Cal, pointing out some detail in the design, had noticed the latter.

'Hold on,' I said. I removed Jon's pint from his hand just as it reached his lips and then walked towards the stage with the three beers. I could hear Jon bleating behind me.

'Far out,' said the biker when he saw me.

'Great set,' I said, handing him the beer. 'Sorry. Couldn't afford a Jack Daniels.'

'Hey. Too bad, man.' Half the beer disappeared in one draft.

'Look,' said Cal. 'Here's the point. How much are they paying you tonight?'

'A score.'

'I'll match it.'

'You're crazy, man. They'll *give* you a gig here if you ask, like.' He laughed. 'This dude'll give anyone a gig.'

'But it's got to be tonight,' Cal said. 'I'm serious.'

The biker finished his pint. With a sweep of his tattooed arm he wiped the flecks of froth from his beard and moustache. He regarded Cal for a moment – I could see the Carter charm was weaving its spell. 'Spider, this guy wants to play after us tonight.'

The other hairy one looked up from tuning his guitar. He was taller, painfully slim and his tight black vest had even blacker chest hair peering out of its every opening. He barely looked in our direction. 'Stuff it.'

'He'll pay twenty.'

Painfully Slim turned round. 'You want to use our gear?'

Cal nodded.

'You better show us you can play then. Don't want it damaged.'

He thrust his guitar into Cal's hands. It wasn't a make I was familiar with. It looked home-made. It was solid but the body was at least five inches thick – more like a semi-acoustic in that respect. Broad fretboard, scratch plate like a serving dish and dials like upturned tumblers, it was massive in every way, heavy too if Cal's reaction was anything to go by. Cal negotiated the thick leather strap. His fingertips must still have been painful but he played like he used to – a little bit of Clapton, a dollop of Page. Although the guitar wasn't plugged in, the other two guys in the band came over to listen.

'No sweat,' said Spider when Cal had finished. 'Five numbers, right. We'll finish a bit early.'

Cal handed back the guitar. Then he pulled a crisp twenty pound note from his wallet.

'Far out,' said the biker. He looked like he'd never seen one before. Like me, I'm sure he'd never owned one.

Spider called after us as we were walking back. 'What you called?'

We looked at each other and then at Spider. All three of us shrugged.

Back at the table, a fresh round of drinks had appeared. 'I hope that was worth my pint, Frankie,' Jon began, a little wounded.

'It certainly was, Jonathan, my boy,' said Cal. 'You wanted to play before we go away and now you will.'

'Great' said Jon, finishing the beer that I'd foolishly put down on the table. 'You've got us a gig.'

'Yeah,' said Cal. He was starting a new pint. 'Tonight.'

Jon choked on his ill-gotten liquor. 'Tonight! Are you mad? I've had three pints.'

'Well have another couple,' Cal said. 'Nobody will know the difference.'

There was about half an hour before we went on stage – long enough to phone Wendy and get her to bring Cal's cassette recorder down. If this was to be a one and only we wanted it for posterity. Now we had the excuse that we were drinking to calm our nerves. Charlie practised on the table-top tapping out rhythms on the beer mats and Jon made himself sick in the toilet. He had sneaked into the Ladies so we wouldn't find him and Cal had had to send Linda in. 'Come on,' he said to me and we went out into the deserted beer garden for a couple of joints.

We had discussed a name before. Cal and Jon in their car keys jangling in the pocket phase suggested souped up bulging bonnet sort of names. I'd vetoed them then and did when, through a plume of whitey blue smoke, Cal raised the subject again.

'Nothing faster than a Go-Kart,' I said.

'OK,' said Cal. And that was it. The Go-Karts. As simple as that. I would love to tell you that it was after a childhood turning point – after a much loved Go-Kart which I crashed and as a result refused ever to drive anything again – but I can't. There's no Rosebud in this story. That Cal was both a Carter and a Karter was a coincidence the full impact of which I'm not sure even he appreciated at the time.

The whole performance went like a dream and I mean that in both senses of the word. We were all too drunk to feel anything much even had there been time to get nervous. True Jonathan dropped the bass guitar and Charlie tripped over the hi-hat stand but that was all before we started. From the first chord of 'Promised Land' to the last cymbal crash five numbers later we had a great time.

Jon was actually in his element. The bassist in the other band had a smaller scale bass than the one Jon owned which meant it was much easier for him to play. This time, when Cal told him to turn the bass amp up he happily tried to comply. Unfortunately what Spider's bassist lacked in guitar he made up for in amplification. There were knobs everywhere and none of them seemed to say anything so simple as 'volume'. Jon looked at it blankly. We were midway through 'Promised Land' – I'd just played the guitar solo as I had been ever since Cal chopped his fingers off. He sang it now instead. What to do? Cal, still strumming vigorously, wandered over. He shrugged too. So Jon did what Cal had done. Jon kicked the back of the speaker in. This one was somewhat more substantial than his own amp but he managed it eventually: the wood cracking in time with Charlie's thudding bass drum beat. At this point, the pub punters, bored at best with Biker's band, came to life. Jenny, Linda and the Bromley crowd came down the front and started pogoing. Jon joined in. Biker's band came to life more than most. Either he and Spider were dancing or they were hopping mad.

I can't remember what we played next – 'Sitting On The Dock Of The Bay', perhaps – but I know it started with the drums and they sounded great. I had to check to see if it was really Charlie playing. As he rolled around the kit our already receding drummer smiled at me as if he'd just got a joke after a long time. A lesson was being learned. Charlie, in his quest for volume, tightened every skin on his kit until it was as taut as possible; these drums were set up to provide a specific selection of timbres and pitches. Charlie realised that drums could be tuned. I kicked in with the fuzz-box and another half a dozen people took to the dance floor.

Vandalising the bass speaker had the opposite effect to that which it had had in the garage. Without a wall behind it, the low frequency notes tumbled out of the back to be swallowed up by the room. Jon was still too quiet which, at this stage of our career, was still a bonus. What's more he was too drunk to notice. The main effect of his playing in the lower registers was to set off the coursing vibration of the delicate wooden stage and through it the floor of the pub. The joint was literally jumping.

By the time we got to 'Rotten In Denmark' with Cal and I harmonising and enjoying our first go at separate microphones, the place was livelier than it had ever been before (admittedly not difficult). Down the front the Bromley crowd were doing a dance that basically involved taking your partner by the throat and leaping around violently. Wearing bondage strides made it all the more dangerous. We got wild, wild, wild. The effect of all this was that Biker and Spider et al could not get near the stage. At the bar I could see them drinking furiously.

When we'd played our five songs there was clapping and cheering and whistling. Linda was roaring for more so Cal obliged. The encore we made up as we went along. It consisted of a backing track of frenetic riffing and Cal yelling 'Do not adjust your set' over the top – it was the birth of the number that we later turned into 'Do Not Adjust Your Scepticism', our second single.

The power-chord crash ending soaring to a double cymbal crescendo coincided with the time-bell which the landlord was ringing like a campanologist gone crazy. 'Time, please,' he bellowed as the final chord reluctantly expired, 'Time, please.'

'Sorry,' said Cal into the microphone, 'No Pink Floyd.' The punks went mad. Meanwhile Biker's band had cut around the back and were now, even as the audience clapped, pulling Charlie from the drum stool. He still had his feet in the pedals as they wrestled him to the floor. Jon grabbed a bit of wood from the backless speaker cabinet and adopted an Errol Flynn style guard. Charlie managed to poke Spider in the eye with a drumstick. As Spider swung a heavy fist, the crowd stepped back, realising now that this wasn't part of the act.

'Grab the lanky bastard's leg,' advised Jon.

'Look, lads, I'm sure we can sort this out amicably,' Cal said as Biker tried to grab the guitar from him.

'I'm a guy of peace, love and flowers, but you dudes are bad karma,' was Biker's considered response. He went to kick Cal in the testicles at the same time as Linda brought a Double Diamond bottle down his head. I was lost for a moment. I hadn't had a fight since I was nine and I didn't know what to do. Biker was on the floor holding his head in one hand and his boot in the other (Cal's height meant that even the best aimed kick could not reach his bollocks without first hitting the solid wood of the guitar). As I stepped over Biker, his band's juvenile drummer leapt monkey-like onto my back. One arm around my neck he began punching me in the side of the head with the other.

'Isn't he under age?' asked Jon.

I began screaming and screaming like the tantrum prone offspring of a whirling dervish and a howling banshee, I charged straight towards the toilets. They had been added, as in so many pubs, as an apparent afterthought, and I knew that the top of the door frame cleared my head by just a couple of inches. As my tennis shoe touched down on the tiled floor, the little drummer boy's head cracked against the jamb like a rim shot and I felt him fall from my back with a thud.

I continued, still screaming, right out of the other door, into the beer garden and back round into the pub that way, slowing down to close the rotting white painted gate and step back onto the High Street just as the police cars screeched over the brow of the hill. I sensed that this was an opportunity that wouldn't arise again and with a skip in my stride I pushed at the heavy door and stepped back into The Roebuck. Amid the mayhem the one discernable image was of Cal waving the guitar around his head like a shillelagh.

'It's the pigs,' I yelled at the top of my voice.

An hour or so later Cal and I were walking back up the hill. I was nursing a bruise on my cheek. He was lighter still further in the wallet department after settling up for the damage to the amp.

'Well, the playing bit was great,' I began.

'Yeah.'

'Jon was right. It's got to be worth doing it again if we can sound like that.'

'There's no time, Frankie.'

'What do you mean? The exams? Well, we can sort that out. We're quite tight now. Don't need so much practice.'

'No, it's not that.' Cal stopped walking. We were near the top of the hill. There was just a hint of sadness as he spoke. 'I'm leaving school, anyway.'

I looked at him. Behind his beacon of blond hair a drizzle of rain was beginning, causing the lights of London to twinkle as they scampered for cover behind the trees.

'I'm going to America. Linda and I...'

'How long for?'

'Maybe for good.'

The King is gone,
Johnny Rotten In
Denmark ...

23

North Wales, 1978

As you will know we recorded the Rotten In Denmark album in Portmerion in North Wales. It's a small Italianate village, the architectural whim of an eccentric English gentleman who wanted to be master of all he surveyed. Its pretty combination of shapes and colours and miniature scale – the arches you can just about walk beneath, the doors you can just about enter – give it the feel walking into a cartoon. Then there are the dense yet cultivated woodlands and the vast bay of a beach with its suntraps and coves. They used the village as the setting for the very popular but very confusing (and therefore very clever) TV series *The Prisoner* and that, perhaps more than any of the other reasons, is why Cal's choice of Portmerion for our recording session was such a shrewd stroke.

We didn't do the recording in Portmerion itself but we made a video and had all the photos taken there. We were staying in a cottage nearby which had a basement and it was this that we used as the studio. With us we took a 24-track mobile recording unit which we parked in the drive. For a while Charlie was trying to persuade us to take Terry Chambers along to operate the thing but Phonodisc weren't having that. They insisted on a professional so we took Wesley Walker who had operated the tape on our single. We were impressed with him because he'd successfully diagnosed the problem with Jon's bass sound as arising from a 'bleeding great hole in the back of the amp'. They were unenthusiastic about the whole idea anyway, Phonodisc. Most first albums are recorded under tight supervision using the label's house producers and engineers. 'They think you're just after a fucking holiday,' said Tony. 'Heaven forbid,' said Cal.

Imagine the five of us in this fantasy village. It was, as Cal later said to some newspaper, 'like a schoolboy dream.' But it worked. Cal understood our collective psyche well. In this make-believe land we could make-believe that we were quality musicians recording yet another album. It also worked because if Portmerion was architect Sir Clough William Ellis's attempt to play God then the first album, here in this toytown where his height for once was just right, was Cal's. Wesley rigged up a voice-back system so that the studio (where the instruments were) and the control room (the back of the mobile where the mixing desk and master tape were) could communicate with each other. With Wesley at his right arm, Cal spent most of the time up there issuing instructions to the rest of us downstairs in the basement, his voice booming with disproportionate size. Usually we recorded the drums first and then Charlie went up to operate the master tape recorder while Wesley engineered and Cal, in his own words, 'produced'. This left me downstairs to help Jon out with any problems.

The pattern became familiar. Jon fumbles. Cal booms 'cut' like some movie mogul. I try to help, showing Jon a different way to play the line or checking he knows exactly what he is trying to do. 'Can't I play a different line altogether?' Jon asks. 'Play the line that's written,' Cal proclaims. 'Written where?' Jon mumbles. With each successive take, Cal would get more exasperated and the chances of getting it perfect would recede.

'Can't you just drop me in halfway through,' Jon pleaded on what must have been take twenty or so of 'Wonderful Moment'.

'But you've only played one fucking bar right, chum,' came back Cal, 'and that was a bar rest.'

Jon got up calmly, climbed the stairs from the basement and, chucking his bass guitar into a hydrangea bush as he went, marched off the premises. I found him in a cobbled street in Portmerion village. He was walking down towards the sea, past the bay window of the bookshop with the vintage petrol pump outside it.

'Jon,' I shouted. He was framed by the imposing Jacobean pastiche behind him which was known in the village as the town hall. To emerge from that light starved basement full of our distorted urban angst to this pageant, this other country, this other century, made the drugs that Cal took seem so unnecessary. I squinted at the slim figure in front of me and waved. Here, the sun always seemed to be out.

Jonathan managed a smile as if he knew it wasn't my fault. 'We thought coming here might make it easier,' I began, 'keep you away from the prying eyes of Phonodisc.' I could see from the way his expression was changing back again that I had said the wrong thing. I tried again. 'Give you your own space, you know. With friends. Only Wesley...'

'We?' he interrupted. 'We? Frank, do you really think you matter?' Then he was walking away again, faster this time, like in a walking race. I laughed but it was uncomfortable. I felt angry now.

'Jon,' I called.

'What?' he demanded, turning round and bellowing while still walking backwards.

I was going to tell him. Unknown to Jonathan Cal had rerecorded three of his bass-lines already, the pair of us getting up early or staying late on some songwriterly pretext in order to do it. Before we finished the record it would happen again. In fact Jon only actually plays bass on, I think, four tracks on the first album – the rest, uncredited, are Cal. The little man may have been a harsh taskmaster but he was loyal.

I was going to tell Jon but I didn't. I don't know why. I could have done – I might have enjoyed it – but I didn't. 'Nothing,' I said, turning my back and walking off in the opposite direction. Cal put it into context at about two that morning. We were redoing 'Wonderful Moment' – Cal playing, me recording it. Up in the back of the mobile, I had the headphones on and, after a successful first take, his voice emerged from the cans.

'He thinks he's my number two, that's why,' said Cal Carter from the basement. Unlike in *The Prisoner* TV series, there was no question about who was number one. 'That's why he's annoyed that we talk about him. It makes him think that you're two i/c.' There was a jokey tone in his voice but more besides.

'And am I?' I asked in a little whiskey laced voice

'Who cares,' said Cal. 'You've seen the TV programme haven't you? Number two is always an administrator, a pen pusher, a know-nothing.'

'Right,' I said. I could hear him putting the guitar down so I removed my cans, took another sip from the bottle. The idea that Jon was in some way a rival both excited and appalled me. I could hear Cal's footsteps first up the stairs and then across the path before he appeared in the control room. Somewhere in the night a car sped past.

'Your contribution's a creative one, Frank,' he said and the fear began to subside. 'That's where it all starts.' He smiled as he leaned over me to rewind the tape machine. 'Let's hear that back.'

Cal wanted to work late that night – he was speeding again – and I was happy to continue. I had a bit of a buzz on too as we overdubbed guitar after guitar, layering them across each other like fabrics, thicker and thicker. I recorded some of the best work of my career that night and, with sweat, we did complete the project within a fortnight – planned so as not to interrupt our touring schedule too much.

The tensions and the problems of the process also helped me when later I recorded my own albums. Where Cal gave them a hard time, I gave Charlie and Jon their parts in advance and often recorded them with them alone eliminating the goldfish bowl feeling which Jon, for one, must have felt. If there was a sacrifice of spontaneity on the sessions for the two Frankie Dane and The Denmarks' albums there was a calmness which was never there on *Rotten In Denmark*. At the sessions for *Stolen Moments* and *Phoenix* we gently joked about the absent Cal – Portmerion was his size of town we said.

One of the few peaceful moments on *Rotten* was the following morning. Cal and I had worked right through; Charlie and Jon woke up early. There was a fatigue slumped over our world like a Welsh raincloud. Jon found me alone in the mobile and struggled to a guilty smile.

'Play me 'Wonderful Moment', Frank,' he said softly.

I rewound the tape and played the song back, easing up the fader on the bass channel to let Cal's freshly recorded line cut through. Jon smiled again. This time a beam.

'It sounds OK. What have you done with it?'

'It's all this little box, ' I said patting the briefcase shaped effects unit which sat next to the mixing desk. 'We gated the sound and added some chorus.'

Jon played a lazy air-guitar along with the bass line. He looked pleased with himself. I found myself yawning and unable to stop.

'You boys need revitalising,' Wesley said and bundled us, mostly barefoot and hardly dressed, into the back of the van and drove us to a waterfall we'd passed on the way up. It was about two hundred yards from the road, the water cascading with a sweep and a rush and a crash over rocks smoothed and greened by its unrelenting. We stood by the back of the van like reluctant workmen smoking, coughing.

'Don't worry about 'Wonderful Moment', Jon,' Cal began. 'I've redone the bass part myself.'

Jon looked at first Cal and then at me. 'Was that necessary?' he asked, enunciating with a plodding precision.

'It was if we want to get to the States this side of the millennium.'

Jon set off up the hill, stamping his cigarette into the grass. Charlie was shaking his head and half-laughing in that nervous, frightened way kids at school had when they saw a thalidomide child. Ahead of us the Go-Karts bass guitarist was removing his T-shirt and tossing it to the ground like a footballer substituted.

'Was *that* necessary?' I asked Cal.

I set off after Jon again, catching up with him where the spume from the waterfall first caught your face. I took him by the hand and pulled both of us in. The water cut through your skin like a rain of tiny knives. It was foaming white with rushing and danced over your nose and mouth with a nimble numbness. Clean, clean water. I swallowed again and again. The water was spewing from Jon's mouth like his first solid food. I think he was trying to yell but the water was too quick for him. I pulled him up the rocks to where it pumped thicker and quicker still. We slipped on the slimy green and stumbled, both falling back so that we were sitting opposite each other, bare feet nearly touching. We kicked at each other, splashed from the rock pools and puddles but these efforts were like a child's spit in this pounding shower of silver. Beneath its continuous crackling cadence you might just have been able to hear us both laughing.

Like I said, recording at the village of Portmerion was a smart move by the boys. Previously we'd made the pop columns of the newspapers but this catapulted us onto the feature pages: 'Looking After Number One', ran *The Mirror*, 'Punk rockers visit the location of 60s egghead psycho-thriller'; 'Playing By Numbers', said *The Guardian*, 'Could the Go-Karts be the first rock band with a sense of cultural history?'; 'Making More Than A Penny Farthing', reported *The Financial Times*.

The album came out in time for Christmas in 1978 and went to number one for weeks.

24

Beech Park, the present day

Do you ever play Desert Island Discs with yourself? You know the idea, choose the X records and Y books you'd want above all others. I've been on the real *Desert Island Discs* so I don't have to play that one. Nowadays I prefer Desert Island Life. This has a material component – imagine you have just one suitcase to take to the island: what would you put in it? – but I prefer the immaterial: which bits of your life would you keep and which would you consign to the celestial dustbin? I play this game lying in bed when I can't sleep.

The fun part is that you then have to reconstruct your life without that bit: how would it have been? Sometimes I wonder what would have happened if I remove my marriage to Wendy. I usually find myself in a gutter somewhere around the age of twenty five.

This morning I am playing Desert Island Life when Wendy wakes me. 'What?' I say.

It is unusual for her to do this – she normally sneaks off to work without a word. She thinks I am sleeping but usually I am not. Sometimes she's out before six. Then I remember that she's not going to work today.

'What time is it?'

'After nine.'

I go to leap out of bed but Wendy stops me with an open palm.

'Don't worry, the kids have gone to school. Anyway, they're big enough to get their own breakfast.'

It is certainly true that since I gave Philip that one thing he wanted – a place at the College – he seems to have suddenly grown up. My morning presence has become largely symbolic. My mother, by contrast, seems to have shed an age or two since the death of my father and her morning presence is very real indeed – she often stops by on her way to or from Keep Fit For the Over 60s, Water Aerobics, nine holes at the Royal Blackheath or Aunty Anne's. She insists on being her sister in law's primary carer even though we could afford some help. She says it's the principle of the thing. I don't argue with her. 'Why break the habit of a lifetime?' Wendy says. Today Mum and Wendy are going shopping. I have been detailed to pick them up later which means I will have to drive for the first time in ages. My mother initiated this yesterday morning.

'Of course, Frankie can pick us up.'

'But I don't drive.'

'Don't drive, no, but you can bloody drive.' She was deliberately mimicking my father.

I don't know how she knew this. My wife must have let it slip. Wendy had taught me in France. Lesson One: circumnavigating the Place De La Concorde. 'But we'll be killed,' I had protested 'So what,' she had replied. It was less than a week after Cal's funeral.

I even tried my usual ploy of claiming not to have a licence – implying its removal for some rock'n'roll like misdemeanour. My mother snorted. 'Of course, you have a licence.'

'It's true that I can drive but I don't like it,' I explained.

'Like it, smike it,' said my mum, 'you can do it for your mother and your wife.' So that was that.

Suddenly Wendy stops speaking. I look up at her and then, following the direction of her surprised expression, turn over in the bed. In the open doorway is my mother. It takes me a moment to recognise her. I could be witnessing one of my own fantastical rewrites from Desert Island Life. Sure, she appears an inch or so taller and her hair a shade or two darker since my father passed on but I've noticed that before. It is the coat she is wearing. The coat is the cashmere I bought her after *Rotten In Denmark* went to number one.

I remember the morning I gave it to her like I remember yesterday. It was a Sunday lunchtime. I had had it gift wrapped, ribbons and bows, the lot but my father must have opened the cans instantly he heard the door being unlocked because as I came into the living room holding this great, glittering gift, there he was offering me a glass of beer. To take it I had to put the package down on the pouffe where, amid the grunts of introduction, it was forgotten. 'It's your favourite, son,' my mum was saying and running through the menu before I remembered. In total, the parcel had sat there in its Sunday best for ten minutes and neither had remarked upon it. When she tried the coat on, my mum looked delighted. 'Fancy,' said my father, between sips and I'd not seen her in it since.

'I thought you'd given that to Oxfam,' I say.

My mother looks at her watch and frowns. 'Time for us to go, Wendy. Frank must be wanting to get up.'

I hear them talking down in the kitchen, arming themselves with substantial holdalls and heavyweight credit cards. 'Buy yourself a hat to go with it,' I shout as I they go out the door.

If I get up I'll only worry about the work I'm not doing so I roll over and try to doze, safe from the expectant cyclops stare of the word-processor. But I don't sleep, do I, you know that already. The family bed is big enough to hold a small tea dance and I try every inch of it but I can't get comfortable, can barely close my eyes. I taste the tea Wendy has left for me but it's cold now and I'm not safe.

I'm still playing Desert Island Life, you see. My case is half-packed and here I am wrestling with a non-Wendy scenario which may not consign me to the gutter. Jody Clarke is her name – the nearest I ever came to an affair. You'll remember her. She did back-up vocals on 'Stolen Moments' before having a couple of big soul hits of her own. She lives in Los Angeles now where she's trying to break into films. You may have seen her. She had a line in the last Bruce Willis movie. Could make it too – she's got the brass neck and balls for it. I'm lying on my back now and trying to relax. Loosen the shoulders, drop the arms.

Once Tony realised that things couldn't and wouldn't go on as 'normal' without Cal, he started to ignore us. He put out *Wonderful*

Moments, that double live retrospective with the repackaged interviews with Cal. Inevitably there had been a lot of press shit after Cal died: like the furore about Elvis Presley and John Lennon all rolled into one. *The Observer* asked if Cal was the most significant teenager since Jimmy Dean. Melvyn Bragg did a TV profile of him. Tony milked it all dry. The album cover is a cut out of Cal with a kind of white aura around him. 'Like radiation,' Wendy says. He looks like a ghost or a kid in that Ready Brek advert. The picture is set against a photomontage of significant events from the 1970s: Watergate, Lord Lucan, hot pants, Bangladesh, a lunar buggy on the Moon, Munich Olympics, withdrawal from Vietnam, Common Market, Thatcher, death of Mao, death of Presley, Muhammed Ali, even the Ayatollah. It is as if Cal in some way ranks alongside or is even responsible for these things rather than merely a chronicler of them. And just in case anybody should fail to notice to whom the cover design pays homage, The Beatles split is shown by a torn *Sergeant Pepper* cover held together with a safety-pin.

He wasn't wholly stupid, Tony. He didn't come right out and say we were crap without Cal – he still had us under contract after all (or in jail as those nobs in the business say) – but by elevating Cal to some sort of deity he certainly implied it. I didn't speak to him for five years.

When I was ready to, I caught the bus up to Phonodisc carrying the master tape in a tatty Small Wonder Records carrier bag on my lap. We'd recorded part of it in my basement and gone into a local studio to do the overdubs – twelve tracks; all Dane/Carter originals – and we hadn't asked Tony for a penny.

Inevitably in reception I was asked to wait. 'Sorry, no appointment, no can do,' said a sulky assistant from beneath a sultry fringe. She reminded me of that woman in the Marquee. I leaned over and picked up the telephone.

'Tell him it's Frankie Dane,' I said handing it to her.

She was brainless, seventeen and listening to Peter Powell on the radio so it was no surprise that she hadn't heard of me. She looked at me like I'd slapped her. 'I'll call security,' she shouted.

Suddenly the broad frosted glass doors behind her desk flew open and a black girl stumbled onto the reception carpet, her guitar in one hand and a portable amplifier in the other. A security guard was helping her out.

'I'll wait,' I mumbled to the receptionist, stepping back.

The black girl was livid. A patent black stiletto crumpled beneath her topple. 'You tell me come and then you change yous mind. Who is he, some sort of fucking airhead? I had to take two trains and a bus, find a baby-sitter. Does he think he's God? Pig thick white boy?'.

'I suggest you make another appointment,' the security guard said softly. When he closed the door on her, it clicked shut and the blur of his suit could be seen receding down the corridor.

I helped her to her feet but she paid no attention, continued to shout after the guard. 'Well, fuck you, Mr. Tony Beale. You ask hear me and you're gonna hear, damn you.'

Then she plugged in her amplifier and proceeded with a windmill sweep of her arm to bash out power chords in the record company's foyer. I couldn't take my eyes off her. She kicked off her remaining shoe. The sulky receptionist turned her radio up.

The black girl, without stopping playing, spat at her – projecting her voice like an automatic weapon. 'Turn that off, child.'

Sulky obeyed and, over the chords, this woman with hair like a cascade of coffee began to sing. Her voice had the gospel singer's depth and power to send it soaring over the amplified guitar yet it had a frail, vulnerable quality like a soft assault.

Then there was a cacophony of strangled language and the door opened again. A drunkard's swaying gait, a double breasted suit, Tony nearly fell out. He was laughing like he was about to have a hernia. That snout of a nose locked into a snarl, those thin lips stretching and smacking and seeping spit. His eyes grabbed her like a fist. The security guard followed him out of the door and took up his position behind the receptionist.

'What the fuck?' said Tony, looking her up and down. 'You see me when I want to see you, sweetheart, and you bring a tape. You got a tape? No you haven't. So you go home. You get back ghetto. Comprendez?' He was pushing her now, shoving her back against the sheet white wall, the guitar swung and her tights laddered against its machine heads. He had a hairy hand on her lapel.

'You don't even have the dots doll, do you?' he began to taunt.

'The dots? For you who don't know shit that is the term what we who do know shit use for the fucking music – those fucking five little lines of magic. And do you have them? Kiss my arse you do. You don't have anything do you?' I couldn't believe the security guard was just standing there allowing this. The receptionist and I at least had the good grace to look open-mouthed but he just stood there pretending not to notice. He was the same colour as the singer and in this situation as powerless.

'You don't have nothing.' Tony's hand dropped to the girl's pencil skirt and pulled. 'Do you have your fucking knickers on. Well, perhaps we can remedy that one, baby doll.'

I grabbed Tony's hand and pulled it away from her skirt. I yelled his name into his ear, roaring like Cal at the climax of our set. He lumbered around, his hand leaving the girl and forming a clumsy fist. I caught hold of it as it sought my stomach. Then his forehead lurched forward as if he were going to nut me. Tony's eyes dived, swam, surfaced and finally focused on mine.

'Who the fuck do you think you are?' he bellowed.

The security guard stepped out but didn't intervene. He for one knew who I was.

Tony swung his other arm and caught me around the side of the head, half a slap, half a punch. I stopped myself against the wall, not wanting to hit the ground. I felt sure Tony Bealc was a kicker.

'Tony,' I said. 'It's Frankie Dane.'

The security guard advanced another pace to ensure that I didn't try to retaliate. Tony looked at me again and with a totter and a cough, great uncle recognition finally staggered into his brain on broken crutches.

'Frankie Dane,' he said, pianissimo and again, with a lick of the lips, 'Frankie Dane,' forte. 'Well, look what the slut's dragged in, Frankie Dane. What is it, Frankie, wondering why the royalty cheques are getting smaller? Can't keep Mrs. Carter in the manner to which she's become accustomed? Take some advice, you should try shagging her occasionally.' He'd completely forgotten about the girl. She was sitting on her amplifier close to tears, deserving them, but not crying. He was edging me back towards the door, half pushing, then he stopped. 'Or perhaps you've come to say thank you. Thank

181

you Tony for giving some value to my otherwise pitiful existence.' He took me by the hand as if to shake it. 'Have you, Franklin?' I was trying to reply but I was only taking in air. 'Because let's face it, you couldn't cut it could you Frank, my boy. At the top of the cock-sucking tree you were and all you could fucking do was turn round and scream for your mummy. Carter dies. Well, he dies. And so you die too, Frankie. Jesus. Well, fucking lick my arse. Kids would kill for the opportunity you had.'

Then he started laughing again and put his arm round my shoulder as if we were great friends. I wondered if he were really drunk at all. 'Don't fucking tell me you want to get back in the studio. Oh no, please I'll piss my pants. You want to do a bollocking Christmas single.'

'Not the studio, Tony. That won't be necessary.' I was trying to shake his arm, heavy as a dead conger, from my shoulder. I held the master tape up in the bag. 'I've already recorded the album.'

'Frankie, mate,' said Tony, changing key, changing tone, changing direction. He was shuffling me back through the security door, his fingers dancing over the fingerboard for the entry code like a concert pianist's 'Grand to see you. I've been meaning to call. How is Wendy?'

And that was how I came to meet Jody Clarke. Actually Phonodisc did pay for one thing on *Stolen Moments* – a week in the studio to put on Jody's backing vocals and to do the final mixdown – but Tony wrote that off and we didn't have to recoup it.

This morning my Desert Island Life has me in LA with Jody, has me writing movie scores but that could never happen. Never could have happened. I never did have an affair with Jody and it wasn't out of loyalty to Wendy. Not if I'm honest about it. It was because of Tony. Jody can sing like an angel and we could have got those BVs done inside half a day had we wanted to but we worked late that night, knew we would. Empty building, Jody and I, a locked door, a soundproofed recording studio and in the control room a bottle of Champagne – Tony's present. When she touched me it was as beautiful as her voice, the same vulnerability and control, but every time I looked at her in that way, with a summer buzz of lust, I thought of Tony and how he had treated her while I'd stood gawping and

182

my desire expired like a punctured tyre.

Recording those vocals we had take after stunning take. Naked on a pine floor where even her sweet nothings had a perfect cadence we tried again – take after take – but there was nothing worth a note. Even now when I think of her as I do on mornings like these, my Saturday night of an erection is followed as surely as Sunday by Tony's leer and a limp feeling inside and out. Sometimes I think of someone else instead but not this morning.

25

I pull into the underground car-park where Jon parked when we came up to see Tony. It was easy as in truth I knew it would be. Driving is just one of the arty-farty fears I have created to mask the real ones. The streets are full of maniacs with wheels but I keep telling myself that I am at least as crazy as they are and it makes me feel less vulnerable. I reverse our car into a parking space and turn off the engine.

I watch as the petrol gauge slides down from full to empty. Here I do differ from Jon. I use a different service station. Jon says he feels awkward calling at Terry's garage these days. I don't. For me it's about the only attraction of getting behind the wheel. Terry is manager there now after all. He jokes with me about my driving. He knows I'm not keen.

'Even when we were teenagers, Frankie,' he says.

'I know, I was scared of the bumper cars,' I say as he leans over to check my oil, a service I doubt he offers his other customers and that makes me feel good.

'I saw Charlie on telly last night,' he continues, standing and wiping the dipstick. 'Local news, you know. Opening that new club of his.'

'Strike Four,' I say.

'Yeah. And that bird he was with. Stunner and a half in't she?'

'Claudia.'

'You know her too? Christ. Well stocked in the knocker department or what? I'll just top you up, Frank.'

I give him my credit card. It's self-service but I'm not getting out. 'You should give him a call, Terry. He'd be pleased to hear from you. I'll give you the number.'

Terry smiles and says he will but we both know he won't. He calls across to the overalled youth by the car wash and instructs him to give my car a quick polish. He's as polite but firm with him as he's polite and deferential with me – a good manager, I suppose. He knows where he fits in now does Terry.

I left early to avoid the rush hour – Philip told me it starts around two these days – so I've got time to kill before I meet Wendy and my mother. Some people are still eating their lunch; I doubt my womenfolk will have left Fenwicks yet.

I'm going to play Product Placement to kill time. This involves going into all the record and CD shops and making sure that my albums are prominent – moving them to the front of the display stand, that sort of thing. I am planning my route around the West End as I walk out of the car park and don't notice Jonathan's gleaming kit car standing just four bays from my Rover.

Over Covent Garden a frostier air descends and I turn up the collar on my overcoat. Given the right hat and a double amputation below the knee, I could be Humphrey Bogart. There are still plenty of tourists, of course, whatever the weather. I stop myself before, like some wizened society dame, I lament how nowadays the season never seems to end. A snatch of German, a sprinkling of French, a volley of heat-seeking American laughter. On the corner a mime artist with a painted face struggles to get out of a box.

I wonder what my grandfather would make of the place where he once used to count vegetables. I like to think he would have had a smile on his face, enjoyed a crepe and a coffee and bought a Tibetan anus flute with his pension. Once, when I asked him if he liked his job, he told me it was 'cramped, cold and smelly'. It's still cramped and cold but now the air is stuffed with patchouli and jasmine and lavender. His nose at least may have sensed some progress.

The beads and the trinkets that were once the bounty of the rucksacked traveller are now set on display for all who can shake a

185

credit card, the spoils of the democratic free market. My mother is examining a copper egg-shaped ornament for holding joss-sticks. If those thick brightly coloured anoraks are anything to go by, the people she is talking to are Scandinavian tourists. She sees me and speaks without surprise.

'Is this some sort of pepper pot, Frankie?'

'No, it's er...'

'Must be a joss-stick holder then.' She returns to her new friends. They utter their thanks and begin to pass the item around the group like an artefact.

'Mum, what are you doing here? Where's Wendy?'

'We've split up. I'm going to a shop called Pineapple to buy some new dance shoes.'

'Right.' I am perplexed. 'Mum, I think Pineapple's more leotards and Lycra body stockings.'

'Well, perhaps I'll try one of those too.'

'Where did you say Wendy was?'

'She's gone to the café at Liberty's.'

'And you've been wandering around on your own?'

A laugh. 'You sound like my mother,' says my mother then she touches my arm with an actressy sort of gesture. 'I'm not your father you know.' And then she is away again. One padded boot followed by another.

'Where are you going now?'

'Pineapple. I'll see you as arranged. Have fun.'

Her red coat disappears into the crowd, scarf swirling like a gymnast's ribbon. I look after her for a second and then turn back. The Scandinavians are buying the joss-stick holder.

Liberty is the West End store I remember best from my childhood. Its Tudor facade looked like something out of a picture book and at Christmas time Charles Dickens himself could have shopped there. I never went in there then but we stood outside a couple of times, my mother taking in tiny breaths, my father champing at the bit. The first time I actually went inside was with Cal when we went up on a Red Bus Rover. We popped in on our way to Hamleys to buy Subbuteo accessories. Must have been about twelve.

I know where Wendy will be. She has a favourite table in Liberty's café – the one in the corner. Wendy says she likes Liberty's café because, by comparison with the rest of the shop, it appears to lack confidence in itself and she's attracted to this quality. Among the opulence of designer labels and carved wood panelling, there it sits with its silly green cushions, tin-topped tables and tea bags, the most English thing about the place. I turn through the books department and am about to call but my words become ensnared in my throat almost before my eyes can register her form. There is someone sitting opposite – smartly dressed in a sunshine yellow blazer. She is adjusting his lapel. I catch the laughter – a laughter as if every other table is frozen in icy silence and their two voices are blended as one, ricocheting around the room, bouncing with the buzzer and bell brightness of a pinball from the ceiling and walls and silent statues. When it reaches my ears it batters my skull like a scream.

I pause, think and realise that I am skilled at this next part. I buy a hat and a scarf and remove my coat in case Wendy should recognise it and then I return. I opt for a chair a couple of tables away shoving the coat beneath the seat as I sit. I'm not close enough to hear what they are saying but I'm near enough to read the writing on the wall. What I witness is like the left and the right hand conspiring. A secret more special for being shared. A deception more complete by its symmetry. Or do I flatter myself? After all, there are other husbands and there are other clients. Careful Frankie, there is a danger that you might start believing your own publicity.

After a coffee and a shared chocolate nut sundae, he rises and with a kiss is gone. As she sits back and savours the flavour of her smile for a second before taking up her newspaper, it is like a scene from a film. A blink and you may never have noticed that satisfaction playing on the lips but the camera catches it all and it is preserved. Wendy is gone behind her *Guardian* when I get up, decline the second coffee I have ordered, and do what I have always done so well: follow. As I leave the café I am pulling my coat on with a purpose.

Sharp clothes, soft furnishings, prints of distinction, fine crystal, oriental mysteries and occidental accessories, I follow through the crowds: the browsers, the buyers, the bored and the wistful. Their shuffling shoes and unpredictable diversions do not distract me as

I pursue a pair of fresh heels. Out on the pavement Jonathan stops. I lose myself in the window display, crawl inside that hollow pumpkin and light a juniper candle. His reflection stretches and yawns, looks bored, and for the first time I feel something nearer anger than despair. He glances again at his watch – the one we gave him when we got married, the one we gave him when he was our best man – and steps out for what must be an important rendezvous. Someone else's wife?

I could go back and confront Wendy but then confrontation never was my thing. I am tossing the emotional options like loose change when Tony Beale emerges from Argyll Street opposite. I duck back inside my hole. Collar up, hat brim down, back inside the head of a vegetable. He crosses the road, trying to hail a taxi. As usual it is hard to tell how sober he is. The cabbies of London spurn him for while he may look rich to you or me, he does not at this often windy and rainswept time of year look rich enough. That is the refreshing honesty our homespun London cabbies bring to their work. With his shambling posture, wayward hair and one-winter-too-many trench coat, they do not see Tony for what he really is.

He is heading under Liberty's arch in the same direction as Jon and my mind is made up. I leave my Halloween window and its white wide-eyed ghosts. He makes a turn and then another. Not so many people here and I need to keep my distance. Ahead I think I can see that yellow sun of a jacket.

They meet on a corner, Tony and Jonathan, and slip into a nearby pub. A gust of wind coaxes another layer of leaves to the ground. The pub's simple sign swings in the breeze – like a film again – and I take a deep breath and step on in. I've given them long enough to order a drink. I intend, if they see me as I enter, to pretend that I was just passing and saw them going in.

The pub is quiet. It is too late for lunch and too early for an after work drink – the briefest of respites in the London drinking day. On the stool, a pal of the landlord reading *The Mirror*, talking about Arsenal. In the centre table a couple of tourists who have wandered from the beaten track, his stubby finger pogoing on the map, her apologising in German. At the table by the window an older couple in respectful silence. Along the side of the bar, four booths. In the second sits an older punter with a trilby and a paper and a betting slip and there it is. Hanging over the arm of the fourth booth, the one at the far end, is Jonathan's yellow jacket. Ducking into the third booth, I pretend I'm a tourist too. I don't want to go to the bar because I'll be seen. After a moment or two the landlord comes across and I order a bière in a fractured French accent.

Behind me, I hear them still slapping and laughing their greetings. When Tony compliments Jon on his new jacket there's a warmth in his voice – the stress of the office is gone and he almost sounds like the younger man we once knew. Then Jonathan is doing what I pay him for.

'It's not that he hasn't written anything Tony, you know that. It's quite simply a matter of quality control. Retaining the standard. There's not yet an album of quality material.'

'Retaining the standard – flouting the contract more like. Well, tell him from me he's a lazy little fucker. '

'I do, Tony, I do.'

'Anyway, point is the dithering must have done something because the British Film Institute want to do a retro on him – Frankie Dane: the movie.' Tony snorts. He's getting into his stride.

'Sounds interesting.'

'You know, archive footage from gigs, old interviews and videos, usual crock of crap. Ninety minutes worth of cinematic excitement and then our Frankie speaks to the audience afterwards and answers questions.'

'Where?'

'It'll be at the National Film Theatre – part of the music in cinema season or some such thing.'

'Nice one, Tony.'

'Don't thank me. It was Ian – you know, Ian Martyn-Baker who suggested it apparemendo. Anyway, point is we could do with some product. Okay so no album but he must have a fucking single.'

'I'm sure that'll be no problem, Tony.'

So I am snookered. I desperately want to join in but I can hardly claim to be just passing now. They can't be seen from the road or indeed from any spot inside the pub itself through which one could be 'just passing'.

I have been standing on the edge for so long that it is now too late to jump in. I finish my beer, get up and leave. On the way back to meet my family I play Product Placement in the record shops and on the walks in between I play Desert Island Life. Perhaps you should be allowed two suitcases.

Outside Charing Cross Station, I help my wife and mother with their shopping. Wendy has a new jacket. My mum in one of her many bags has a new pair of dance shoes. They both moan a bit about the long walk to the car but they are satisfied with their day's work. This time I do notice Jon's vehicle but my wife's eyes don't flicker. Down in this gasolene alley she's modelling the new jacket for us. I tell her to let her hair down, it will really suit the casual cut of the jacket I tell her and she does it and I fancy her.

26

Beech Park, Autumn 1977

I placed my packed lunch in my briefcase. As my dad always took
the newspaper, it was the only thing of any interest or value in there.
Just a couple of biros and pencils, a slide-rule I never used, my
personal copy of the department's procedural manual and my daily
bread: a round of cheese and tomato and one of peanut butter. My
mother was dabbing on my tie with a damp cloth and wittering on
about being more careful with my corn flakes when the doorbell's
tiny fart interrupted.

'Now, who's that at this time in the morning?'

Cal was wearing the same all-American threads as he had been
the night before in The Roebuck, was smoking the same soft-pack
Marlboro. I blinked and it wasn't caused by the sunlight.

He yelled 'Morning, Mrs. Dane,' and then, to me, 'I've come to
give you a lift to work.' Parked outside was the red Ford Escort that
he had had before he went away.

'Still driving the Chevvy, then?' I observed.

'Hey, it's been garaged these twelve months and had a full service
yesterday.'

'That should be satisfactory.' Solemnly I straightened my tie and
the creases in my suit. 'So you going to tell me some more Elvis
stories then?'

'The time for stories is over,' Cal replied. In the street he executed a breakneck three point turn, peering over the dashboard with an intent that wasn't for the road.

'You're going the wrong way,' I said.

'And you're looking a bit queasy,' he said. 'Russian flu, I'd say. My prescription: a day down on the coast.'

The Carters' second (or was it third) home was on the south coast in one of those villages near Brighton. We drove it in little more than an hour. It was a cottage – 'an artisan's dwelling,' Wendy later told me – with a mossy slate grey roof and white pebbledash walls buffeted and made bald by the sea breeze. The gate was attached by a single hinge and the garden had a gay abandon which I far preferred to my parents' antiseptic affair.

'They've let it go a bit,' Cal said as he stumbled through the wooden doored pantry searching for the mains switch. There was that musty smell of history in the air. I dumped my briefcase on the table which was metal-legged and formica-topped like the one we had once had in our kitchen at home. 'There's years left in it,' my father had said when my mother suggested chucking it out. 'That's what you said six years ago, Derek,' she had replied.

'I wish I'd brought some civvies,' I said, fingering my pinstripes distastefully.

'We can go shopping,' said Cal. 'There.' The lights came on like after a power-cut. He tested the electric cooker and then he put the kettle on. I'd visited the cottage a few times as a child – the odd weekend and for a week one summer holiday – but this was my first adult visit. We both had to search the pantry to find the tea-bags. They were in the flour container.

'For freshness, I suppose,' Cal scoffed. He had been away for the best part of a year and over tea he began to explain.

'You know when my father first told me I was going to go to Oxford University, Frankie?' He sounded like that old woman in the hairy purple cardigan who used to come and tell us stories of a Friday afternoon in primary school. I shook my head.

'When I was six years old. When I was this fucking big.' He held his hand about six inches from the floor. 'So since failing the A-levels wasn't an option as I'd already passed the entrance exam, it was a case of leaving the country or bust.'

'Yeah, well thanks for all the postcards,' I said. I had them plastered across my wall. Long distance information like it says in the song. I didn't understand what he was talking about – my mum would have been made up proud if I'd gone to Oxford.

For a minute I sounded adult. 'But you've got the ability, Cal. Isn't it a waste?'

He carried on, scornfully. 'And he was appalled I was going to the States because of course the family don't go there any more. That's beneath them since they decided to buy a gîte.'

'A jeep?'

'A gîte – it's a French peasant house. They want to buy one in Provence – it's so fucking unspoilt, apparently. They've got a poxy caravan nearby for the time being so they can search for the right little one in the right little spot. Well, a pox on your unspoilt. America's spoilt to death. It's a spoilt brat. Just like me. And you know what spoilt brats have got. They've got everything. You call it ability. I call it privilege on a plate.'

He expected a response. 'How did Linda like it?' I asked.

He looked at me like I was way behind. 'Linda? I'll tell you about Linda. In Las Vegas she walked up to the first fruit machine she saw, put in a quarter and watched as the coins rolled out. Poured and poured like in a cartoon. She'd won a pile of money, an absolute fucking heap of the stuff, bags full. Nearly pissed herself she was so thrilled, people around clapping, free bottle of champers and a plastic smile from the hostess. She's hugging everyone and they're saying 'well, whaddaya know, missy?' and stuff. Me? I couldn't give a fuck. Took a cab to the Hilton Hotel and gatecrashed a Presley gig.' he shrugged. 'We covered the bed in dollars later and shagged in it. That was quite good. But gleaming gold? What do I need that for? I'll take a chance on the buried treasure any time.'

'But if you'd kept it you could have stayed longer.'

'We stayed another nine months. How much longer do you want? How long does it take to get the message?'

I looked blank.

'There's a vacancy at the top, Frank. Has been since August the 16th 1977.' Another shrug. 'I've got to give the music a go.'

I wasn't sure for a moment whether he was about to burst into song or tears. 'So, how does he feel about that, your father?'

'Let's just say, as they say stateside, we've cut a deal.' He winked. I finished my tea.

'Come on,' said Cal. 'Let's shop.'

I was about to protest that I had no money but I knew from the way that he was looking at me what he meant. He had pound signs for pupils.

The sea front was quiet. The tide was out, the water's edge off in the morning mist somewhere. Three silhouettes of men were digging for worms. We walked across the prom and jumped down onto the beach, the stones yielding with a crunch. I wasn't really dressed for this. Further out the sand was still damply brown, drying to an ooze of ochre beneath our feet as we walked. Down here, the wind was more vigorous, sweeping at Cal's blonde locks with a singing rush and even disturbing my civil service short back and sides. I turned up the collar on my suit.

I felt like a particularly stupid incarnation of Dr. Watson. 'The one thing I don't understand, Cal,' I said, 'is what's so bad about going to Oxford University, anyway?' (I wasn't about to give my right arm for anything but if I was the right-arm giving sort, Oxford University was the sort of return I would have coveted.)

'Nothing if that's what you want to do.' he said. I kicked at a pebble. 'If it isn't there's no point. It doesn't make you happy. Look at Wendy.'

'What about Wendy?'

'A good job in the family firm, a husband in a suitably high-flying job but believe me, Frank, she's not the contented honey you might imagine from that heart melting smile.'

'But she doesn't work for the family firm.'

'There's family and there's *family*,' he said mysteriously. 'It's a different publishing house to the old fella's agreed, but these people are like the Mafia with dust jackets. It was father who opened the door. And the guy virtually pimps for her.' With the weight he was giving his words Cal ought to have been becoming sombre but he appeared unmoved.

'Your dad pimps for Wendy?' This, I was laughing at.

'Well, I'm exaggerating for dramatic effect obviously but if your

194

father throws you a twenty-first birthday party to which he refuses to let you invite any guests and the only person there of your own age is the son of your father's schoolfriend who also happens to be a broker in the square mile, you'd get the message, wouldn't you and you'd reap the rewards – the money, the house, the society wedding.'

'Is that true?'

'Sure it is. She's daddy's golden girl now but a happy bunny she ain't. Look, come on, those shoes of yours are letting in water.' Then Cal was running.

As a civil servant I spent every working day processing paperwork in a manner that was ostensibly as egalitarian as possible. But even the dumbest clerical could not fail to be struck by the uncomfortable fit between this principle and what was really going on in the world. Cal's words scratched at this feeling but as I took off my sodden shoes and hurled them out to sea I realised that I still wasn't understanding it.

'It's about getting inside people, Frankie, moving them, communicating with their souls – you, me, everybody.' He was looking up to the clouds appealing to them with his arms like a supplicant. 'We must transcend the material.'

We climbed onto a breakwater and, like a balancing act on a beam, walked pigeon-toed back up to the promenade, Cal, leading, kicking at the limpets as we went.

I cut quite a figure in the village, barefoot in my city suit. In London you have to be murdering someone before anyone notices and even then you need to be doing it clumsily, noisily and with a callous disregard for the spray of blood. Down here heads turn and eyes lock at the drop of a hat. My appearance attracted much of this and, from some, the accompaniment of a low-level tutting sound. One old lady leading a sausage dog and wearing a clear polythene rain hood and heavy blue mackintosh despite the clemency of the weather asked me if I was cold, dear.

'No thank you,' I said. 'We're just going to buy some shoes.'

'There's a Clarks round the corner,' she smiled.

'Thank you.'

'Excuse me,' said Cal. 'Can you remind me where the bank is? I need to cash a cheque.'

The woman pointed out a flint-fronted Lloyds.

He went in and I waited outside trying to keep moving so that nobody would think I was begging. Apart from being shoeless, my trouser turn-ups were covered in sand and I'd managed to get chalk on my jacket. I read the parish noticeboard. I picked up a discarded sweet packet and put it in the municipal litter-bin. I read the headlines on yesterday's Argus through the newsagent's window. I counted the number of jars of sweets on the three shelves behind his counter. I thought briefly of Mr. Parker; I wanted to hear more about Wendy.

'Where's Linda, now?' I asked when Cal emerged with his fistful of fivers.

'At home I should imagine but this is not relevant, Frankie. We have a band to get back together. Just as soon as we've stopped you looking like old man Steptoe.'

I looked across the square to the village's one clothes store and winced. 'Can't we go to Brighton?' I asked. So we did.

That morning I bought my first pair of straight jeans, drainpipes. They still had flared ones in the shop but you could almost see them skulking off shamefacedly to the back of the store. I got sports socks and a pair of maroon baseball boots to replace my faithful but ageing Dunlop Green Flash tennis shoes. Cal bought baseball boots for everyone: turquoise for himself, black for Charlie and a golden orangey colour for Jon. In one of those print your own T-shirt places I chose one that said 'Too Thick For University'.

'What did you want that one for?' asked Cal. We were on the pier now playing Air-Hockey. I smacked the puck goalwards and it spun off the blue playing surface towards the Penny Falls machine.

'Well, I never took the poxy A-levels either, did I?'

As Cal sent the puck back up the table on its millimetre cushion of air so the machine cut out and the puck died.

'I never sat the exams,' I explained. 'I don't know why.'

'What's that got to do with the T-shirt?'

I put a coin in a fruit machine, didn't answer. Cal started on a trivia machine.

In the boot of the car, Cal had both our guitars. We spent the remains of the day writing the balance of what became the Go-Karts set and planning how to put it all back together again.

Charlie, incredibly, had got into art school. He'd persuaded the school to let him retake O-level Art which he had passed and then he'd persuaded the college to accept him on the basis of that, two A-levels in other subjects and the portfolio he'd put together. They admired his work, his paintings almost as thick as sculptures, and agreed to take him provided he paid for his own paint. We didn't foresee any problem with him. Camberwell College was just down the road from Beech Park. 'Everyone at art school's in a rock band anyway,' said Cal. 'That's what they're there for.'

Jonathan was more of a problem. He'd passed his A-levels and gone to Durham University. We talked about it over fish and chips sitting on a covered bench on the prom. We could have got another bass-player or one of us could have switched to bass but neither of these options felt right. At ten past closing time we loaded the guitars back into the boot of the car and set off on the long drive north to kidnap Jon.

'Aren't you too tired to drive?' I asked.

'No,' said Cal and handed me a small sandwich bag containing white powder like sea salt, a handbag mirror and a razor blade.

'Be careful with the blade,' said Cal, making a chopping motion on the dashboard with his hand. 'They're dangerous.'

27

The National Film Theatre, the present day

I finish my pint. It mixes with the taste of panic in my mouth. Wendy knocks back her second Scotch – for some reason this evening is making her nervous too. Perhaps it's on my behalf. This is my first public appearance for donkey's years.

At the next table a guy with a dog called Rotten is trying to make it sit down. I wonder if he's going to try to take it into the cinema. His thick dog collar is jet black, heavy with studs and partially coated in saliva. Rotten's is slightly smaller. Both have long, straw brown hair with a centre parting.

The guy asks Rotten if he can be trusted not to get heavy in the one and nines. Those who recognise me try not to stare but they can't help it. They get themselves into uncomfortable positions and casually look over. They almost smile. I feel awkward, shuffle in my seat. It's like the school playground when you've trodden in shit or got piss on your shorts.

Ian Martyn-Baker drags himself away from a cute black girl half his age and half his width and saunters over – he'll be asking the questions tonight. He places his porky hand on my tightening shoulder. 'All set, Frank old son.'

He sounds like Jonathan's older brother, a sort of pipe and slippers around the swimming pool voice. His brief sojourn as presenter for yet another possible replacement for *The South Bank Show* never got to second series – Ian's girth is not camera friendly – but he's made it as far as most could want to. Matched his inheritance and then some. He's shaking hands around our table, gives Wendy a peck on the cheek and a squeeze on the arm. His greetings are as to fellow members of a club. Finally he pats me on the shoulder again. 'It'll be fine, old boy – you'll get no curve balls from me I promise.' He's still smiling with a Cheshire glow. 'And now, ladies and gents,' he says to the assembly. 'The show commences.'

Jonathan has seen the clips although not in their final edited form. I didn't want to – I would have got too involved and then I wouldn't have wanted to see them again on the night. My only request was that they keep it chronological. I like chronological. I wish I could do it.

'So, Jonathan,' asks Wendy as we rise. 'Are we in for a treat tonight?'

When Ian reappears at the front of the gently raked auditorium to welcome us all to '"Dane Framed", part of the BFI's *Rock On Reel* season, to be followed by an interview with the great man himself', every seat is full. He calls me the Godfather of grunge and the favourite uncle of Brit-pop, mentions my unpretentious unswerving style. There is the soft buzz of laughter at his self-deprecatory parting gag and the lights go down. Wendy takes my hand and squeezes it.

My heart is pumping like an amphetamine rush and as Cal's face, six feet tall and fresh, appears on the screen beside my own I am back there. Nights when the world existed in a demimonde. Nights when my heart beat just like this, a hammer pounding in my sternum like a clockwork drummer, my insides as taut, tight and tender as the toughest drum skin. Sometimes Cal looked that big then.

On the screen the credits are rolling over some Electric Ballroom footage. Cal and I are back to back, leaning on each other. We're the same height. He's standing on the drum riser watching Charlie's tendon charged forearm as it brings the stick down with a whip-crack back beat on the snare. Our arms whirl in a swirling unison. Cut from one grin to the other. As the shot pulls away from us it moves from black and white to colour and we break, me striding Chelsea-booted, Cal almost dancing, to our respective microphones. The camera is level with his turquoise baseball boots looking up, examining every fold of Cal's jeans and T-shirt as his Adam's apple rises and falls. It must have been mounted on the monitors, the camera. I try to remember but I can't. I'm right back there, you see, empty headed and frantic.

Suddenly we, the audience, are on the stage, the camera framed to something very close to what must have been, back in 1978 or whenever it was, my point of view. Was the cameraman crouching at my side or shooting over my shoulder? I still can't remember, can only guess from the angle of the shot. The crowd are leaping and dancing as far as this artificial eye can see. There is a lot of sweat and spit, some wayward glasses spilling lager and then an ID parade of female faces. I know from the direction of their pleading eyes that it is Cal for whom they pine but the caption doesn't admit that. 'A portrait of Frankie Dane' it says over their evocative young faces preserved forever in freeze-frame. Wendy squeezes my hand again.

And just like those nights, my heart just won't slow down. It wants to overtake itself. I want a drink. There's a taste in my mouth like white spirit.

I think I like the film. The assault of images: the live stuff when we were cooking, the studio shots with Cal and I calling the tune, the jabber-jabber of the young talking heads, some of which turn out to be ours. It has no commentary and doesn't really try to tell a story which I appreciate. It accepts the great holes in my output. Inevitably it concentrates on the Go-Karts – partly because of the immortality of death but also because there is no live footage of Frankie Dane And The Denmarks. In a sound-bite I've not seen before, this fact enables Tony Beale, having compared Cal to Dean and Lennon in the usual way, to compare me to Brian Wilson of The Beach Boys. I should feel complimented but in the back of my racing mind there's a little ticker tape message that says Wilson's overweight, certifiably insane and plays in a sandpit. I really want a drink. I wish I had prepared properly by reading the list of questions that Ian Martyn-Baker provided but then what can I tell him or anyone about anything?

Although there is studio footage of us cutting 'Stolen Moments' and 'Phoenix', it's pretty tame stuff. It shows the putting of the final touches rather than the heart of the creative process. The 'Stolen

Moments' material was actually taken by Jon on Super 8, I think. At one point they resort to panning over newspaper cuttings and even throw in a bit of Jody Clarke on *Top Of The Pops*.

The pace has been quick fire but suddenly we're in a slow silent pan. It's a dressing room I recognise and from somewhere off in an alleyed recess of my mind in a cobwebbed cabinet marked ancient history, I dredge up that specific night. The camera slowly moves the length of the room. It's long and thin and it's got graffiti on the wall. I am adding to it. Finally there is a commentary. It's the voice of Ian Martyn-Baker. 'Frankie Dane has written his name large in the annals of rock,' he begins. I know that night. It's mere weeks before Cal's death and in three hours time the Go-Karts will write their wills. The camera, while it crawls like a snail, feels like a vulture circling.

There's Charlie, his baseball cap dripping with sweat, inserting his tongue into a welcoming orifice – the girl with the thighs – and with his fingers on her bottom still drumming a beat. There's Tony, talking with dripping gestures, arms expansive, clothes expensive. Jon's similarly suited cronies. Cal. Cal's tickling out little licks on his unplugged Telecaster, tossing jokes to the couple of girls squatting on the floor nearby and to all beyond. The camera is going on crutches now. The white door at the end of the room opens inwards and chalked on a blackboard mounted on the outside just below the frosted window you can make out the word Go-Karts. In the doorway, two figures hover in a half-light the camera can barely penetrate. The light from the room's what, two, three, naked bulbs plays on the folds in their clothes as they slowly make motion – a female flare quivers like a denim curtain, a slim-fingered hand slides to where only a lover's caress should be. Comfortably bold, edging forward now, bodies touching, the tip of a golden orange baseball boot.

In our plush upholstered seats my leg is hard against Wendy's. Again she squeezes my hand. To me it is an involuntary confirmation. It feels tight as a shackle and my palm begins to perspire. On the screen her hair, so much like Cal's, cannot help but be caught in the light as she sweeps it back to incline her head upwards.

The picture is changing shape now. Compressed to half their

natural width the doorway shadows are forced to continue their hazy, crazy tale still closer together. On the other half of the screen, over a golden hue selected to match the baseball boots, the credits begin to roll. My throat is arid.

Then the auditorium is drenched in white light and I am in a pounding drumming of applause, physically struggling against it as I descend the stairs to the front of the auditorium. Ian Martyn-Baker has his left arm out stretched towards me. It's nearly as long as his grin. A seat has been produced and gratefully I fall into it. I know now that I should never have agreed to do this.

'Thanks for coming, Frankie,' Ian is saying. 'It's a real privilege because you're so notoriously reluctant to have any truck with us journalists. Why did you agree to do this one?'

I cough. I feel sick. It's not my heart pounding now its my head. I feel the tear in my eye and I find myself talking about my father. I don't know what I am saying. 'Tribute' and 'died earlier this year' I am saying. There's a sea of eyes and an audience of fishes. They're all so far away. The words 'great' and 'man' appear adjacent to each other and without a 'not' before them. 'Terrible' and 'loss' and 'had an honest heart'. Then I'm talking about all the things he didn't have. Privilege and patronage and choice and the sense to see it. It's like two loose wires have finally connected and suddenly I'm buzzing. 'Enlightened self-interest in the market place,' I snort. 'What opportunities did he have, my old man? – the free market in fucking driving licences?' These sound like Cal's words. Cal's words but my emotions. I feel my tongue racing like a child's when his father's hitting hand is over him. They're not just words any more. I feel like Steve Jones when Bill Grundy told him to say something really outrageous. I have moved on to back to back housing and outside toilets and I am standing up now. I am haranguing. Usually I can barely tell one person what I think and here I am telling hundreds. 'The 1980s, that's when I became someone,' I declaim. 'And what else did that emotionally empty decade give us?' Privatisation, recession, unemployment, xenophobia, union-bashing, I conjure them all up – a collection of clipped images: the evil a third of our society vested upon another third while the middle third watched television and, four times in the twee English privacy of the ballot box, pretended not to notice. 'If that's what they were fighting for in the second world war, Dad, you were better off out of it.' And then it happens. I go beyond the boundaries of what is publicly acceptable. I mention the C-word. Yes, I've definitely done it. I am talking about class. I know this because Ian Martyn-Baker is looking at me as if I have just farted. 'And you?' I point at the audience and hold my finger there even as my hand begins to shake. 'You know which third you are. You can break down all the barriers you can find, sup free market poison or carbon-dated culture till you choke, have all the riches you can take or make or fake, be a free spirit and recycle your rubbish as often as your fucking opinions but you can't change what's between your ears and you can't change where you come from. So sit back and be comfortable in your designer labels and designer lifestyles. Cuddle up to your credit cards and feel smug and good about yourself. Be centred. Be shopping centred. Tell yourselves that you've made it and pat yourselves on your fat little heads. But don't tell me class doesn't matter any more. Don't tell me this is a classless society because I might, just. Fucking. Puke.' I stumble to a stop. That is it.

I note my silence, note Ian's toy dog nodding head. I can see Wendy and Jon. They turn to each other. I look at them, I watch and it all stops: the rush in my voice, the pound in my head, the clock in my heart. Then they turn back, face the front and smile at me. Wendy and Jon lead a standing ovation which lasts and, as my faculties slowly click back into gear, lasts. I slump back into the chair like a boxer finished. 'That's why I wanted to do this,' I mumble to myself.

When the hullaboo dies down Ian says: 'And if that's not the spirit of 1977 I don't know what is.' He asks me a couple more questions but I know I could start reciting nursery rhymes and they would clap. I tell him about our collaborative approach to songwriting – Cal's and mine – and just what an honour it was to work with him. I explain that this is what at first made it so difficult to write alone. Then I tell him about how one day I remembered the first night, the two song night and about the importance of keeping it fun, keeping it young. I smile at Wendy and the kids. I tell Ian how once I had learned that lesson then I knew I could take my time. Pop music doesn't have to be a race to die before you get old.

'And now,' he asks, 'another album?'

'No, the book, the autobiography first.'

'And you'll come back and see us when you've finished that?' he says like he's still on telly.

'Sure will,' I say. They clap and Ian extends his arm towards me again. I feel calm and I smile and when a tiny tear returns I dab it away with a handkerchief.

The audience slowly begins to leave. I can see Wendy, Jon, Tony and the kids standing at their seats waiting for me. I wait until I have a clear route to my wife then I walk slowly up the stairs and take her in my arms. We kiss passionately enough and long enough for a few passers-by to clap *this* and for Rebecca to tug at my sleeve and hiss, 'Dad.'

I can feel my erection like an eighteen year-old's growing inside my trousers and forcing itself against the fresh cotton of Wendy's dress. As we break she allows her open palm to brush across my fly.

'Frankie, you were excellent,' says my manager.

'Thanks,' I say. 'Jon, can I just have a word with you?'

I sound like a character in a soap-opera. He puts his arm around my shoulder and leads me away.

'See you all outside,' I instruct.

The auditorium is nearly empty. Ian Martyn-Baker claps me on the back yet again as he leaves, bet I'll have a bruise in the morning.

'If you're getting the flavour for these Frankie, we could do plenty more,' Jon is saying. 'There's dozens of independent film theatres up and down the country. We could do a tour, package it like a rock tour – T-shirts, videos obviously, a single would be nice...'

We've climbed the stairs onto the stage now and, black-suited both, we stand stark against the white movie screen as if we're in the poster for *Reservoir Dogs*.

'That reminds me Frank, I did sort of promise Tony a single to coincide with this bash. I didn't want to mention it before because I knew you were nervous about doing it anyway. I was thinking, if you really have nothing at all, a cover in the classic Go-Karts tradition would be more than acceptable. But I'm sure you're just being modest.' He pokes me in the stomach. 'I'm sure there's another 'Rotten In Denmark' hidden in there somewhere.'

'Jonathan, how long have you been having an affair with my wife.'

He looks at me, activity like a hive behind his eyes. For a second I think he is going to deny it and in that second I hit him as hard as I can in the stomach. As he doubles over I bring my knee up into those big deceitful eyes. When Jon lifts his head his nose is bleeding. I draw my fist back and aim at the softly pumping puddle of red. He falls back like a star, arms wide apart, legs splayed, and collapses straight into the cinema screen. Supporting him for a fraction of a second, it then gives way, splits and tears and swallows him up like a black hole. Drops of crimson scamper across the vast brilliant screen like first blood in a painting by Jackson Pollock. There is the thud below my feet of rapidly moving flesh against dead concrete and all that is left on the stage in front of me is Jonathan's mobile phone. It rings twice and then his voice-mail answering service clicks in. An American female offers to take a message – she says it like massage.

Outside Tony has bought the drinks. 'Fucking magic, Frankie sunshine.'

Already Wendy has taken my hand and I feel her heat tight against me. The other hand flashes across my fly again. My erection is back. Or perhaps it never went away. I feel her stare. I feel her squeeze my hand.

'I think we should skip food,' says Wendy, 'I'm bushed and these kids need to get to bed.'

'Where's Uncle Jon?' asks Philip.

'He had to go,' I say. 'Someone called on his mobile.'

28

Undulating, ululating fields swoop and soar, bank and arch. A fence, floating, cats-eyes pouncing, a stile swaying like a seesaw, the red hot punch of a postbox. Yes, the countryside is fast but I am faster.

I think Cal is talking in the front but it's simple chatter. The words go over me like birds. I'm lying across the back seat and the window pane is cool as I press my smouldering nose against it. A road sign looms: a pyramid headed extraterrestrial. A village sweeps past in a blink – just catch sight of the church spire puncturing the shawl of night. Stars like glitter on a witch. When Cal pulls into a lay-by, the front wheel churning grass as we halt, we take some more. The razor blade catches the tinny glow of the car light and shines like a guillotine. Here's some we made earlier. Cal tips the powder onto the mirror and forms it into two white stripes like racing trims. He rolls the fiver into a tube, finds a nostril, covers the other and sniffs. I copy and my nostrils roar.

Cal's old Escort had a top speed of little more than fifty but at times that night I'm sure it felt like we were taking off. After the initial buzz along the A23 I sat up and played acoustic guitar. I seemed to have hours to find the chords yet only seconds to play them. Up the M1 we sang at the tops of our hoarse voices every Go-Kart song and every cover we were going to play, discussing the running order and the exact arrangements, who would do what, even what the between song patter might be. I made notes until I started feeling sick. By the time we reached Darlington and were making jokes about their football team, dawn was peering tentatively over the horizon.

Durham town, then, came like a slap: Cathedral and castle soaring towards the sky, the turrets and towers climbing above the houses and a thick collar of green grass, majestic in the mist-streaked morning light.

'You really need to see this from the train,' said Cal.

'Right,' I replied.

The road snaked round with the river and we were in the palatinate's narrow streets. The road led to the cathedral as sure as sanctuary. At the castle we enquired of the gatekeeper which hall was University College and he told us we'd already found it.

'Isn't this a castle?' I asked.

'Aye, son – a castle and a seat of learning.'

After a brief search we discovered our quarry, knife and fork poised over bacon and egg. Outside the great hall in which the students dined was a notice 'Open To The Public'.

'They don't watch you eat, do they?' I asked.

'Sure but they have to stand up there,' said Jon, pointing up to a gallery running around the room. It reminded me a little of the Horniman Museum but this hall was much bigger, the balcony much higher and it seemed infused, like the rest of the town, with a kind of divinity.

He didn't quite smile but I think Jon was pleased to see us, putting his arms around our shoulders and leading us off to his room as if we were a playground gang. He was busy for much of the day with lectures, tutorials and, would you believe it, bass guitar lessons so Cal and I passed the morning trying to sleep – taking it in turns to use the bed.

I felt tired but my eyes wouldn't sit still long enough to close. Jon's vast chair – a lumpy re-upholstered affair – wasn't comfortable either. I realised how much my throat hurt from what must have been three or four hours of raucous singing. Tossing, turning, rearranging the blanket's oppressive checks, I noticed the washbasin in the corner of the room. I had a glass of water but it tasted stale and I could hardly swallow anyway. There were Jon's familiar posters, strange in these new surroundings, and an old bookcase racked with books I'd never heard of. Some of the titles I didn't even understand. I thumbed a few but the paragraphs assaulted me like cudgels.

Looking out of Jon's bedroom window I was dimly aware that my mother's home village must be near here somewhere but any idea of visiting it soon passed. It seemed irrelevant to me that morning – something that someone else should do. At midday we got up, took some more speed and went to the students' union. At least, I think it was the students union.

We had a couple of beers, Jonathan declining because he had work to do. We asked where the dart board was. We asked if we could go whippet racing or stick ferrets down our trousers. Cal got talking to a Geordie girl, cracking her alleged northern impenetrability with easy charm. He told her he was in a band. She told him she was coming to London at the end of the academic year. He told her we would be playing the Marquee then.

We spent the afternoon walking around the town. We knocked on the cathedral's monster of a door knocker. Inside I picked up a leaflet. Apparently, the knocker is a copy but a faithful one right down to the hole made by a Scottish arrow.

We had another line of speed on Palace Green and then we walked along the River Wear engaging with the autumn colours and the tree-framed views, kicking the leaves. Cal talked. He was full of plans. We crossed a bridge at Kingsgate and another at Framwellgate. We walked until the day began to lose its battle with night. Then we took some more speed and returned to find Jonathan.

'We haven't eaten much have we?' I said and Jon took us to a pub called the Dun Cow where we ordered pie and peas. Jon fed the dog with polo mints.

Cal started to outline his plan. There was a time-frame built in. If we hadn't made it within two years we'd pack up but he was sure this wouldn't happen. Jonathan didn't agree. Jon was enjoying his degree course and didn't flatter himself that he could play the bass. Two years seemed like an eternity to me – surely everybody would have made it by then.

By the time we reached the Queens Head the debate was raging and to my mind Cal's unfailing powers of persuasion appeared to be failing him. There were dozens of people there, some student faces I thought I recognised from lunchtime but also plenty of what Jon called 'townies' too. Some of them looked like they might even have been working in one of those fields Cal and I had surveyed that afternoon. In the corner a dodgy band were chugging away.

'We must be better than them,' insisted Cal, resorting to old arguments, his arms waving vaguely.

'Probably,' said Jon, 'but you're asking me to give up my day job. This lot are prison warders. Plenty of security in that.'

Cal snorted, took another drink. 'Even her?' he asked pointing at the mousy female singer bopping acceptably in her leather jacket.

'Yes, even her. Durham has a heavy duty female nick too, Calum.'

We were leaning on the bar and although behind us I could sense the crowd swelling, our heads were edging closer together in that familiar way. I was enjoying the claustrophobia, the smell of the beer, the chatter around our heads and the rising temperature. All that mattered was that bar towel and the three pints standing on it. I don't think Cal had expected this. He assumed everyone enjoyed the same confident indifference as he. Then a wave of sweat-shirted, scarf-wielding youths hit the bar. I noticed the Geordie girl just as she peeled away from the group and touched Cal on the shoulder.

'Hello,' she said.

Cal turned a fraction, registered and gunned her down with his eyeballs. He carried on talking to Jon, cajoling, animated.

The girl took a step back. 'We met at dinner time,' her small voice began.

'I know full fucking well when we met but right now, I'm busy.'

'Cal,' said Jon. He touched the girl on her shoulder.

Cal shook his head. He took Jon by the arm. 'Come on you. Frankie,' he instructed, pointing at me. 'This is Karen.'

Jon hesitated for a moment.

'This is important,' said Cal, picking up both pints in his free hand by putting his thumb in the top of one and his fingers in the other. There was some spillage as he ushered Jon away. 'Universities, prisons,' I heard him saying. 'They're all the same, Jon. Total institutions designed to bleed you of your soul.' Left at the bar were me and Karen.

'Hi,' I said. 'I'm sorry...'

She shrugged. 'Do you want to dance?'

I saw Cal just once more that night when he dragged me into the toilets with him to take some more speed. We did it in a cubicle, using the half-broken bog seat as a table for our paraphernalia, trying not to kneel in the piss. 'He's cracking,' said Cal. 'Here take a third line. By the way, I've had to offer him a place in our flat.'

'What flat?' I was still kneeling on the floor, head over the mirror.

'Explain later,' he said and I felt his hand brush the top of my head as he left.

More dancing. More drinks. I can't remember leaving the pub. Next Karen and I were at some party – the whole corridor seemed to be involved so I guess it must have been another hall of residence. We were in a kitchen I think – there seemed to be about seven toasters and a smell of lentils and dirty socks. Karen pressed a bottle into my hand.

'Bottle of dog,' she said.

I suffered a blink of sobriety. 'Did you say dog?' I asked, remembering the black-brown mongrel and his polo mints.

She smiled and took my other hand. In the bedroom I opened my bottle of Newcastle Brown Ale with a sharp downward movement against the edge of a desk. Half the contents ejaculated over an essay, the words swimming and drowning in the piss-brown liquid.

'Sorry,' I said.

'It's not my room,' said Karen. She was on the bed.

I took a deep breath and slugged the rest of the bottle. In the mirror on the wall I could see black rings around my eyes like a panda's. Karen, sipping from a bottle of Liebfraumilch, moved over. I was still standing when she began unbuttoning her top. It was a violent violet cardigan with wool-covered buttons. My Auntie Anne had something similar but she didn't have CND earrings and a tight white New York Dolls T-shirt. I realised that Karen was quite sexy.

'Lock the door, pet.'

I looked at the push-button locking mechanism on the back of the cheap wooden door and tried to fathom how it worked. There were no French-polished finishes here as in Jon's hall. I shook my head. 'I don't think I can manage this *and* a bra strap.'

Karen laughed, spilling wine all over herself and the bed. 'I suppose you think that's sexy?' I said.

Things were easy with Karen. She was relaxed with a simple kind of warmth that made you feel safe. It wasn't like you had to impress. My tongue was in her ear, my hand scampering up her thigh but there was no po-faced exhibitionism about our lovemaking. We were laughing all the way through like a couple of kids face-painting each other.

I managed to knot my shoelaces and she had to pull my boots off for me. On the bedstead, her tights, thick black things, laddered in great lacerations to a degree that would have satisfied Jacob. We laughed about that although neither of us were sure who Jacob was and as a result she managed to snag the zip on her matching black skirt. When we were finally naked we ran our hands over each other in a soft silence before I slipped inside and we were at it again: talking, joking and laughing.

My cock felt strangely distant as if it were making love next door or we were using a tarpaulin condom. As we continued, the tiny bed rocking rhythmically, only Karen, writhing as much as giggling now, seemed to be feeling anything. There was none of that rippling tingling climbing in my cock. I felt as if I could go on all night. I was absolutely confident that she would come first and I began to enjoy it – we rolled over into a new position. Then another. Tongues. hands. Caressing. Kneading. Her tits above me, rising and falling. Hip bones, Bezier crescents gently rocking. My heart was pounding though. Was that because of the exercise or because I'd only just realised? I was back on top again. My staccato heart – beating with stabbing hemi-demi-semi-quavers. We were kissing our lips raw. Her hands on my back and bum. Her fingernails in my flesh. My fingernails gouging splinters out of the side of the bed. My cock was numb and it was like my heart was coming instead. Then just as it seemed about to explode it changed gear, dropped a cog or two. Its natural gentle pulsebeat re-established itself after the briefest of struggles and as it did my erection left me like a fracture and the sleep that I'd denied myself for so long washed over me.

I collapsed on Karen. 'Just like dead weight,' she wrote. She had had to struggle out from beneath me like a crash victim. When I woke up some time in the afternoon the following day, the lad from Birmingham whose room it was was getting very angry. Karen had left me a note and a packet of Alka Seltzer and gone to a lecture; Jon had agreed to join the Go-Karts.

I never really took drugs seriously again. I smoked joints and had the occasional line of speed before going on stage but I never took anything in a quantity that could be dangerous. I had had the benefit of a warning that was denied to Cal.

29

If I wanted Wendy in the foyer of the NFT, the moment has passed by the time we get home. Sure, she gets the kids off to bed with all haste, reawakens my now limp cock with her usual grace but it's like making love to a ghost. Words unspoken circle our contortions. It's as if we have a routine and are simply running through it like two dancers in rehearsal. Wendy wants me to eat yoghurt from her but I am not hungry any more.

When we lie leg by leg in solitary silent pleading for sleep, I could choke on the weight of what I want to say. It's trapped in my throat like a snared beast. As Wendy's breathing softens and lengthens and her body jerks into sleep I play Desert Island Life – packing my suitcase. I know I won't say anything. Will she to me? Does she know I know? And if so, know what? Did she see me in Liberty's restaurant? Did she see what I saw in the film? And what did I see? I've replayed that footage dozens of times in my head – rewinding, rewinding – and I know there must be thousands of meanings to be found in those shadowy shivers of shapes but only one can I see. Thanks, darling. This is doing wonders for my insomnia.

I can't say that I'm surprised when she is up and gone before six-thirty. Jonathan never was an early riser but now I wonder if he's changed his habits. I wait for the first thumping and bumping of the children before I too rise and execute my paternal duties. By nine I am down in the studio. My manager said something about a single and I am wondering if I can eke something out. The cupboard feels bare but I run through some half-remembered chord sequences, play some old master tapes.

Then the entry-phone buzzes. I swivel around from the mixing desk and pick up the receiver.

'Hi, it's me, Jon.'

I'm alone and absurdly, my first thought is whether or not he is armed.

'Come on down,' I say, casual. 'I'm in the studio.'

I find a blank cassette and put it in the Portastudio – the little four-track recorder I use as a sort of musical notebook

The door opens a little tentatively. I don't look up – I'm rewinding the reel to reel machine. 'Are you decent?' Jon asks. He's in, standing beneath the red light which when illuminated reads 'Live'. The door closes with a click. I turn grudgingly. His face is a mess. Right now, Jonathan, to me, feels dead or is it me? Do I feel dead?

He is armed only with the morning papers.

'Ah, the 'Phoenix' tapes,' he says. He taps his foot, shakes his long frail frame a little. 'Great stuff. Listen to that bass-playing.'

I considerably prefer watching Jonathan grope for words to watching him grope my wife. I simply smile and don't show him the vacant seat beside me. He looks around like he's never been in here before and then perches on the Yamaha keyboard – the bass notes register a discordant fart as he sits.

'Jazz bass?' he asks, twisting to turn the keyboard off.

'Slap bass,' I say. 'The setting's on Slap Bass.'

'So, we going to make that single?'

'We?'

He shuffles. 'Look Frankie, yesterday you asked me a question.'

Beneath my sock is a switch, a drop-in switch. It enables you to operate the cassette on the Portastudio by using your foot. It's designed to let you record all by yourself while playing guitar or some other instrument and, of course, it operates silently. I ease my toes forward and feel it bite.

'What's the answer?' I ask.

'Well I've sorted everything out with the British Film Institute. I told them that I was epileptic and had had a fit.' A croaky nervous laugh. 'Was that a bit politically incorrect? I suppose it was really. Still, needs must. Anyway I paid for it – the screen. My money obviously. Said they could throw in a set of curtains too if they wanted.'

'Jon, what's the answer to the question?'

'Well, it's not as straightforward as all that. A bit complicated.'

I leap from my chair as I've been waiting for the opportunity to do. Jon's nearly my height but he's not much broader than Philip. I want the pleasure of intimidation. I think I deserve it.

'A bit fucking complicated. It could get a lot more complicated, Jon.'

'I don't know what you're getting so het up about, Frank. It's nothing,' he hesitates. This isn't Jon's sort of territory – a bit too kitchen sink: 'You and Wendy are good together. But well, it wasn't always that way, was it? When she was with Julian.'

'Do you think I don't know that?' I turn back into the centre of the studio, take a step, another. The clock on the wall circles silently.

Behind me Jonathan gets up and coughs. That deep breath sounds like one of relief. 'And we can always get that bit cut from the movie before we do the next one,' he says. 'I tell you, Frank, immediately after I left you I spoke to the BFI...'

'You didn't have a lot of choice, did you?'

'Yeah but I suggested a tour and they jumped at it – some of these regional theatres are desperate for bums on seats and you'd be just the man, Frank.'

''But what's so complicated?

'Nothing. Like I said, we run it like a rock tour.'

'But what's so complicated about your relationship with Wendy? What's so complicated?'

'Well, nothing, I suppose. It was just seeing it in the film and I know how fond you are of her.'

'Fond, Jon? I love her.'

'Yes, of course, you do. That's right, I knew you'd be upset. Was embarrassed really – wished I'd told you before.'

'Told me what, Jon?'

Next to the mixing desk is the drum machine with its little black plastic drum pads. I punch out a roll with my fingers and the beats ring round the room like shots from a gun.

'You've been taking fucking liberties, Jon,' I say with the pronounced menace of a TV gangster.

'What do you mean? It was years ago.'

'Liberty's.'

Silence. In the Portastudio the cassette continues to roll. I can't imagine why I should ever want to listen to this again. 'It's a shop off Regent's Street, Jon. Surely your good mama is a frequent visitor...'

I turn and face him. I have psyched myself up to look him straight in the sockets. I focus on a spot just behind his rapidly blinking eyes and hold my gaze. 'Do you take me for a fool, Jonathan?'

'We just ran into each other. Surprised you didn't...'

'Do you take me for a fool?'

Jon coughs and looks away. He bows his head a little. His hands snatch like they're just itching for a cigarette. 'The families have been friends for years. Well, you know all that. Most of the time she was with Julian I was very close to her.'

'And?'

'And Wendy's got a special place in my heart. Always will have.'

'Now we're getting somewhere.'

'But she loves you.'

'Yeah, yeah, yeah.' I'm sneering now like a great bloated, snarling Tony.

Jon reacts, takes a step forward, ups the ante a fraction. 'Don't knock it, chum. When somebody loves you, you don't knock it.'

'And who loves you, Jon?'

He looks at me as if I am a foolish child. 'I can't believe you're asking me all this stuff. Wendy is gorgeous. Always has been. And she is crazy about you, Frankie. You saved her life. That's what she says.' He turns, lets his fingers tumble across the keyboard – discordant, descending notes. 'She says Cal's death would have finished her if it hadn't been for you. Not me, someone she'd known since she was was child, but you. You. Simple as that. Has she never told you? Well, I tell you, she's told me often enough.'

I don't know what to say. But Jon now can't shut up.

'She adores you. Of course, you've never believed it, have you?' He looks at me incredulously. 'You never had to change for her,

Frankie. That Open University degree. All those books. There must have been fifteen rooms in this house full of books.' He laughs. 'Even this studio was. Your conversation. That wasn't you. That stupid Christopher Marlowe interview you did. All that stuff was crap. I don't know if you've got a chip on your shoulder. Perhaps you do thinking about what you said last night. But if you do Wendy loves it just as much as she loves the rest of you.' He quietens, rocks back on his heels. I can *feel* all this. 'You know what she said to me one time in the middle of it all?' His eyes ask the question insistently. 'She said to me "If I'd wanted another one of *them*" – meaning a Cal or her father or a Julian – "I'd have come to you." She was joking, Frank.' He pauses. 'She was joking because she knew.'

I can't take in the subtleties. My shoulders twitch. 'Jon, are you shagging my wife?'

He laughs shortly and looks wide eyed for a moment. 'No, Frank. Is that what you think?'

'Yes.'

He shakes his head in a patronisingly paternal manner. 'It's a bit complicated.'

I do what I swore I wouldn't do. I take Jon by the lapels and slam him against the door. The solution of violence, unknown to me for so, so long, is becoming achingly attractive. I don't want to hit him again but there's anger swelling like a storm inside and I am fighting against it, trying not to go under. I slam him again. 'Just fucking level with me, Jonathan,' I scream. This time I slam him so hard that the 'Live' sign falls from its hinges and onto his head and everything changes. We both, after a dotted quaver of quiver in the lips, laugh like we haven't laughed for years.

With this moment we are teenagers again. In this room with its soundproofed walls there's a purity about the quality of our laughter. It has a richness and a depth. We are doubled over till my sides hurt more than my heart. We end up sitting on the cork-tiled floor on opposite sides of the room, our feet almost touching in the middle.

'Wendy,' Jon says through the tears, '*is* the only woman I've ever slept with. But it happened when I was still at primary school and it was in the back of the Carter's car coming back from the coast.'

I blink – consciously blink – and this time when Jon starts to talk

217

he sounds like he did before Durham, like he did when we were all together at school and all the differences between us seemed to be little ones. This time he is telling me something I don't know yet I believe every word. He keeps saying 'I thought you knew' and 'How many girls did I have at school?' and pretending to count on his fingers. Half way through I stop him and get us both bottles of beer from the small fridge in the corner. We throw the bottle opener back and forth.

Jon tells me that he was at Durham when he had his first relationship with a man but he'd wanted one for ages. That, he explains is why he could never entertain the idea of not going away to University no matter how much Cal, the band or I meant to him. He just had to go away somewhere. He laughs. 'North Staffs Poly, if necessary.' How could he have come out at home with Terry Chambers peering over his shoulder? How could he have told his parents?

I smile. 'Your dad would have had to resign from the drama group.'

'More like they would have made him president,' says Jon.

'So what is it with you and Wendy?'

'She was the first one to know, Frank. The first person I told. That's a special thing but it makes no difference to your special thing.'

Now Jon and I can laugh like schoolboys. We can remember when we were those schoolboys and we can desperately want to feel like that again. Yearn for it. But we can't have it and we won't because now we're the men we are, not the boys we were. He's nearly forty and I'm the first straight man he's told.

If you just look, Jon's face now is not the face he takes to business meetings at all. This one is soft and childish not hard and adult. They could be different people. But we aren't 'just looking' – I'm not staring hesitantly at Mr. Parker's confectionary stand now – we are right in there living and for most of our marriage Jon has been as close to my wife as I have been. Fact. So we drink some more and we joke and laugh.

'You know the old cliché about how a straight woman's best friend is always a gay man,' Jon says. We both know there is more to it than that so why don't I feel so bad? Even as he tells me about their occasional coffee mornings of which I have heard diddley squit before. I feel a little uncomfortable but not angry. What is it that the thought of Jonathan's prick could do to me that his comforting arm and Wendy's reciprocation cannot. Why is the idea of them fucking so painful when genuine companionship and emotional support are not. Aren't they more important? Touching people's souls, isn't that what Cal said mattered but it's the sex thing that really matters – it's nothing but it's everything. Then something clicks into place.

'Jon, what about Tony?'

'As a nine bob note.'

'Are you two?'

'Don't be absurd.' He laughs. 'Tony's conversation may be chocker with sexual imagery but his life certainly isn't. He can't accept what he is. Wanted to be macho, ended up sad and celibate. Anyway, can you imagine getting it on with Tony Beale?'

'Not while there are dogs in the street,' I say.

'It helps though. That I know about him. To be honest most of the industry knows but he doesn't know that. Or isn't prepared to acknowledge it anyway. That helps. You must have wondered, Frank. An album every decade, come on. Your contractual obligations are somewhat stiffer than that. I smooth them over.' He chuckles.

As I watch him drink and listen to him talk, the one image that keeps returning to me, much as I don't want it to, is of a drama lesson nearly three decades ago. I search through the battered black metal box in front of me. It's full of cassettes. I read the labels and try to remember when they were recorded. Eventually I find what I am looking for. It is an old Maxell thing, scratched and without a case. I blunder across to the Portastudio which has long since switched itself off and put it in.

'I've got it by the way, Jon. The new single.'

It's a cassette of The Roebuck gig. The tape rattles and it hums but beneath it you can hear what we are playing well enough. We are playing 'Sitting On The Dock Of The Bay'. By fiddling around with the sliders on the machine I can affect the mix slightly. Jon's bass doesn't seem to be there but I track it down. We listen. I turn up the volume. Not one of his notes is in tune.

'And can you play it in the right key this time?' I say.

He laughs – laughs again, long and deep. 'This takes me back,' he says. Then he sips shortly like taking a quick puff on a cigarette. 'Not the music, Frank – the laughing.'

I look at him and I try to place how I feel. I find an answer in a stutter and smirk from our playground past. There is anger in me and it is coming from all those quips, all Terry's jibes. It comes from the fact that I didn't know umpteen years down the road what the dumbest teenager knew at school: Jon's gay. As 'Sitting On The Dock Of The Bay' comes to a stumbling end it's clear he doesn't know why I'm playing it and if the song means nothing to him why should I let it to me? I earmark it for the B-side. It's like watching yourself grow up. It's wisdom dropping like pennies.

Jon's talking about Cal now. We look at each other across the floor and through our collective haze our eyes manage to meet. There's a morning glow about us and I feel on the level with Jon. Cal's name on our lips and I feel on the level. But I am wise enough not to ask the one question that remains, wise enough to know that the wrong answer could hurt more than I could understand.

'Jon,' I say. 'I'm sorry I jumped to the wrong conclusion.'

'And I'm sorry I've never told you before. You don't know how often I've wanted to, even when we were at school. Especially when we were at school. I was always on the outside and I thought it would bring us all closer but I couldn't take the risk and...' He trails off. For the first time ever in his life Jon is inarticulate. And for the first time in mine, he feels like my friend.

I smile and clink my bottle against his. He smiles too and pushes the newspapers across the floor to me. 'You seem to have struck a chord,' he says.

'Frankie Dane's Masterclass', says *The Guardian*'s arts page, the reviewer welcoming my contribution to the social debate while wondering if my analysis is not oversimplistic in post modern Britain. 'Class Act' says *The Independent*. 'Is Dane On Drugs?' asks that idiot columnist in *The Mail*.

'You've even made the editorial in your favourite tabloid,' Jon chuckles. He opens it for me and there it is in block capitals reversed white out of black: 'Dane Has Brain Transplant.' 'There's no class in this newspaper and has-been rock star Frankie Dane's ludicrous suggestion that there is in this great country of ours...'

We're both laughing. I don't care what they say about me. I don't care about any of it because now Jon's words, Wendy's words, are beginning to ring like church bells in my mind. 'If I'd wanted one of them I'd have come to you.' These words are headier than any brew. They are an inspiration, an affirmation.

30

It started going wrong when the band went to America in 1979. Since Cal had returned from the States all those short but sweet months earlier it had all been plain sailing and no-one had been more surprised than me. I'd had my spotty teenage head buried in enough rock biographies to know that it wasn't supposed to be that easy: a question of doing the rounds, the pubs and clubs, halls and balls, looking for the break and riding your luck. For us, it was a piece of piss.

Midway through the British gigs we recorded the album. As with most bands the material for this first album wasn't a problem. You've been preparing for it for so long. The songs have been around. The band know them. The audience know them. You can take your pick from your whole repertoire. Cal and I wrote some of those first songs in the lower sixth. We were three years older when we recorded the album and in between we'd got every note of every arrangement sorted. The recording took a fortnight and it was to be rush-released so that it would be in the shops before the end of the UK dates. Already Tony was creaming himself over the advance sales. We were beginning to think we could do no wrong.

Cal had been talking about doing some American dates ever since we'd walked off the stage at The Roxy and now he wouldn't shut up about them. Tony sorted some out and then tagged on a couple in Europe too. We started talking about our World Tour. 'Do you think it will be over by Christmas?' asked Jon.

I felt a rare moment of sympathy for Tony. His job was not made any easier by Cal's insistence that the US dates should follow a bizarre itinerary of his own devising. He didn't discuss it with me but then Cal knew America, I didn't. Tony took one look at the list and said that the least we could do was to begin in New York.

'But I've been to New York,' moaned Cal.

The result of all this was that we were booked to play what looked like some pretty strange places.

We travelled light – the formula that had worked for the album. We took just a couple of roadies and a sound man. Tony had arranged for one of Phonodisc's men in America to be tour manager. He was meeting us at JFK airport. In the plane Charlie had a map open across the seat and was scouring it for the towns in the tour schedule. 'Which state's that one in?' he asked every five minutes. While the names were sometimes familiar to me I didn't actually know the answers. Nor, I suspected, did Jon, hiding behind a Henry James novel. 'Georgia,' Cal would reply, 'Alabama', but without interrupting his own monologue on the delights of the USA. It took a stewardess with the two bottles of champagne he'd ordered to do that.

Cal began to get irritated at customs. He couldn't wait to get into the country but we had to hang around for ages to get through immigration. He appeared to think that his sundry previous visits entitled him to express treatment.

On Charlie's insistence Tony had reluctantly booked us into the Waldorf Astoria.

'Do you realise how fucking much it costs just to fart in the lobby at that bloody place,' he demanded. 'And you haven't made me a cock-sucking cent yet?'

'Think big. Think globally,' said Cal. 'We've made you plenty of pounds sterling and there's no reason the States should be any different.'

Tony raised his eyebrows. 'It's a fucking ball-breaking business to penetrate the States, like Jodrell bloody bank or Mary Whitehouse's knickers, especially if we can't get airplay. No one knows you from Mrs. Mills over there.'

'No one knew us here six months ago.'

Tony was getting hot under the collar.

'Why exactly do you want to stay in the Waldorf, Charlie?' I asked.

'I want to order a salad.'

'Oh, very fucking rock'n'roll.' Tony did his indulgent uncle laugh – 'One night only, savvy?' – then he disappeared before we could make any more ludicrous demands.

At the airport there was a message from Phonodisc saying that the tour manager would meet us at the hotel instead. We tried chatting up the cabbie on the way but he didn't speak English. As he pulled away I noticed him looking up Park Avenue on the map. He was a slight mustachioed man who held tight onto his steering wheel as if to let it go would be fatal.

'Musicians. We're musicians.' Charlie was shouting at him trying to make him understand. He demonstrated his own particular art by pounding vigorously on an imaginary drumkit. In the rear-view mirror I could see the shock of recognition dart across the driver's eyes.

'Oh, you policeman,' he said and refused to utter another word thereafter.

The four of us checked in and adjourned immediately to the lobby bar where Cal summoned a bellboy. Cal was determined that we should all try the cocktails. The hotel was all Chinese carpets and colonnades. Even time was beautifully fashioned in the Waldorf Astoria. There was a lobby clock like something from a church. Charlie ordered his salad. From his pocket he produced three sachets of Heinz salad cream that looked as if they could have been stolen from the café near the school and drowned the thing.

The crew arrived. They'd waited at the airport to collect the gear and pick up the two vans Tony had hired for us. They were moaning. Tony had booked them into some fleapit near the venue. He had told them that it was for reasons of convenience but one look at where we were staying told them it was for reasons of economy. Mac, the beefy Glaswegian roadie, who seemed to be their foreman was saying that an act like us, who'd had a number one single 'by the way', should be providing something better.

'We haven't had a number one in America,' said Jon.

'Och, details,' said Mac.

The three of them looked around the lobby: Mac, Nev – his younger but equally substantial Jamaican sidekick and Ant – the partially deaf sound-man. Ant's line was 'Brian Wilson was deaf in one ear, you know'. He would repeat this mantra dozens of times daily, partly because many people queried Ant's aptitude for the job, and partly because, as Ant could rarely hear what they were asking him, he repeated himself a lot.

Mac flexed his nostrils and took a sniff of glamorous old New York. He noticed our cocktails and the absence of anyone who could really be said to be 'in charge'.

'D'ye want a wee drink, mates?' he said appropriating a seat at the other end of the bar. He was talking to Nev and Ant not us. I felt awkward enough anyway in this hotel drinking a cocktail the name of which I'd had to ask Cal to pronounce but I truly felt my palms sweating now.

So we drank. After a couple of rums Nev was telling the lobby how the hotel reminded him of the days of slavery.

'That would make you over a hundred,' said Charlie. He had walked over to share his second salad with them.

'He works like a man of a hundred,' said Mac.

'Pardon?' said Ant.

Jon and Cal took it in their stride. 'The tour manager will sort them out,' said Jon as if he was talking about children or, at least, people who weren't in earshot. Scampering nervously between the two groups, I was the obvious one to respond when the reception paged 'Mr. G. Karts'. The message was from the tour manager saying that he would meet us at the venue.

By the time we set off we'd all had too much to drink. The crew followed in the two vans. I could see them snaking about the road behind us. I don't know if it was alcohol or the fact that they were still laughing over the valet parking service and the white bellboy who had had to say, through gritted teeth, 'have a nice day, sir' to Nev. 'Don't worry, Frank, these people can hold their drink,' said Jon.

'But can you?' said Cal.

Unfortunately, the tour manager couldn't sort it out. He wasn't there. Mac and Nev set the stage up while Ant deafened the rest of us with some unscheduled feedback. We were playing CBGB's, the punk venue in Bovary: sleazier than anything the good madame of the same name might have imagined with a great sound-system to boot. Except there wasn't going to be any booting – at least not of the sound system, Cal reminded Jon.

In the event, Jon could have done all the booting he wanted. Nothing would have saved us. Hardly anyone turned up. I don't think the Americans actually knew what a Go-Kart was. The nearest thing nomenclature-wise was Go-Cat so God knows what the punters of New York thought – perhaps they thought we were the house-band for a pet food manufacturer. Nobody else seemed to find this notion funny except Nev but then Nev found everything funny.

If we had had a crowd, I probably would have moaned about the sound which was appalling. We all know your hearing gets impaired by alcohol and it's even worse if you only have one ear to start off with. Moreover, Ant was a one venue man. He knew the mixing desk at the Greyhound inside out and used this knowledge to disguise his aural shortcomings. After we came off stage to a trickle of applause and a swelling squawk of feedback worthy of Hitchcock's *The Birds*, he revealed he had worked at the Greyhound for nine years and nowhere else.

'Why the fuck didn't you say before we left?' demanded Charlie who after an hour's fruitless labour on his drumkit was looking for a more profitable outlet for his hitting activities.

'I fancied a holiday, like.'

'So you heard that then.'

'Pardon.'

One of the many people who didn't turn up to witness our US debut was the tour manager. Back at the hotel there was a message that he'd catch up with us at the next venue.

We sat silently in the bar – heads bowed over our glasses. At length, Cal looked up at me. 'Well, there's only one way we're going to survive this isn't there?' Without a backward glance he disappeared out of the lobby into the night and the following morning he began consuming copious amounts of speed.

31

Beech Park, the present day

Jon has to get a cab home. I walk to the supermarket, hope it will clear my head but it doesn't. I think only a bazooka can do that job. Instead I opt for sleep. Wendy comes home in the middle of the afternoon.

'I would have thought you were dead but I could hear you snoring out in the drive,' she says as she wakes me with a touch that tickles my nose. 'I was expecting to find one of you dead. There wasn't much on at work so I decided to come home and clear up the mess.'

I don't ask how she knows because I don't care.

'We talked. We had a lot to drink,' I say. 'Anyway, I wasn't snoring in the drive.'

Wendy smiles. 'I'll make a pot of coffee.'

I get out of bed. I have that 5am taste in my mouth. I feel heady but in an empty way like after a dope party. I edge hesitantly towards the mirror. My tongue looks like a slice of red sponge. Beneath each eye is a sack of coal. A rush of water courses through the cistern as downstairs Wendy puts the kettle on. I want a shower – a shower beneath a waterfall like we had that day in Portmerion when we were recording the album. That day the water was so cold it cleaned right the way through you. I put on my bath robe. On the way downstairs, I check on my watch and pause at the bathroom to clean my teeth.

Wendy is filling the big cafetière – the eight cup one for when we have guests. I guess she is expecting a long talk. From the fridge I take one of the three family size pots of yoghurt that I bought at the supermarket. I take two steps and am right behind her. I place the yoghurt in front of her on the work surface, and join my arms around her tummy. It's soft. I let my own stomach nestle against her back. My erection rises, opening my loosely belted bathrobe as it does so. I lower my head and kiss her at the point where proud neck becomes gently curved shoulder.

'Can I help you?' asks Wendy.

She twists round and we are facing each other. She is smiling, unbuttoning.

'We haven't done it in the kitchen for ages,' I say.

'You're right. Must be at least a week.'

Later, we are in bed watching the clock when I have the idea. I allow my hand to slide down Wendy's torso, her chest rising and falling with life, her tummy gently yielding to the touch, her navel complete with a sticky residue of strawberry yoghurt, her soft mossy mound of pubic hair.

'The kids'll be home soon,' she says.

'Let's go on a second honeymoon,' I say.

Wendy levers herself up on her elbow. She's interested. 'You mean, no kids.'

'Just that. Mum keeps nagging about having them. We could send the three of them off somewhere.'

Wendy giggles. 'Do you think your Mum's having a second childhood?'

'Probably. She's certainly young enough to mother pre-teens again. I suppose I'm not saying we couldn't all go to the same place. We'd just need a few ground-rules...'

As we dress, my wife and I play Desert Island Life together and even add a practical dimension by fetching our suitcases from what I still call the box room. We discuss the duration. Will three weeks be long enough? Will it be too long at our age?

'Your age, sweetheart,' I say. At this point Wendy takes a break from folding the swimming costume she is already packing to kick me. I love to see her like this.

We discuss the location and conclude that it isn't where that matters – 'there are plenty of beautiful places in the world if you have money in the bank, sweetheart,' Wendy says in a cod accent – but when. We want to go immediately. I am detailed to visit the travel agents first thing tomorrow.

'We don't want some toffee-nosed affair,' I say 'We want somewhere for normal people.'

'So you're not coming then?'

I spend the rest of the afternoon and evening in the studio. It stinks of beer so for the first hour I chain-light joss-sticks. Then it smells like the 1970s and I am ready to work. Settle myself into the swivel chair, guitar and keyboard both close to hand. To one side stands a pile of old manuscripts and lyric sheets. On the top is the list of questions Ian Martyn-Baker provided before the NFT interview. My gaze hops down the page. There's a cliched familiarity about most of the contents. How did you get into the business? What characterises your approach to songwriting? How did you and Cal collaborate? But one question causes me to pause. Have you ever done anything evil? it says. I stop. That's getting close. That's the sort of thing that keeps me awake at nights. I'm still thinking about Jon too. I've got the tape of our conversation playing in the background. His words are chasing the image of his bloodied face around my mind like a kitten chases it tail. For a moment the two things gell. I sit back and the footage being playing in my head is as vivid as anything the NFT could provide.

Cal has been dead a few months and the balance of the Go-Karts are walking in the West End. We walk slowly. None of us thinks a night out is a very good idea but we are determined. This time there are just three but we intend to do it like we used to. Train to Charing Cross, walk to Trafalgar Square, feed the pigeons if it's afternoon, pint in The Chandos if it's evening, walk up Charing Cross Road, past the National Portrait Gallery and the theatres, cut through Leicester Square, past The Talk Of The Town and the Empire (The Ray McVay Band so it must be Saturday Night), round the back of Piccadilly Circus bathed in the red neon of Coca Cola, wander beneath the giant disembodied arm mounted on the Peter

Stuyvesant advertising billboard to Wardour Street. The church and its courtyard, a small green sanctuary where little save litter congregates, an amusement arcade, another pint in The Intrepid Fox. The Marquee. Nights to die for.

Except that this time, as we emerge from the forecourt at Charing Cross Station into the autumn sun, I already have cold feet.

'I'm not ready for this.'

'No,' says Charlie. He kicks at a pile of unsold *Evening News*es. It's as if half of our lives have been taken away, buried in that coffin with Cal.

'Oi,' says the news vendor. The grille on the front of his stand contains a poster hastily inserted and hastily printed in black block capitals: MAGGIE'S DREAM FOR BRITAIN.

'We could go to the pictures,' says Jon so we walk back down Villiers Street, past the Duke Of Buckingham, past Gordon's through the Embankment tube and up onto Hungerford Bridge. Trains rumble in and out of Charing Cross. We are small in their wake. Small and argumentative. Jon wants to go and see *Taxi Driver* at the National Film Theatre.

'I just think we want a good laugh,' says Charlie, glumly.

'We're angry aren't we,' says Jon. He sounds very angry. 'This will be a cathartic experience. It'll purge all the shit from inside.'

'What do you think, Frank?'

'Without Calum, Frankie doesn't think anything, Charles.'

'I'm easy,' I mumble, thinking that Jon might be right. I light a cigarette.

'Cathartic, eh, Mr. College?'

'It's using drama as an outlet for emotions, particularly those to do with pain and suffering.'

'I know what it fucking means but this isn't ancient Greece and you're not fucking Socrates. This is real life.' Charlie is trying to light himself a cigarette but the words keep on coming. A pleasure cruiser passes beneath us. 'Did watching all those gigs purge your desire to get on stage yourself? No, they fed it. You wanted to do it. You have to do it. Not watch it. Not read about it. Do it.'

Ahead of us are the steps that lead down to the South Bank complex. A man wrapped in a blanket sits at the top of them. I can't place him but then I haven't been up town for an age. He's got a small wooden cigar box open in front of him. Taped to the lid are what look like large coins – presumably to show the tourists what he wants. Inside are a couple of coppers and a few silver pieces. I dredge in my pocket. His overcoat is torn and almost black with dirt and grease. So is his flat cap. As he peers up from beneath it and we take another stride closer I recognise him. Bermuda Shorts. I pull out some change. 'I didn't recognise you with your clothes on,' I say.

The man smiles just as Charlie lands his first kick. It catches the tramp's outstretched arm, sending the money flying and completes its journey into his breast bone. I don't know if it's a crack I hear or a wheeze. Charlie sweeps the hat from the old man's head and kicks the cigar box down the steps. More money flying. Three steps from the bottom the box cracks and breaks on the concourse below. The old man pulls the blanket tight around him and tries to make himself into a ball. Charlie kicks him again. Jon picks up his cap and tosses it onto the railway.

Charlie is yelling like the mad man he has become. 'You have to *do* it, Jon. You have to fucking do it.'

Jon takes the tramp by what remains of his hair so brutally that it seems his head will be torn from his body. I see his shocked face closer than ever before. Weathered lines, the folds and creases hanging heavy, he's older than I thought. Jon punches him as hard as he can in the middle of the face. The sound is a sickening soggy crunch.

The tramp slumps forward, face down on the bridge and there is a dropped beat like the night inhaling before blood emerges from beneath his cheek bone and trickles away down a crack in the concrete. Jon and Charlie are halfway down the stairs. I take a weekend's worth of notes and put them in Bermuda Shorts's pocket. As I do I can smell his snatched breath and feel his clucking heart. I know he's not dead. I follow Jon and Charlie. At the foot of the steps they're completing the demolition of the cigar box and chucking the pieces into the Thames.

'Havanas,' says Jon. He holds the lid up and it catches the street lamp with a slight shimmer. As he pulls his arm back, cranking up for the throw, I take it from him. Taped to it are not coins but two ribbonless medals. Once silver they are now nearly brown. Beneath the dirty twisted tape they barely shine. I walk back up the steps and place the lid, its hinges bent and twisted from where it was torn from the box, beside the unmoving body. Then I hear an asthmatic wheeze and a cough as a passing train shakes the bridge and disturbs the dust, dirt and grit.

We didn't go to a film. We went to the pub, that hole in the wall by Waterloo Station, and we sat and we drank and we talked about Cal and how we felt and in our way we cried for him and for ourselves bound by an unspoken shame of what we'd done and the surge of life it sent through us. I awoke the following day with a bad taste in my mouth. Wendy and I returned to France and didn't come back for years. Don't think that when I had Jon by the lapels in the NFT that night wouldn't have gone through his head. Catharsis? I should co-co.

But we've all survived. Five years later when I went up to Phonodisc to present Tony with *Stolen Moments* who should I trip over in a Soho doorway but Bermuda Shorts? He smiled like a fat cat when I gave him a couple of fifties and thanked me in a Laurence Olivier voice. He'd got a new suit by then. The odd thing is that he'd done exactly the same thing to it: cut the legs off at the knees. But then perhaps it's not so odd. Experience plus gimmick equals survival. It's the free market in begging.

Real evil is systematic, premeditated and planned – not some individual act in a moment of madness. Cal would have argued that the most evil thing I witnessed that day was not Jon and Charlie losing their heads but the foreboding of the flyer on the newspaper stand. I think about that and what I said in the theatre and then I do a 'Rotten In Denmark', produce a series of images. This time from the 1980s not 1977. Paratrooper abseiling down office building to reveal privatised share price, mounted policeman clubbing female protester during miners' strike, People's March for Jobs T-shirt stretched across fat chest of man who has never walked anywhere before, heartless witch squealing newspaper headline Gotcha as po-faced civil servant announces sinking of Belgrano, poll tax riot in Trafalgar Square.

I felt a churning inside as like a pestle to a mortar Jonathan's fist ground into Bermuda Shorts' nose and that's what I use for the chorus – a repeating refrain of Jon and Charlie and an old man in the dirt. I shuffle the images around, rewriting over and over, juxtaposing each simply descriptive verse against violent images of clockwork kicking and fists that aren't for turning. Today in little low-skill England we all grope in the dirt. It's enough to drive anyone mad, Dad. If you can't exploit it. But I can – it's the spirit of the age. I've got a new single and I title it 'Anything Evil'.

Then I pick up the guitar and begin searching for some chords. I have a buzz about this song – a unique buzz – and as I work on through the night, I feel the occasional echo of that churning inside but it's so watered down by history that it's little more than the nausea of an empty stomach.

I am still at it when Wendy leaves for work the following morning. Apart from half an hour's kip on the futon in the corner of the studio I've worked right through.

'You are mad,' she says as she sticks her head around the door. The bare bones of a backing track pounds from the speakers. It's got a dance backbeat: 4/4 with a heavy thud on every beat. It's the first thing I've ever done like this and the beat, I must admit, is something else. It's a simple bass drum mixed with the sound sampled from the cassette of the 'Live' sign falling from above the door onto Jon's head. I've compressed it, phased it slightly and added a cocktail of EQ but that basically is what it is. Crash, crash, crash, crash. On Jon's head. It amuses me. Cal would have loved it. Think how much he would have welcomed the sampler – Jon would only have had to play one note right then. Over the top I've put the familiar Carter/Dane jangling guitar. It's like The Byrds playing on a building site. The words will be spoken – not quite rapped, something less certain. Wendy nods like she likes it.

'Travel agent,' she says as she turns to leave.

'Wendy.' I approach her and we kiss with a passion. My fingers run down her spine, over her bottom, supporting her buttocks, hers stroke the back of my neck and knead my shoulders. Our tongues explore with the desperation of thieves.

'I'm only going to the office,' says Wendy. 'You should work all night more often if it gets you like this.' She pats my bottom and with the words, 'love you,' is gone.

Choices, choices. What to do? I keep it simple – a single line of vocals with a double-tracked chorus and some sequenced saxophone. By the time I am upstairs breakfasting with Philip and Rebecca I have made my choice. The song is finished and a rough mix already on DAT tape.

'Dad, are you getting older?' Philip asks me, looking into what I imagine must be hangdog eyes.

'No, but you two are,' I say.

'Sadly none of us is aware of the passage of time,' says Rebecca. She gets up from the breakfast bar and kisses me on the nose just like her mother. 'You need some sleep, Dad.'

'If you want to go up we're quite capable of getting off on our own,' says Philip.

I put down my orange juice. 'I know. It's not that.'

So I watch my children get off to school. I enjoy seeing them looking for lost books and pens, bickering and arguing. Just as they are finally about to go out of the door I call them both over. 'Hey, I love you both, you know.'

'What is this, pops, The Brady Bunch?'

'Working all night seems to have addled his brain.' Rebecca tugs at her brother's sleeve. 'Come on.' I laugh and get up to go back upstairs. Then as she is about to shut the door, my daughter turns and whispers, 'Love you too, Dad.'

Finally I go back upstairs and complete the packing Wendy began yesterday.

32

You couldn't swim at Virginia Beach. At Raleigh, the birthplace of Andrew 'Stonewall' Jackson, the Confederate general killed by 'friendly fire' in the civil war, had been moved. 'How can a birthplace move?' Cal demanded. He was interested in the story because he reckoned the friendly fire had been supplied by a slave or two. Soulless Charlotte had music but it was only jazz or country. We seemed to be the only rock act in town. After every number, one hick yelled 'Ya got som'ing a little more country, boy?'.

Things weren't going well. Ant was getting increasingly frustrated and increasingly drunk. We'd given up on the man from Phonodisc and kept having to check out of our hotels before Tony ever got round to returning our calls. Audiences were nonexistent. We had consoled ourselves that after New York things would pick up – word of mouth. Cal had shaken his head. 'You're wrong – we're going to another country.'

He was right. South of the Mason Dixon line, word of mouth was unlikely since nobody opened their mouths wide enough to emit any discernible words. Nevertheless, we remained hopeful about Atlanta. Cal told us that in 1974 the city had elected the nation's first black mayor and he knew for a fact that Martin Luther King's birthplace hadn't moved. But Atlanta's most famous son is not called King but Cola, Coca Cola, and by the time we walked off stage, Cal was cursing: 'Sherman had the right idea: torch the fucking place.

Jesus, I'll never laugh at *Gone With The Wind* again.'

The minibus broke down on the way to Birmingham, Alabama and Cal seemed determined to blame it on divine intervention, retribution even. The American Dream was letting him down. While the rest of us hung out in MacDonalds, he stood beside the road appealing to heaven like a farmer desperate for rain, his arms waving like the robot in *Lost In Space*. 'That does not compute, that does not compute.' We made it to downtown Birmingham in time for the gig but once again the audience didn't.

Ironically we sounded great that night – the best on the tour. Sitting in MacDonalds, Nev had come up with the answer to Ant's problem. 'You need some cans, man. Put everything through the desk and use some cans.' This Ant did and, by miking up every instrument and putting them all through the PA desk, he was able to mix the sound pretty accurately using a headphone over his good ear. Cal, I'm sure, never heard the difference. His arm hung over his guitar like a sullen scarecrow, he barely moved all evening. After the show, I tried to cheer him up with a pair of tickets to visit Elvis Presley's Graceland mansion in Memphis (our next stop) and a Presley Sun original single I'd bought in Bleeker Bob's Golden Oldie shop in Greenwich Village. I told him our album was still number one back home. He asked me for a bag of fizz.

I can't remember going to bed that night (but then I can't remember going to bed on any night of the American tour). I do remember getting up. I knocked on Cal's door and there was no answer. We were in a small hotel – it was painted white and looked like an old plantation house – and it was soon apparent that he had disappeared.

'He'll be back,' said Jon. He'd found a browning copy of an old English newspaper in the breakfast room so he was happy.

'He won't,' I said. The thought of pancakes with maple syrup again was making me feel bloated. I poured myself a massive mug of coffee instead. 'Actually,' I said, in a voice I barely recognised as my own. 'I think I know where he's gone.' I sounded like Cal when he insisted on a particular arrangement – absolutely certain. Our next stop was Memphis where we were booked to play some bar on Beale Street, the street where according to the Tennessee tourist authority the blues were born, but it wasn't there that I thought Cal had gone.

'I'm going to find him,' I said. 'If I'm not back when it's time to go, get on to Memphis without me.'

'Isn't this a bit melodramatic?' asked Jon.

'Everything about this fucking country's melodramatic,' said Charlie without looking up from his breakfast. 'I hope you find him, Frank.'

At the Amtrak Station I checked which trains he could have caught and when I discovered that he wouldn't have been overendowed with options, my initial suspicions were confirmed. It wasn't the midnight flyer but the modern equivalent – I knew why some of the names of the places we'd been playing sounded so familiar. I looked at my watch to see when it would arrive and then telephoned the ticket office at the destination. The ticket clerk seemed happy enough to page Cal as I requested and even offered to call me back as the Bell phone began to chew up all my quarters. He seemed glad of something to do, kept calling me 'sah' and remarking on my accent.

The train arrived as he was taking down my message and he kept me on the line giving me a running commentary on the various passengers as they got off. 'Only one more now, sah. Some geeky looking little chile, sah. Looks like he ain't got a cent to make groceries.'

'That's the one,' I said.

When Cal came on the line he knew exactly who he was talking to. 'How the fuck did you find me?'

'Well, we're playing the birthplace of the blues – you take off to the birthplace of jazz.'

'Bullshit, man.' He'd been snorting.

I started to sing. 'I left my home in Norfolk, Virginia, California on my mind – I straddled that Greyhound and rode him into Raleigh and on across Caroline.'

A black guy who'd just bought a ticket for Atlanta with a collection of dog-eared dollar bills he'd produced from under his hat joined in doing a doo-wop as I sang. He managed to do this perfectly while smoking a cigarette at the same time and every time he caught my eye, he inclined his greying head towards me and winked.

'We stopped at Charlotte,' I sang, our voices blending. 'We bypassed Rock Hill, we never was a minute late. We was 90 miles out of Atlanta by sundown, rolling out of Georgia state.' The black cat was dancing now. So was I. With our rolling arms and synchronised steps we must have looked like an anaemic, economy sized version of The Four Tops. I'd only ever sung with Cal before. I was surprised at how much better I sounded with this bloke.

'We had motor trouble that turned into a struggle halfway across Alabam – And that hound broke down and left us all stranded in downtown Birmingham.

'Right away I bought me a through train ticket riding across Mississippi clean – And I was on the Midnight Flyer out of Birmingham smoking into New Orleans.' I stopped singing. 'Or should I say "N'Awlins",' I said imitating the ticket clerk.

'Who's a clever boy?' said Cal.

'Remember, I used to sing 'Promised Land'.'

'Well, I don't know about you Frankie but I'm taking me in a set of cool trad at the Preservation.'

'What about the tour?'

'The tour's over. It's been a fucking disaster area.'

'There have been one or two hiccups, it's true.'

'Hiccups? What do you call the H-bomb, Frankie, a fucking firework?'

'Why did you chose such daft venues?' I asked. 'Elvis Presley aside.'

'To prove we could do it.'

'We don't need to prove anything, Cal. We've been meteoric.'

'After I've been to the Preservation, I'm getting the next flight back. If you want to do the same I'll be at the cottage. You talk to the others but don't bring them. I'll sort it out with Tony. And Frank,' he said just before he hung up. 'You can't put Presley aside.' His voice faded away.

The doo-wop bloke was still standing there. 'You've a voice like an angel,' he said. 'Would you see your way clear, my boy, for a loan of fifty dollars.'

'Loan?'

'Well, gift.'

'I thought it was supposed to be "say buddy can you spare me a dime". What is this, inflation?'

'One needs to be frank when embarking upon a journey, my boy and plan for the unexpected.'

'How much have you of your own?'

'Three bucks, sah.'

I peeled a pair of fifties away from the roll of notes in my jacket pocket and handed them to him. He stuffed them under his hat with the grace and speed of a conjurer. 'You sing like an angel too,' I said.

As I walked away he began singing a song I didn't recognise, a chain-gang sort of song. His face may have been pockmarked and lined like old leather but his voice was pure as morning. Me, Cal and any number of white boy wannabes could have practised eight hours a day every day and never been in the same league as that old boy.

Back in the hotel, Jon and Charlie were philosophical. I agreed that we'd all meet – all four of the Go-Karts – at our flat in a fortnight's time. My departure was more substantially delayed by the need to convince the crew that Tony would pay them for the full tour. I've never been the most persuasive of people but in the face of a real crisis I managed it with a succession of assurances that I had no reason to believe and of promises that I had no idea if I could keep. 'We'll take you all on the World Tour, promise. We'll give you an annual retainer.' The whole business took longer than it needed because of Ant's habit of uttering 'pardon' whenever Mac, Nev or I drew breath. When I left Jon and Charlie had agreed on going to California for a holiday but were arguing the toss between Venice Beach and San Francisco.

We hadn't played 'The Promised Land' since our early gigs but Cal had used its story of a boy's journey across the United States as the basis for planning our tour. On one level I suppose, it was as good a basis as any but given that we were totally unknown in America, surely doomed to failure. Perhaps it was our deviation from the song's route (Tony having vetoed some of Cal's suggestions as 'absolutely fucking ridiculous') that had brought the heavenly wrath of the King of rock'n'roll down upon us or perhaps we were simply trying to sabotage our own careers.

33

Sussex Coast, 1979

Cal began with four lines of speed for medicinal purposes. He was snorting off the kitchen table.

On the kitchen floor where they'd been dumped on arrival were the only belongings we'd thought it important enough to bring: our guitars and our bags of tricks. We both had jet lag – mind-numbing, body aching, throat-wrenching, eyeball-busting jet lag. America was half a day behind us. Walking down onto the beach we started on another bottle of Jack Daniels. It was nearly lunchtime. The Go-Karts were at a crossroads.

We hadn't said much. The odd burst of laughter, too loud and too long. The tide was out and so were the fishermen after worms. We walked all the way down to the shore and tossed a few stones into the sea, trying to make them skim but each in its turn was swallowed by little waves. In the wet sand we wrote the Go-Karts in great three foot high letters.

While we were working I could see a figure walking slowly towards us – at first a speck on the seascape, then a suited man, then a suited old man with no shoes on paddling in the sea.

'Morning,' he boomed from fifteen yards or so. Cal and I both stood up as if we had heard the voice of God himself. We exchanged glances and Cal pretended to pinch himself. Were we looking at a ghost? Walking towards us was the headmaster of Beech Park Grammar – a few years older and apparently a good deal more eccentric but instantly recognisable. We waited for him to recognise us but it never happened. He looked at us briefly before turning his proudly held head out to sea. His suit wasn't as tatty as Bermuda Shorts' but it was on its way.

'Bracing morning, isn't it,' he observed. 'For a constitutional. The rush of the wind, the call of the gull. Sand soft between your toes.'

'Good morning, Mr. Hart,' said Cal.

He reacted as if everybody knew his name – smiling benignly at the pair of us and moving to proceed. Cal stepped into his path. 'Cal Carter, Mr. Hart.'

'Calum Carter,' he savoured it slowly – adopting the longer form of Cal's name but without giving any indication of recognition. Then it was as if he clicked into a different gear. His voice, hitherto airy and light, assumed a deeper more rigid tone. 'Beech Park. You're a long way from Beech Park, boy.'

'I've come a long way since Beech Park, sir.'

'Have you now? Well, that's very pleasing to hear.'

'And this is Frankie Danc, Mr. Hart.'

We weren't that long out of school. It was absurd that he shouldn't know me but he didn't. I was looking straight into his thin brown eyes and there was nothing there – not even a shimmer of familiarity denied. Nothing at all.

'Good day, boy. You must forgive me. I cannot recall.'

I wondered if this new tone was largely one of embarrassment. He appeared to have become an old man over night.

'Well, good morning to you both.' He went to tug at a hat that wasn't there and walked briskly away. As he did so his footprints shivered and died in the wet sand behind him.

'He didn't recognise us,' I said.

'Neither for who we were or for what we've become,' said Cal in a spooky voice like a parody of a horror film.

We were sitting on the breakwater when Cal started to speak. He returned to a subject we'd discussed before – his conversation with his father after he went to America. 'Give me a chance of a career with the band.' Cal had said. His father had scoffed and Cal had left

241

the country. 'By the time I came back, he had mellowed a little. Of course, initially he assumed that I would be off to Oxford but when I made it quite clear that I still wasn't going, he gave me a day to stew and then came back. The old schemer already had a contingency plan. "You want to be a musician, Cal? Then let's do it properly. Let's take a businesslike approach." He took me into his fucking study and pulled out a chair.'

Every time Cal talked about him, his father became bigger and what Cal told me this time was shattering. Most people think our story is the story of four school-friends and so it is, but these friends are not Cal Carter, Frankie Dane, Jonathan Waters and Charlie Ball, they are Alexander Carter, Anthony Waters, Gerald Beale and Ronald Baker. We're not talking 'bout our generation but our masters' voices. Cal's father had arranged it all. He called in a favour from an old school chum who worked at Phonodisc – Ronald Baker. This meant our deal was sewn up before we played our first gig. It also explained our very tame contract – it was the sort of indulgent contract you'd give to a friend when you weren't really expecting anything. Tony had always claimed it was his belief in our talent that had enabled him to persuade Phonodisc to offer us such friendly terms. In fact he'd been lumbered with us. He couldn't say no when Ronald, who had given him the job as Gerald's son in the first place, told him to take the Go-Karts on. Not that he wanted to say no. Not with the PR and publicity budget he was being offered. That the decision to take us came from higher up the corporation took the pressure off Tony a bit and enabled him to display all that apparent brinkmanship when signing us which earned us all so much publicity.

Meanwhile Alex gave Ronald's son Ian a job on the *New Rock Journal*, the UK's leading rock weekly which happened to be published by Mr. Carter's publishing house and instructed him to cover every activity of the Go-Karts in full and glowing detail. This wasn't difficult for Ian to do because Mr. C. let it be known to the editor through the appropriate channels that the Go-Karts were to be given the 'next big things' treatment. All this ensured that Ian Martyn-Baker's name became very prominent too – prominent enough to attract the attentions of the *NRJ*'s teenage punk rock correspondent Miranda Paxton. Ian and Miranda were married shortly before *Rotten In Denmark* hit number one – a happy by-product of the whole business and, given Ian's egocentric personality and over-extended girth, perhaps the biggest miracle of them all.

If by any chance we still didn't make it, despite all this 'investment', Anthony Waters construction company had been prepared to underwrite Phonodisc's losses. They were putting up offices in London ten a penny back then but they sold for a little more than that. If we'd bombed there would have been a block or two with Phonodisc's name on the deeds.

It was a win-win package. All the fathers were able to help all of the sons. Cal and Jon became pop stars, Ian became a top rock journo noted for his nose for talent and Tony went from being a new boy to the A&R man handling Phonodisc's hottest property.

When Cal finished I knocked back the rest of the Jack Daniels.

'So we haven't achieved anything ourselves?'

'Well, we got the gig at the Roebuck.'

I thought about that for a moment. It was some consolation, I suppose, that that had been the best night of them all. 'And you've known about all this business since the start?'

'Yep. The last time we came down here, I knew what they wanted to do.'

I sat up. 'What *they* wanted?'

'Yeah but I didn't want it – not then – and I didn't think the rest of you would.'

I threw a big stone. It landed with a spark and sent a flock of seagulls scattering. 'Jonathan?'

'It was the only way to persuade him to leave University.'

'Why didn't we just get another bass player?'

Cal looked at me. He picked up the whiskey bottle and inverted it. Not a dribble. 'I don't know.'

'So America was your attempt to do it on your own?'

'Exactly. And what a fucking catastrophe. Now do you understand why I'm so miserable?' He looked left and then right like a kid crossing the road and then he boomed: 'He's doing it again, the bastard.'

I got down, taking with me the empty bottle. The sun was coming out and the breakwater cast a shadow across the beach. 'I'll get another bottle,' I said.

'Nice one,' said Cal. 'I think I'll have a kip down there.' The other side of the breakwater was out of the wind and in the sun. There was a strip of dry sand which the tide had never reached. He jumped down from the breakwater to join me.

'My stash is in the kitchen, Frank. You know where. Can you get it for me?'

'Taking more drugs won't help,' I said. That was the sort of thing his father ought to have been saying. 'We haven't actually lost anything, yet.'

'Except our self-respect.' He rolled his jacket into a pillow. 'OK. Except my self-respect.'

When I came back Cal was curled up on the beach, snoring, sand in his hair. I had another two bottles of whiskey, eighty cigarettes, the tobacco pouch containing Cal's speed and a large jar of generic paracetomol. My head was pounding now and while I wanted sleep more than anything in the world I knew it wouldn't come. I took two tablets and knocked them back with a swig of bourbon.

As Cal slept I looked out to sea. I followed the familiar gait of the headmaster as he walked back – his morning constitutional having transmuted into an afternoon stroll. Strangely sad and prematurely wizened. It was all too much to take in.

The swoop and squawk of seagulls on their way inland. The distant chattering chuckles of the fishermen as they repaired back to the pub. A bird – a tern? – pecking at the sand. A couple walking. Behind me the trundle of a wheelchair being pushed along the promenade. The sun slipped behind some clouds again and a grey shadow fell over the whole beach like a cloak over a cage. The temperature dropped a notch. Cal stirred, sat up. 'I could eat a fucking horse,' he said.

I remembered that I hadn't had any food since that curling, yellowing ham sandwich on the plane. 'Good idea.' I patted my stomach and it emitted a hollow holler. We laughed.

'Hold my coat up,' instructed Cal.

I held his coat as a wind-shield as he snorted more lines of speed. He got to his feet gingerly like a man who has been kicked by an elephant. 'This stuff is burning my brains, Frank. I've never had anything like it. Must be stale.' He coughed, clearing his throat. 'Got anything for a headache?'

I told him I had paracetemol but that he shouldn't mix it all. He took four tablets and washed them down with whiskey.

'Did you bring that back from America?'

'Don't be daft. It's the rest of the stuff I had down here last time,' he laughed. 'It's actually the other half of my first ever stash.'

We walked back along the front into the village. My head felt heavy with lack of sleep and too much drink. With the sun appearing then disappearing behind the cloud, the beach was brightly lit one moment and in the shade the next. I was losing track of the time. Cal was walking next to me – a yard away that seemed like a mile. We carried a bottle of Jack each from which we sipped intermittently.

'Did you go to the Preservation Hall?'

'No, a prostitute,' he replied breezily.

'Really?' I said, lazily. (Nothing could surprise me now.)

'Her name was Cherry. She was the one my father introduced to me. '

(Yes it could.) 'Your father?'

'Frank, my father's fortune, success and power has given me everything except a challenge.' He paused for a moment, looked away. 'Except this time I couldn't get it up anyway, not for all the baby-oil in all the brothels in all the world. Cherry was good about it. She said I wasn't always like that. Quite the opposite as she recalled.' He laughed with a boom. 'She had a better memory than the fucking headmaster. Or she was a better actor.' His voice and that old man's laugh were whisked away on the breeze and he was fading into someone else. 'But she's nice, Frank. Too nice for that.' He turned and looked at me and wiped his hands on his jeans as if he was ready to go somewhere. For a moment he reminded me of my mother in her prim readiness. 'I was fifteen when he first took me to her,' he said. 'On a family fucking holiday would you believe? Yet another present, another step on the inevitable road. They had an argument about that one though – Alex and Faye.' He turned his nose up with each name.

'I'm not surprised.'

'You think about something of substance? No, she thought he should wait until I was sixteen. He said that I probably would have got it for free by then and that we didn't want any mistakes. She didn't say anything but I bet she was thinking about my height – not this little one, she was thinking. And he was thinking they'll shag anything with a bank balance these tarts today. My virginity was just like another insurance policy, a question of when to cash it in.'

The first time I had seen vulnerability in Cal's eyes, heard it in his voice, I had lifted him up into the window seat outside Beech Park Station. This second time, much longer was the moment and nothing so simple the solution. He was sliding away and I was silent.

In the village, hidden among the charity shops and beside the window displaying knitting patterns, we found the one café. However even this, behind its greasy spoon curtains, had some pretensions of an afternoon to being a tea house. As we collapsed in the wooden chairs, we were offered cream tea for two.

'Are we too late for a fry up?' asked Cal.

'I'll just ask,' said the waitress. She was barely out of school, thin and anaemic-looking in a starched white coat that made her resemble a lab technician rather than a waitress. I could see Cal eyeing her up, calculating whether he wanted to shag her enough to completely fuck up her life. 'Can we have two large teas?' he asked as she disappeared through the frosted glass door into the kitchen. The café was decorated in that 1930s art deco sort of green like the old Deptford cinema. There were a few lacy flourishes belying its aspirations but the menus – they were hand corrected and falling from their torn PVC holders – gave it all away. That and the tomato sauce in a plastic tomato on every table.

An older woman stuck her head out of the kitchen – her hair-up, her apron greasy and egg stained. The owner's wife, I think. 'Full English love?'

'Thanks,' said Cal.

'And what about you love?'

'Just an omelette thanks.'

She disappeared and the waitress appeared with our teas, a dull brown residue swilling in the saucers.

'You're in that band, in'tcha?' she said to Cal. She sounded like she'd taken a deep breath to do it. 'The Go-Karts. My brother's got your records.'

Cal laughed as if this was the best joke he'd ever heard. 'No, sweetheart, you must be mistaken.'

'Yes, you are and so's he.'

I shrugged.

'Curses, foiled again. Look, we're just staying one night,' Cal said conspiratorially then the star sat back expansively and smiled. 'Bring your brother's record round and we'll both autograph it.' He gave her the address which she wrote on her little notepad, young hand and yesterday's nail varnish shaking with excitement.

I looked at him distastefully. Nearly as distastefully as I looked at his fry-up: bacon, sausage, eggs, mushroom and fried slice all floating like flotsam on a puddle of grease. 'Are you trying to kill yourself,' I asked.

He shook his head. 'The material's good. Our songs. I still believe that. I mean you can't make people buy records, can you? It's where do we go from here. Where do I go from here?' He regarded me curiously for a moment, a fatty sliver of bacon clinging to the end of his poised fork. 'How do I get out of this?' He didn't look that convinced of anything. I wanted to free him. 'Did you really think it was just luck?' he asked.

'No, Cal, worse than that: I thought it was just talent.'

He didn't say anything for a moment, ruminating thoughtfully over his breakfast. 'Talent, sure we may have made it on talent. But how long would it have taken? My old man only invests in sure things. Anyway if we wanted to make it on talent, we definitely would have needed a new bassist.' He laughed. He seemed to be perking up as he warmed to the idea that all we had really done was to save time. I knew how fast his brain could move – accepting an idea and moving on while I was still trying to work out the first thing. I'd get there eventually but this time I wasn't sure that I wanted to. Then I figured he'd been living this lie for months. I wondered if he had rehearsed this in his head before.

We ate on in silence and by the time we emerged into the

afternoon Cal was well on the way down again. We returned to the cottage so that he could take some more speed. Line after line of it. Gorging. I sat in the armchair gently sipping whiskey from my bottle and when I woke up it was still in my hands. The evening had drawn in tight as a noose and the room was shrouded in darkness. My neck ached from the way I'd been sleeping with it hanging over the top of the armchair. My mouth was open, my tongue like broken glass. In fact, I think it was the pain of swallowing which woke me. I had no idea of the time.

Gradually I became aware of that distinctive creaking sound floating down the narrow staircase of Mr. and Mrs. Carter's two up, two down cottage. I pulled myself to my feet struggling with an overwhelming gravity. I stretched. At the foot of the stairs hanging over the slim pine bannister was the waitress's overall. The bedsprings creaked manically. The strangled puffs and pants and squeals of human contact swirled like dregs in the salty air. I walked straight past the stairs – I needed some freshness in my lungs – picked up my own coat from the table and slipped out of the back door, night lapping me up as I emerged. I breathed, taking great gulps of air, fancying that I could smell the wild neglect of the Carter's little garden mingling with the fresh saline salute of the sea. I walked and walked and to my eternal regret I never turned back.

I walked back down to the seafront and along the beach. The tide was higher this time but on its way out, leaving its ebbing print upon the sands. I had a beer in a pub with formica topped tables and a dartboard which hadn't been turned in thirty years. It reminded me of The Roebuck back in BC – Before Carter. I discussed the superiority of deep-sea fishing over the freshwater variety with the landlord despite not having a clue about either. Then I walked to the station and got on the next train home. I felt as if I had been awake for half a lifetime and I wanted my mother's cooking and a fresh bed.

I still had a key for my parents' home and I let myself in. In fact, like Jon, I didn't see the flat as my home, more a rehearsal room with beds and beer. I still did much of my everyday living – the eating and sleeping stuff – at my parents. The flat was Cal's really –

after all, it was his Dad's gift. Despite the hour, my mother appeared in the kitchen door within moments of my arrival.

'Frank,' she whispered.

'Hi, Mum. America finished early. It didn't really work out,' I managed brightly.

'That'll disappoint your father. He's told everyone at work that you're going to be on the *Ed Sullivan Show*.' Perhaps she was chuckling to herself. 'Do you want some stew?'

The next morning when I walked round to the flat, the police were already there. It was Wendy who told me and comforted my tears when they came. The waitress had gone back the next morning, that morning, to show her brother where Cal Carter lived, found the back door still open just as she'd left it and Cal lying at the foot of the stairs.

'He fell down the stairs, Mr. Dane. But we don't believe it was that what killed him. We're working on a suspected drugs overdose,' said the police officer. He was writing my name in his notebook. 'Of course, there'll have to be an inquest.'

'Why was the door open?'

'She said he told her to leave it open for you, Frank,' said Wendy. I felt sick down to the soles of my shoes.

I answered all the policeman's questions sitting on the wall holding Wendy's hand – our heels kicking against the brickwork like kids – and I went into the flat for just a minute. My head was pounding and I needed a glass of water. I put my hand into my coat pocket for my paracetemol but they weren't where I thought they were. I found the jar in the opposite pocket and it rattled shyly like a broken toy. Inside there were just two tablets left. I took them and, as I went back outside to where Wendy had her car, I gave the jar to the policeman.

34

South of France, 1979

The road had been pitch black for some half an hour and now we were turning off it onto a dirt-track. The grit spat and cursed beneath the tyres. The sky was clear; the stars silver. When we stopped to lift the entrance barrier the only sounds were the rustle of trees and the distant rushing of the waves across the sand.

The barrier had to be pulled back like a great single barred gate. It was heavy and I was tired. Wendy smiled at me through the windscreen of the hire car as I struggled with the thing, her hands resting on the steering wheel. When the paltry light from the single lamppost caught her wedding ring it sparkled like the eye of a beast.

The dirt-track became narrower still, the branches tapping on the windows like long fingers, one after the other as if a coven of witches were lining the road. You couldn't see the caravans – just the little blue numbered plaques standing in the soil marking the bays like flags on a putting green.

'Nearly there,' said Wendy, peering forward into the gloom.

I was never numb. Quite the opposite. My emotions were in overdrive, demanding attention where they were normally so subdued, as close to the surface as another layer of skin. I listened to Wendy as she spoke. She listened to me and we drove on through the night. She mentioned the 'I told you so' pleasure her husband seemed to find in Cal's fate but apart from that we never talked directly about what had happened. Somehow, tragic and terrible and everything else as it was, we didn't want to consider death, Cal's or anyone else's, yet it underpinned everything we said. Me – with the taste of real human suffering on my breath – I'd never felt so alive.

We turned into the parking bay by the Carter's caravan. Silence as the engine died. We both slumped back in the seats. I lit a cigarette and crumpled the empty packet. Wendy looked across and our eyes met in the rear view mirror – an inquiring eyebrow. I took a puff and then placed the cigarette between her lips. In my pocket I found the second of the two packets I'd bought when we stopped in Paris. As I exhaled I became aware once more of the sea in the background like a low level wow and flutter on the intro groove – the waves breaking with the rhythm of a record turning.

'Is that the Côte D'Azur?' I asked.

'Côte not Coat. I think technically it's called the Golfe du Lion.'

'Technically?'

'Well obviously all the English tourists think it's the Cote D'Azur and the French see no reason to disabuse them.'

'Marketing.'

'You sound like Cal.'

'No, you do.'

The windscreen was steaming up inside.

I got out of the car and walked towards the caravan. 'You got the key?'

'No, Frank. I thought we'd break in.'

I took another step. 'Looks like someone already has.'

The door to the caravan was open and the window nearest to it smashed. I pushed at the door and it swung open heavily. Wendy reached round and found the light switch and the strip light overhead stuttered into action.

We stood in the middle of the caravan. We both looked around. Not having been there before, I wasn't sure what I was looking for. It wasn't particularly big and not dissimilar to the sort I'd been used to on caravan holidays as a child: pull down table, tiny fitted kitchen, foam-cushioned wall-mounted seats doubling as beds, that sort of thing. The burglars hadn't trashed the place.

'Is anything missing?'

'The microwave, the TV,' Wendy opened a drawer, 'and the radio.'

In the car we had a box full of food. As I unpacked it and flattened the box to repair the window, Wendy looked around for the bedding.

'Here,' she said, tossing me a sleeping bag. 'You can have the big room.'

In other words, she was having the bedroom and I was on the couch. But when I was lying there alone half an hour later it wasn't like it would have been had these circumstances befallen me before Cal died. Even though I'd yearned for Wendy for the best part of a decade, I didn't interpret her decision as a sexual slight and spend half the night poring over the evening looking for where I went wrong or beating myself over the head because of it. I thought about other things and despite everything I enjoyed the sea in my ears and a feeling of space and, when I closed my eyes, Cal's face in happier times before me. Despite the narrowness of the bed, the thinness of the foam and the hardness of the plyboard beneath, I slept long and late. I was thinking of Cal when I went to sleep and it was of him that I dreamt with a bleak shocking vividness. When I woke up I had that disorientating feeling when you're not sure where you are and what's dream and what's reality.

We lived on baguettes, cheese and wine, exchanged the occasional 'bonjour' with our neighbour (I couldn't help thinking that he or someone else on the site was probably watching our telly) and took long walks on the beach. Outside the caravan we set up the deck-chairs and read. I had Down And Out In Paris And London. As I turned the pages, the sea hummed softly in the background beckoning. Meanwhile, on the south coast of England there was an inquest going on into the death of a pop star.

We were chain smoking and a bottle of wine was always open. At midday on the second day, Wendy looked up from her book. It had been written by someone I had never heard of – Wendy was reading it because he was one of her authors.

'What will you do now?' she asked me.

'Not the civil service, that's for sure.'

'Well, I never thought that for a minute.

'No?'

Wendy closed her book. 'Do you want to go for another walk?'

I nodded. I suddenly had an overwhelming desire to swim. The bottle of wine was freshly opened and we carried that with us. On the beach, I stripped down to a pair of mauve underpants. Wendy was teasing me, telling me that I'd freeze to death but I didn't feel self conscious, dumping my clothes in a heap and charging into the waves with a scream. There wasn't any dipping of the toe, I simply ran and ran until the weight of water made running impossible. The water was icy. My thighs turned purple and then as I waded deeper and deeper slowly numbed and warmed and then felt barely attached to my body at all. I dived, fell forward into the blue water, my hair going under, my ears burning in the cold. Underwater I ran my fingers through my spiky hairstyle until it had lost all definition. I swam a few strokes, slow breast stroke. Back on the shore, Wendy had disappeared. Out to sea I could see nothing at all except a blue that never ended. I was tingling all over.

When I got out I wasn't shivering, I was wondering where Wendy was. There were a couple of French kids playing with an inner tube which must have come from a tractor or truck tyre. I essayed a word or two with them but I don't think they'd seen 'une femme blonde et belle'.

She reappeared as I was looking through my pockets for a cigarette and she threw me a towel. 'Here, Mark Spitz – we don't want you catching your death.' I put the towel around my shoulders and my arm around hers. Inside my sodden briefs, my shrivelled cock was struggling back to life. 'You'd better get dressed,' laughed Wendy.

We were walking along the beach when I started talking about the dream I had had. Cal and I were at school, in assembly listening to the head tell his stone mason story. In the story there are two stonemasons both producing beautifully crafted work for the local churches and nobles. But one stone mason works faster than the other so he gets more work and becomes richer. The people assume he works harder and pay all sorts of tribute to him. His work looks perfect, his figures so lifelike that you expect them to rise from the stone to greet you. One day a great fraud is discovered in the church finances and everyone assumes the slower, lazier mason is responsible. Until one day the vicar takes a closer look at the work in his church. The master mason's work may be wonderful indeed but only the parts which can actually be seen from the nave of the church. Everything behind, everything in shadows, has been left unfinished, untouched. The reason the other stone mason is slower is that he completes every detail with the same care and skill whether it will be seen or not. Who is the fraudster? Although the story was confused, in my dream as in my memory, its message still frightened me. Don't examine anything too closely, it seemed to say, or you'll see the flaws. I'd lived my life not examining anything too closely.

As with most of his stories, the head told this tale once a year but in the dream we were adults, all dressed up to go on stage as the Go-Karts. As I was watching him speak I became unable to move, as if I were turning to stone. Then, as happens in dreams, I was suddenly out of my body, watching like a camera. We had all become models, waxworks I suppose but with great macabre faces like ventriloquists' dummies: Jon, Charlie, Cal and me. Cal, so much shorter, so much like a child physically, began to spin slowly like a little doll on a podium, his fixed pose, hand over his guitar, his hair seemingly caught on the breeze and then frozen. But me I couldn't spin. I tried but I couldn't. I couldn't move at all. My dream camera floated above my dummy. I could see my eyes struggling but nothing was happening, my torso and limbs strait-jacketed within wax. I was fixed to the wall behind me and the ground beneath me by a slag heap of molten wax like the stalagmite deposits of a billion candles.

Then I was on a beach and the wax had turned to stone. The waves were lapping over my toes. Mr. Blake was there saying to me over and over, 'The head's very fond of you, you know, Frankie' and then the head himself was next to him, now as the old man we'd seen on the beach, nodding but with that nothing in his eyes, misty and distant and then he turned into my father.

Wendy snorted as a laugh suppressed escaped. 'Are you making this up,' she asked but in a way that made it clear she knew I wasn't.

In the dream the headmaster's words repeated over and over. In the dream I was not on the beach I was walking on with Wendy but on that other beach near the Carter's cottage with my father. In the dream at the end, just before I woke up, it was my father mouthing words. I'm very fond of you, Frank.

When Wendy spoke to me, acknowledged she understood, I could feel something animal growing in my jeans. Doesn't the fact that we fancy people who seem to understand us prove that we just want to shag ourselves?

'Sometimes,' I was saying, 'I feel like I'm still standing by Mr. Parker's confectionary stand. You know at...'

She finished my sentence for me. 'Beech Park Station. In his bow tie.'

'Standing there looking at the Mars Bar and knowing I can only afford the bubble gum.'

She stopped walking and removed the packet of cigarettes from the breast pocket of my T-shirt. 'That's rubbish. You can have anything you want, Frankie.'

'No,' I said. 'You can't change what's between your ears.'

She looked up at me – a clipped look of recognition and of not wanting to dwell. 'Anyway,' she said, fiddling with the cigarette packet, 'you're an artist. You're creative. You're supposed to have these painful insights into the human condition.'

We were walking again, sucking on little sticks of comfort, when she started speaking again. 'I know what intellectual inferiority is all about, Frank. Cal was my little brother.' She took a deep breath, more resonant than a sigh, silkier than a groan and it flickered down my spine. 'Of course, I took Daddy's job – I'm no fool – though I insisted on a different publishing house.' She paused, inhaled deeply. Listening to the seagulls we could have been in England, France or anywhere. 'But then of course I am the fool. I married to get out of the house because it was suffocating me.' She was speaking slowly. 'But a soulless relationship is suffocating too. It's a death so slow you wouldn't notice.' The wind was whipping up and I put my arm around her. 'Driving down here whenever it was – two, three days ago – I was thinking Cal was the lucky one. At least it was quick.' She trailed off but I knew exactly what she meant. Sometimes I'd thought that of my best friend too – death as a favour.

There was a pause. 'You're a long time dead, Wendy,' I said. I could hear my mother's voice rather then my own.

'Yeah, I have been,' she said, walking away.

That night we ate out at a pizza restaurant where the oven was a five foot square flame blackened hole in a white wall. The devil's own cauldron could not have been brighter, warmer, deeper or more golden. The candle on our table flickered in deference and we ate in a companionable silence pizzas the size of LPs.

I was woken by the sound of the caravan door rattling in its frame. I could see the handle rising and falling. Wendy and I met in the middle of the kitchen just a yard away from the door. She had a giant T-shirt on. Outside I could hear someone breathing. Then he uttered Wendy's name. We were speaking with our eyes. The burglars were back. She gestured for me to step back. As I did so, Wendy with a deft hand unlocked the door. It flew open propelling the intruder into the middle of the caravan. Wendy brought a stale baguette down onto his head like a cudgel and he slumped to the floor. The figure had a heavy black great coat on and from beneath its tailored hems protruded a pair of golden orange baseball boots.

35

The baguette was getting on for four days old and as solid as a shillelagh. On the floor Jonathan stirred, rolled over and rubbed his head. He looked up. Wendy was still standing over him, open-mouthed, the lethal loaf in her hand. He rubbed his head again. 'What is this, Miss Scarlet in the caravan with the lead piping?'

'Perhaps you'd like a sandwich, Jon?' I asked. 'I was just about to make one.'

He ignored me. 'Wendy, the door's not usually locked.'

She explained briefly about the break-in.

'So you haven't heard anything then? No radio.' said Jon. He was sitting up now. I lit a cigarette and passed the packet around.

'Thanks, Frank.' Laughing, he took off his coat and handed it to me. 'Here, cover yourself up – now's not the time.' I realised that I was completely naked.

Jonathan had been to the inquest. Cal, he said, had died of hypoglycaemia resulting in liver failure. His low-blood sugar level had been caused by the cocktail of alcohol, amphetamines and paracetemol that he had consumed. The verdict: death by misadventure.

'It seems they think that he must have taken at least some paracetemol himself because even if the speed itself was contaminated it would have been hard to ingest the amount he had.' We all knew with what reluctance suicide verdicts were handed down, particularly in the face of prominent families with strong feelings. We all knew how Mr. Carter's were rarely otherwise.

'Well that's true. He was complaining of headaches, wasn't he, Frank?' said Wendy.

I nodded. 'I said all that in my statement.'

'They thought you'd be there, Frank,' said Jon, turning to me.

'I wouldn't let him,' said Wendy.

'They nearly adjourned it but Alex insisted. Did his magnate routine. He waved your statement and said: how much more do you want from him?'

'Quite,' said Wendy.

I faced Jon. 'The amount of time before he was discovered – that was a factor?'

'No, Frank,' snapped Wendy but Jon was already answering me. 'Yes, if he'd been found sooner – well, insulin, stomach pump.' He was mumbling. Wendy looked at me as like Jon I bowed my head.

I lit another cigarette from the one I already had, buttoned up Jon's coat and stepped out into the night. The gravel crackled, hurting my bare feet as I walked on it. The caravans had gone to bed for the night. As I walked past the only one that still had a light on behind its orange curtains I could hear whispers. They were in a language I didn't understand but their gentle messages were universal.

As I walked, I felt the texture change and soften beneath my feet. I tossed my dog-end out towards the sea and it died on the sand with a hiss. I began looking through Jonathan's pockets for his cigarettes. In his inside pocket, close to his wallet, close to his heart, I felt a folded document printed on heavy vellum paper – the type where you can still feel the grain. Just the feel of it gave it away. I took it out. It was cream and folded in three. It was too dark to read easily but I knew what it was all right because I had one just the same. Its first line would say: I, Cal A. Carter, a citizen of the UK, being of sound mind and disposing memory, do hereby make, publish and declare this instrument to be my last will and testament. I refolded and replaced it.

I felt sick. When, a moment later, I found the cigarettes I contemplated burning the will but I didn't. I sat on the beach smoking and watched the sun come up over the sea. From that day on, I didn't write another note. I couldn't. Every song on *Stolen Moments* and *Phoenix* was written before Cal died because when he died my creativity died too.

I watched the sun rise, watched it slowly beguile the sea, taking it deeper and deeper – from the greys to the blues. I felt empty and purposeless until the moment when the ocean turned the same rich blue as it had been the previous day and it reminded me of Wendy. Then I tossed Jon's heavy coat to the sand and plunged in.

Here in my study I begin to make up the two parcels: the DAT tape which I will address to Tony and this manuscript and computer disc which I will address to my editor. Then I will walk round the house – the kids' bedrooms, Wendy's study, the kitchen in which we made love yesterday. I will probably wash my hands and then leave with two cases – my suitcase and my briefcase, the old one Cal gave me back in the days when I lived my life, briefly, in colour. At least the monotone black on white of this VDU will soon be behind me.

I will walk down the hill to the station but I won't catch a train – they don't stop here outside the rush-hour now. At the old Victoria Regina postbox opposite the station entrance I'll stop and post my letters. Perhaps I'll look around – hear the fragments of old conversations, the ghostly bounce of tennis and footballs and the rustle of a sticky bag of bubble gum. I'll notice the station window that has been boarded up for five years now but I won't try to climb up and sit in it. Whatever it was I thought I was looking for when I used to sit up there I've finally got a chance to find. Then I'll walk, a case in each hand, down to the minicab office. It's not called Park Cabs any more. I don't think it's called anything. It's just a nameless, faceless shit-brown shopfront with a grille at the counter, a peeling lino floor and overflowing ashtrays.

The controller now is still a woman but it's not the fat controller. It's not Janice. She retired to Guildford according to my mother. She informed my father of this with a note of glee. With a note of glee and, as it turned out, excellent timing because about two weeks later he pissed himself in the Horniman museum. Perhaps I'll think of my father when I sit down to wait in the office. Perhaps I won't.

Perhaps I'll think of Cal's father and the stunting weight of success that he placed on his son's shoulders and wonder what I am doing to my own children. Perhaps I'll think of another person.

When the driver drops me at Heathrow, I'll tip him well – not extravagantly but substantially enough for him to mention it when he gets back to Beech Park or over a pint, perhaps in the Roebuck, tonight. Maybe I'll even tell him who I am so that he can boast about who he had in the back of his cab. I don't know but I feel the need to make some small mark before I get on the plane.

I insert a piece of card into the envelope with the manuscript and disc so as to protect them in the post. Then I seal it and write the address of the publishing house. Beneath that I write FAO: Wendy Carter.

Before I leave I open the old briefcase. In it is every song that Cal ever wrote and the handful of teenage lyrics that were in truth my only contribution to the oeuvre of Dane/Carter. As well as the Go-Karts numbers, it includes all the songs that I have arranged, recorded and released under my own name over the past decade. Many may have credited Frankie Dane as the writer (if I'd honoured my pub promise to Cal they would have at least said Dane/Carter) and they may have been legally mine (he honoured his in his last will and testament) but, in fact, if accuracy matters, they were all written by Cal. The lot. Every one. I didn't write 'Rotten In Denmark' in my bedroom in 1976. I couldn't have – just look at the words. I didn't write any of them. What I have done is to prove what Cal still doubted on the day he died. I have proved, with two of the best-selling pop albums of all time, the strength of the material.

If Tony releases 'Anything Evil' that, at least, like this autobiography, and for the first time, will have been all my own work. I riffle through the loose pages as I have done a thousand times before – music manuscripts, tablature, lyric sheets, each of them on feint-lined paper torn from a Beech Park exercise book and loaded with fountain pen strokes in Cal's rounded, open caress of a hand. I close the tired leather and fasten the buckle. I pat it like an old friend. The devil does have all the best tunes.

The briefcase was in the kitchen where I'd left it, of course – as thick with his invention and creativity then as it is now. Sleep clogged my eyes and I had to rub them like a child. For a moment I thought it was just the creak of the bed springs but it wasn't. With each stroke I could hear the waitress gently coming to the boil. I felt sore all over – my head, my neck, my legs, my prick. In the kitchen, I paused. The hammer, incredibly, was still on the table. The mistake of a mediocrity. I put it back in the larder where I knew it was kept. Then I opened Cal's sports bag. Inside, as usual, was a thick sheaf of papers. I looked through it for anything new but there wasn't much. America, this time, had not been inspirational for Cal. I transferred the pile of papers to my briefcase and walked out of the cottage.

I checked the times of the tides by the peeling blue noticeboard on the promenade below which the lifebelts hang. It was going out. I walked down onto the beach circumnavigating the broken bottles, tar and turds. The seagull that was scratching around took off, soared up over the waves, swooped and effortlessly disappeared. From my pocket I took the duster in which that morning when I'd returned to the cottage alone, I had wrapped virtually the entire contents of the bottle of paracetemol before crushing it into a white powder that even an expert like Cal could not distinguish from speed. This time I wrapped it around a stone and hurled it out to sea where, for one blink of time, shorter than a heartbeat, it stood out against the cloud like a little yellow sun before plummeting into the rocking greyness.

There. That's the truth. I wish I could report that Cal's drug-induced death had some glamour about it – heroin or cocaine – but it was just everyday paracetemol that I used to adulterate his stash of speed and he, with his drinking and his housewife's headaches helped it along. It was all so ordinary. Like dying on the toilet. For me ordinariness comes as no surprise but for him perhaps this revelation is the unkindest cut of all. He would at least have enjoyed the irony.

I read the news today ...

Police Take Possession of Rock Star's Autobiography

(From the morning papers the day after Wendy Dane passed this manuscript to the police)

The autobiography of musician Frankie Dane, who disappeared five days ago, has been handed over to the police. The manuscript is believed to shed new light on the death from a drug overdose in 1979 of Mr. Dane's songwriting partner Cal Carter.

The manuscript was addressed to Mr. Dane's wife, publisher Wendy Carter, who is the sister of the late Mr. Carter and daughter of the publishing magnate Alexander Carter, at her workplace. Mrs. Carter is employed by publishers Big Blue where unofficial sources have suggested that the envelope was addressed by Mr. Dane and bore a postmark from Beech Park, the area of south-east London where Mr. Dane has lived since childhood.

Mr. Dane's manager Jonathan Waters held a brief press conference yesterday morning at which he appealed for Mr. Dane to contact him. He informed the media that Mrs. Carter was unavailable for comment and that an injunction had already been taken out preventing the press from approaching the couple's two children.

Tony Beale, a representative of Mr. Dane's record company Phonodisc, was more relaxed. He said 'This is just the sort of crazy thing Frank would do. He's always felt guilty about Cal's death but that's not the same as being responsible is it?' He added that the new Frankie Dane and the Denmarks single would be released on Monday.

Rival record companies have dismissed the whole thing as a publicity stunt. A source close to one said 'the only thing that's been murdered here is the truth. Dane, Waters and Beale are all in this together. They're probably having a big laugh about it right now.'

Missing Musician's Final Release Breaks All Records

(from the same paper a few days later)

The song 'Anything Evil' recorded by the missing rock star Frankie Dane is set to top the charts after selling more copies in its first week of release than any other single in the history of popular music on both sides of the Atlantic. If sales continue at the present rate it will be the quickest million selling record of all time. In the meantime the record's creator Frankie Dane has not been seen for over a fortnight.

Tony Beale of the successful record company Phonodisc told a packed press conference at the label's West End offices, 'Frankie has eclipsed Elvis, the Beatles, the Stones, Michael Jackson, Madonna, The Spice Girls and anyone else you care to name. He could be the biggest star ever now. If you're listening Frank – it's time to come home. We all miss you and we all need you.' He declined to answer questions about whether Mr. Dane had or would receive any royalties for the song.

Mr. Dane's autobiography *Rotten In Denmark* due for publication next week is expected to break similar records in the world of publishing.

Earlier yesterday the metropolitan police issued a warrant for Mr. Dane's arrest.

- *Leader comment*, p.16
- *Where might Dane have gone?* – Ian Martyn-Baker, p.18
- The serialisation of *Rotten In Denmark* begins in this newspaper on Saturday

Also by Jim Pollard

All Right, Mate?

An Easy Intro to Men's Health

'I first had the idea for this book while lying on my back with my underpants around my ankles and some sort of jelly substance smeared all over my testicles.'

Jim Pollard claims that this experience came completely free on the NHS. Amazingly enough, he's telling the truth. In fact, it was a perfectly routine procedure. But then he wouldn't have a clue about that, would he? He's a man.

There's a need for easy, accessible, honest information about men's health: a book for blokes who are too busy, too lazy or too scared to go to the doctors. So here it is: everything you want to know about the male body (but are too strong and silent to ask).

published by Vista, price £7.99

Smith/Doorstop Books

Independent publishers of poetry and fiction

Another new title on our fiction list

Eating a Sandwich

Felicity Skelton

An extraordinary collection of stories about ordinary people dealing, or failing to deal, with the trivia of their trapped lives.

'I love Skelton's odd lonely characters, the strong individual flavour of their lives and views, their vividly realised worlds. She writes with beautiful precision.' – Jane Rogers

She speaks for those whose voices 'sound loudest inside their own heads'.

Felicity Skelton spent twenty years in the professional theatre, directing and backstage. She has an M.A. in Writing (Distinction) from Sheffield Hallam University.

She is married to the actor Terry Skelton, and they run a tea shop and B&B in a small town in the Peak District, where she is well placed to observe whims and idiosyncracies.

Paperback Original
Price £6.99
ISBN 1-902382-08-0

Publication June 1999
198x126mm; 192pp

Smith/Doorstop Books

Independent publishers of poetry and fiction

Our latest poetry titles include

John Harvey   *Bluer Than This* £5.95
'He sings the blues for people too bruised to carry the song
themselves' – *New York Review of Books*

Kath Mackay   *Anyone Left Standing*   £5.95
'Bags of spread and energy' – Michael Laskey
Winner of The Poetry Business Competition 1997

Michael Laskey   *The Tightrope Wedding* £6.95
'Engaging warmth ... remarkable imagination'
– William Scammell, *Independent on Sunday*
Poetry Book Society Recommendation

Jo Haslam   *The Sign for Water* £5.9
'Her poems surprise and delight' – Maura Dooley

Joan Jobe Smith   *The Pow Wow Café* £5.95
'Humming with vitality ... a rich collection' – *Poetry Wales*

Dorothy Nimmo   *The Children's Game* £5.95
'Sly skill ... ardent singlemindedness' – Frederick Raphael
Poetry Book Society Recommendation

All are available from The Poetry Business